Lisa was born and raised in North Norfolk in the UK, where she grew up with her two older siblings and parents. At the age of 24, she decided to travel around Australia, where Sydney soon became her new home. She has grown her love for writing over the past six years and amongst other things, she is a qualified nutritionist and a proud mum to her three children.

This book is dedicated to my family and friends for always being there for me when I needed them most. Thank you for all your support, reading, feedback and cherished words. It has given me the confidence to keep writing and publish this book.

Lisa B

NEW BEGINNINGS

AUSTIN MACAULEY PUBLISHERS™

LONDON * CAMBRIDGE * NEW YORK * SHARJAH

A CIP catalogue record for this title is available from the British Library.

ISBN 9781398441248 (Paperback)
ISBN 9781398441255 (ePub e-book)

www.austinmacauley.com

First Published 2023
Austin Macauley Publishers Ltd®
1 Canada Square
Canary Wharf
London
E14 5AA

Monday, 8 June

As Annalise woke from her emotional roller coaster of dreams, speckles of light shone through the curtains, making her aware that it was morning.

Her life had been a whirlwind recently. Not only had they moved from her lifelong hometown. Penelope had started at a new school, and now it was Annalise's first day at her new job. As she lay in bed, mustering up the motivation to get up. Excitement and Panic went running through Annalise's mind.

A burst of doubt came crashing into her muddled brain. She wondered if she was going to be good enough for this role. What if they knew she was a fraud, that she had never worked for such a large company. She had written a few white lies on her resume. But Annalise knew it was the only way for her to be able to get a role like this.

She thought about how much she needed this job, not only for her but more importantly for Penelope, her daughter. This was their fresh start away from everything. The two of them against the world. She could do this she thought. She had to do it, for both their sakes. She was going to make something of her life, to make Penelope proud of her, and it all began today.

As she lay there pondering about her day, even procrastinating knowing she had to get up and get ready. She heard someone creep into her bedroom and before she could look up, a bundle of long brown hair was heading straight for her face.

"Today's the day, today's the day." She was all messy hair and cute in the mornings. And with it being her first day of school, Penelope was even more excited. She fell on the bed, falling headfirst into the pillow next to Annalise and was smiling from ear to ear. Her eyes were dark and sleepy. They always reminded Annalise of Penelope's father, it was a strange feeling that she always got when looking into them.

A short flashback of her life before. The life that she wanted to forget and move on from. Although Penelope had certain features of her dad, everything else about her face was different, and it reminded Annalise of her when she was younger. Penelope had the loveliest round face with little chubby cheeks. They were always rosy, and she had a small dimple on her right one.

She had a gorgeous smile that would light up any room. Her hair was light brown and came to her mid-back, and she had the longest of eyelashes. As she lay there looking at her daughter it brought back memories of herself as a child. It instantly made Annalise think of her parents, something she tried to avoid as much as possible nowadays. Deep in thought, she was soon snapped out of the memory by Penelope jumping on her and singing it was breakfast time.

After being jolted up and down like she was some kind of trampoline, her thoughts about the past had ended, and she felt relieved. She didn't need any distractions today. Today was the start of the rest of her life, and she wasn't going to stop anything or anyone getting in the way of that.

Penelope was talking to Annalise, and she tried to shift her focus back to her daughter.

"Mummy, it's my first day at my new school today, do you think everyone will like me? What if they are mean to me, and I don't make any friends. I do hope I make friends, Mummy. I really hope that I have a best friend named sunshine. No! Rain. No, rain makes me sad. I don't want a best friend that makes me sad. I like sunshine, yes, I'm going to have a best friend named sunshine, and we are going to be best friends forever."

Annalise loved the way Penelope would ramble when she was nervous and how she looked at life. so young and carefree. Before they left their old life, Penelope didn't have many friends. Other children were not very nice to her because they knew about Annalise's past. They would make jokes at Penelope. That's part of the reason Annalise wanted to move away. To give Penelope a fresh start. Penelope was being so brave and positive about starting a new school, something that inspired Annalise. If her daughter of 7 could do it, then so could she.

"My little treasure. You are going to make so many friends at school. Everyone is going to love you, and I am sure you will meet a best friend. Maybe not one called sunshine! But I'm sure they will bring sunshine to your life as you do to mine."

Annalise reached over and pulled Penelope into a big cuddle, taking in every special moment with her daughter.

"I do hope so, Mummy. Now, can I have pancakes with lots of yummy berries and chocolate sauce for breakfast?"

As Annalise looked at her daughter, those big brown eyes looked at her with pleading. How could she refuse on this special day? She would do anything to make Penelope happy. They had both been through a lot, so today could be an exception. They would have pancakes!

"Only if Mummy can have them with you?" She smiled sweetly at Penelope.

"Of course! I'm having pancakes before school, this never happens! I'm going to tell all my new friends that I have the best mummy in the whole world!"

This filled Annalise's heart with nothing but joy and love. She knew children could be fickle at times. But she didn't care right now. She needed to hear those words. Annalise needed to know that she was needed by someone. This is where her insecurities came into play. She quickly locked them back in her Pandora box and carried on like everything was OK.

Annalise looked at her phone and knew that if she didn't get up now, she would definitely be late for work. She still had to get Penelope ready, make breakfast and sort herself out. She had to remember tomorrow to give herself more time in the mornings.

"Right missy, you need to get ready for school. Mummy will go and make the pancakes and then we can have some breakfast together before I drop you off at school."

"Yum, they were the best pancakes ever."

Penelope had chocolate sauce all around her face and Annalise couldn't help but laugh. She always managed to get some kind of food over half of her face and clothes right before she had to be somewhere important.

"Oh, Penelope. What do you look like! You have chocolate sauce all over your face! Go and wash your face again while Mummy gets ready for work. We have half an hour till we have to leave so we need to be quick."

Annalise thought that she better get on herself otherwise she would be late, and she didn't want to give a bad impression on her first day. She had the perfect outfit ready to go. It was smart and sophisticated and perfect for her first day. She had treated herself to it when they first arrived in London, a week ago.

She thought back to when they first arrived and had collected the keys from the estate agents to their new house. It didn't take her long to choose the house on Rightmove. She had organised one weekend to come down and see it on her own while a family member looked after Penelope. As soon as she had entered the front door she knew that it would be their new home.

It had the most amazing wooden floorboards throughout the house, with large Georgian windows that brought so much natural light in giving her a warm feeling. A feeling that didn't happen much anymore. The kitchen was open plan into the dining area and had a cute little breakfast bar where she could see Penelope and herself sitting and eating breakfast together each morning. It had a quaint little garden with enough grass where Penelope could play outside.

Once she had finished the viewing, she had gone straight back to the agency to sign the contract and arranged to move in a week later. Now they were all moved in, and she was starting her new job. It was crazy how quickly it had all happened. As she thought about the life that she left behind, anxiety-filled her body. She reached into her bedside cabinet, pulling out a bottle of pills. And popped one in her mouth. She hated that she relied on a pill to help her get through the day. But, if it meant that she was stable and happy for Penelope. That's what she needed to do.

Annalise caught a glimpse at the clock and panic hit her. She needed to stop thinking and start moving. How was she going to get ready in 5 minutes!

As Annalise looked in the mirror, she almost didn't recognise herself. It had been a long time since she had tried with her appearance. She had straightened her hair, and it now lay soft and sleek over her shoulders and down her back. She had curves she had forgotten about and her dress clung to them in all the right places. She hoped it wasn't too much for work, but deep down she didn't care. For once she felt good about herself and nothing was going to change that for her today. She slid her black heels on, grabbed her jacket and handbag and walked out of the bedroom feeling confident about the day ahead.

"Penelope, are you ready yet? We have to leave otherwise we will be late, and we don't want that today!"

Penelope was sitting on the sofa dressed in her school uniform, waiting to go with a huge smile on her face. Annalise looked at her little girl and wondered how she could be so brave when she was scared herself. Penelope always looked at the bright side of life; she wasn't scared of anything and this helped Annalise get through in life. Penelope was her sunshine and that's all she had to remember.

"Right missy, time to go, let's go see what the world has in store for us today."

Monday, 8 June
Hunter

Hunter's day started off the same each day. He would wake up at 5:00 a.m., head straight to training with Tyrell. Shower, breakfast and then head to the office. It was his daily routine that he had been doing for as long as he could remember. It's what he needed to do every day to make sure he was focussed.

It had kept him sane for this long, and he wasn't going to change anything now. He ran a successful business with over 5,000 employees who relied on him every day to make sure they had a job. It was a lot of pressure. He knew he had it in him to keep growing the company; he had been doing it for the past 10 years. It had been hard work at the start and a constant battle, but this was his life, and he was not going to let anything or anyone get in the way of it. He had come too far to let that happen.

He thought back to when he had left home. He was 18 and couldn't get out of there fast enough. He hated his parents. He hated his house. He hated everything about the life that he had grown up with. All he wanted was to make sure that he would never feel like that ever again.

For him to achieve this he would; WORK. TRAIN. EAT. SLEEP. AND REPEAT. That was his life, and he liked it. He could be happy that way. He knew he could. It had worked so far. He didn't need anyone else involved in his life that was going to complicate things. Especially a woman.

He saw the kind of relationship his mum and dad had, and he couldn't think of anything worse. He remembered the arguing, the objects being thrown at each other, the resentment in their eyes every time they looked at him. He knew he had been a mistake from the start and that he had ruined their lives. He knew it, and they knew it.

"Harder! Come on Hunter where's your head at today? Stop thinking about work, hit the pads! That's it get that aggression out! Jab, cross, hook, uppercut, repeat but faster this time."

Hunter loved his boxing sessions with Tyrell, it always gave him pure satisfaction. Along with clearing his head for the day, and keeping his body in great shape. He had been training with Tyrell ever since he had left home. Hunter had so much anger in him when he first started, and Tyrell had taught him how to control it over the years. He had become much calmer and had managed to resolve his temper by channelling it to either work or training.

He owed Tyrell so much. He didn't know where he may have ended up if he had never started boxing. He remembered all the times where he would get into fights at school. He never cared about getting into trouble if it meant that his parents would acknowledge him. Hunter knew that it would just disappoint them more, but at least it reminded them that he was still alive. That's all he wanted.

"Sorry, Tyrell, I've got so much on at work at the moment. New contracts to sign, deals holding on by a thread and my personal assistant left me in the lurch by deciding to have a baby. I have a new person starting today, but there was no handover. No doubt she will be asking me questions non-stop all day." He threw a punch toward Tyrell but missed him.

"Hunter. Calm down! You say this to me every day. This is your life. You love it! And well, your new PA, I'm sure will be fine. You stress over the smallest things. Has she worked for a big company before?"

Tyrell kept hitting punches at him while Hunter was trying to concentrate and move at the same time.

"I'm not sure of her story. Charlotte organised it all with the agency, and I trust her decision. As long as she does a good job then there will be no problem."

Hunter was moving, but Tyrell was just too quick and kept catching him by the tip of his glove.

"Well, Charlotte did always have good taste!" Tyrell smirked at Hunter knowing that his comment would hit a nerve.

"Tyrell if you ever try and hit on one of my staff members again, you will only last one round in this ring!" Hunter's frustration grew, and he powered his energy again at Tyrell. This time clipping him on the jaw.

"Ooh, good one! Anyway, I never heard Charlotte complaining! OK, well maybe her fiancé didn't like it. You need to start having a life Hunter before it gets away from you. It's all good having a successful business but try flirting with some of those gorgeous women who throw themselves at you daily, you might even like it."

"No. You know the sort of parents I had. All I think about when I look at women and relationships is how hard they are and not worth the time or effort. I am happy with the way things are going. Work is enough for me. Well, training as well, I definitely need that in my life."

Hunter hated referencing his parents, but Tyrell knew some of the stories when it came to them.

"Fair enough, but one day it might not be enough and what will you do then?"

"Tyrell, enough! I don't want to talk about women, relationships or how I may feel in the future. All that matters now are my future plans for the business. Now let's finish up, I have to go and run a successful business, and well, you have to look after this place." He teased Tyrell, knowing deep down that this place was just as successful as Hunter's business. On a more personal level.

"Hey, man, this place saved you! Remember that before you start belittling it!" Tyrell clocked Hunter in the ribs, making Hunter let out a grunt of pain.

"I know, sorry! I owe you my life. Come on I need to clear this head of mine. Let's do another round."

As Hunter drove down into the car park of the building, he always got a buzz as he drove into his parking space seeing his company name 'Hunter recruitment' on the sign. He had built his company up from nothing. Having over 5,000 employees working for him now, across 33 offices in 15 different countries. It was a life he had always dreamed of. And now he was living it.

It was a new day, more business to be done and Hunter couldn't think of anything better to be doing. No matter how stressful work became; he couldn't get enough of it. This was his life. He could control this, and it made him happy. He loved the fast-paced and competitiveness of recruitment. He enjoyed the hunt.

Negotiating with companies on their recruitment needs, setting up retainers and gaining PSA's for future business, everyone he employed had to have the same passion as he did, it was key to maintain a strong name in the industry and to keep the business thriving. He was currently one of the top 4 recruitment companies globally, and he wanted to become number one. It may take time and sacrifice, but he didn't care. This filled the void that he had felt for so long now. It made the pain become numb. Bearable.

As Hunter entered the building to his office, he was greeted by the concierge Mike. He gave him a broad smile and polite nod while opening the security gate for him. Mike was always so happy and Hunter wondered what put a smile on his face every day. A family? Career? It always amazed Hunter to find out what drives people.

"Morning, Mr Maguire."

"Morning, Mike." Hunter was heading for the gate when Mike continued talking, which made him stop and walk towards him.

"Your new member of staff is already here. I have given her a security pass and told her to wait at reception for you."

"Thanks, Mike. How long ago was this?"

"She has been here for about 20 minutes, Mr Maguire." Hunter wondered why she was here so early. He thought that Charlotte may have told her to come in once he had arrived. Now he wondered what she had been doing for the past 20 minutes.

"Thanks, Mike." He proceeded to the elevators, pressed level 50.

Monday, 8 June
Annalise

As Annalise pulled up to Penelope's school she could see how much Penelope was bursting with happiness. Eager to see what her new school had in store for her. The headmaster was polite and welcoming, confirming he would take Penelope to her first class and introduce her to all her classmates. Annalise was nervous to leave her, unsure whether it was down to Penelope or it may just be her nerves from starting a new job. She pushed that feeling to one side, and embraced Penelope into a huge hug, kissing her on the top of her head.

"Good luck today sweetheart and remember just be yourself and everyone will love you."

"I know Mummy. I can't wait to meet everyone. Will you pick me up from school as well?" Penelope smiled at her sweetly, while looking around at the other children. She could see the excitement in her eyes.

"Of course, Penelope. I'll come straight from work. Enjoy your day."

Penelope ran into the school with the headmaster slowly trailing behind her. Annalise was so proud of Penelope; she had so much courage and nothing seemed to faze her. She thought back to their life before and how she had put Penelope through so many difficult moments, but Penelope surprised her every time. She always seemed to see the positive in everything and Annalise wondered how she had such a great child considering how her life was so messed up. But that was all about to change. She hoped. Annalise started the car and headed towards the city, hoping she wasn't going to get stuck in traffic and be late on her first day.

As she pulled up to her parking space in the underground car park, she checked her face in the rear-view mirror making sure she still looked fresh-faced. She stepped out of the car, straightened her dress and set off towards the main entrance. She was so thankful she had managed to negotiate a parking space with the job. It hadn't been easy, as the previous personal assistant didn't get one.

But because they were desperate and short-staffed, she thought that may have been why they had agreed to it. Hopefully, her new boss liked people who negotiated and didn't just settle. He was in recruitment after all. She didn't know what she would have done if she had to get public transport into work, it would have been a nightmare with dropping and picking Penelope up from school. She must remember to thank him again for adding that into her contract. She would mention it the second she was settled.

Annalise headed for the lift to the main entrance. As she walked across and approached the concierge desk, she was greeted by a pleasant man. He was fairly handsome she thought to herself. Taking the sight of him in, he was tall and lean with soft blonde hair that was cut short. He was wearing a fitted black suit and was smiling at her as she approached him.

"Good morning, Madame, How can I help you today?" he greeted her with a handshake.

"Hi, my name is Annalise Smith. I am due to start work today for Mr Maguire at Hunter recruitment. Would you mind telling me which floor I need to go to?" He smiled knowing all too well who she was referencing.

"Ah yes, I have your name on the list. I will just set you up with a security pass and then you will be able to go straight up to the reception area. Mr Maguire hasn't arrived yet, but I'm sure the girls upstairs will be able to look after you until he does."

"OK, great, which floor do I need to go to?"

"Level 50. Just swipe your pass in the elevator and press level 50, once you get to the floor the reception desk is just straight in front of you. Candice will be there to meet you." He passed her the pass and asked her to always have it on her for security reasons.

"Thank you. Have a good day."

"You too, Mrs Smith."

Annalise thought about correcting him, that it was in fact Miss and not Mrs but decided it didn't matter either way. It was no concern to her, and they would only ever know each other on a professional level, so it didn't matter. As she proceeded to the elevators, she noticed the lobby of the building was starting to fill up with gorgeous well-dressed individuals. Something she wasn't used to.

She was from a small city. It didn't even come close to the size of London nor the companies that did business here. She liked the idea of being a small fish in a big pond. No one knew who she was or where she had come from. No judgement when she entered a store. Or walked down a street. She now lived in a world where she was just a stranger, like everybody else. She could get on with her life with Penelope and try and be happy.

The elevator pinged when she arrived on level 50, the doors opened, and she stepped out onto the carpet leading to the reception desk. The reception area was light and airy, with large floor to ceiling windows. As she looked to her right, she saw the most magnificent view of the Themes. They hadn't visited many places in London yet, but Annalise made a note to take Penelope there at some point. There was artwork on the wall that complemented the décor of the room.

Black leather chairs and glass coffee tables on either side with beautiful bright coloured flowers. Glass doors leading off the area to meeting rooms and Annalise wondered where her office would be. A very attractive woman with long blonde hair, dazzling blue eyes and lavish eyelashes was smiling at her as she approached the reception desk. Annalise made a note that everyone that she had met so far was very attractive and extremely presentable. She hoped she was going to fit in.

Annalise knew she was pretty but in a non-descript kind of way. She had always been the sweet quant girl growing up. The girl next door so to speak. She never really dressed up and mainly just wore jeans and a T-shirt if at home or out with Penelope. She didn't have anyone to dress up for she thought, so there wasn't much point. But today she had made an effort, and she was glad that she had with everyone looking the way they did. She just hoped that her attire was enough to give a good first impression.

"Good morning, do you have an appointment with one of our consultants today?"

The receptionist had a posh London accent; however, her tone was friendly and polite. Her name tag read Candice and Annalise thought what a lovely name it was.

"Hi, yes, I mean, no. I'm actually starting work here today, I am Mr Maguire's new personal assistant." Candice's reaction instantly changed. A warm sense of familiarity crossed over her face, and she walked round to greet Annalise properly.

"Ah yes, Annalise is it?"

"Yes. That's correct. Mike the concierge informed me that Mr Maguire wasn't in yet, I think I may be slightly early." She looked at Candice with an apologetic smile.

"Always better to be early than late! My name is Candice, I'm one of the receptionists here at Hunter recruitment. Yes, that is correct, Hunter. I mean Mr Maguire is on his way in; he just had to pick some contracts up first so he shouldn't be too long."

Annalise focussed on the part where Candice had slipped up and said his first name, Hunter. She had never heard it before and thought it was such a strong name. Very powerful. No wonder he was a successful businessman with a name like that.

She wondered if all of his employers called him by his first name or was that just Candice? Did they have a thing happening between them both? Annalise brushed the thought out of her head. It was an inappropriate thought, and it was none of her business either way. She didn't need to be getting into the office gossip, let alone start making rumours up. That's the last thing she needed. She was here to do a job. That was it.

"Annalise. Do you mind me calling you by your first name? all of us around here are on first term names. We work together after all. We are like family. You will soon get to know that. I'll show you to your office so you can start settling in. Then later Jo from human resources will come and find you so she can go through your orientation and work health safety. Now, Mr Maguire has been extremely busy recently, Charlotte has left you some handover notes that I know you will want to go through. But if you have any questions then please come and see me, rather than bothering him today."

Annalise was a little confused. She did work for Mr Maguire after all. Why wasn't she allowed to ask him questions? Surely, that's how they would build up a professional relationship. Get to know how each other works. They always did say that PA's are the work wife of their boss.

"OK, I'll make sure to do that. Candice, what is Mr Maguire like to work for?"

Annalise had been told by the agency how he had built the business up from the ground, that it was now one of the top 4 recruitment companies worldwide, that he was a charming but a hard-working individual who didn't take any crap from anyone. She wondered if he had a soft side and if they would form a good working relationship together. It was a great opportunity for her to work for such a global company, it would do wonders for her resume. Candice looked at her for a moment, something changed in her eyes that Annalise didn't recognise; she thought it looked like lust, but it was probably in her mind and soon they were back to normal when she started talking again.

"Mr Maguire is a very professional man; he expects his employees to work hard, and in return, he will reward them if the business does well. He is a private man, so don't go asking him any personal questions. Purely professional, OK?"

It hadn't really been the answer that Annalise was looking for, but it was still an answer. It gave her a bit more of an insight into the man that she would be working for. Candice showed her to her office, then where to find the toilet and kitchen area for lunch breaks. Every part of the office was kept immaculate and to a very high standard.

As she walked around, she noticed a few people looking at her, wondering who she must be. Was she their next competition? She laughed to herself, knowing full well she would never be any good at sales. She just didn't have it in her DNA.

Annalise went back to her desk after being shown around. She removed a picture of Penelope from her bag and arranged it next to her computer. She then turned the computer on, hung up her coat and decided that she would go and get a coffee before Mr Maguire arrived. That way she would be here to meet him when he came in. After all, she didn't want him to think that she was slacking on her first day.

Then she would come back and start going through the notes Charlotte had left for her, then go through Mr Maguire's daily calendar and confirm all his appointments and check if there were any meetings that she needed to attend to take down minutes. Annalise enjoyed organisation, that's why she became a personal assistant along with other reasons. It wasn't her intention to always do this job. She had higher hopes for herself, but life didn't work out that way.

Annalise never looked at it as a negative. She had gained Penelope and that was the most important thing for her, no job position could come close to how Penelope had changed her life. She was still happy with her career outcome, and she was hoping that working for a large global company such as Hunter recruitment would keep her going in the right direction. She would keep her head down, work hard and show everyone she could be a mother and a successful business woman, and it all started today, right now.

Annalise noticed out the corner of her eye that someone was walking towards her getting closer by the second and wondering who it might be. Could it be Mr Maguire? She had never even seen a picture of him before so wouldn't even know if she had walked past him already. She couldn't stop herself from looking straight at this man. He walked with meaning and power.

Gradually getting closer to her by the second. He was medium built, tall, strong with broad shoulders that were defined by muscles. It made her think that he must work out a lot to maintain a physique like that. She knew she was staring right at him, but she couldn't stop herself; he was mesmerising. Annalise felt a strange feeling deep inside her, something she hadn't felt before, and she couldn't quite work out what it was.

The feeling was soon pushed to one side when the man who had been walking down the hallway towards her, was now standing in front of her and looked as if he had been asking her a question. She didn't actually know what he was saying as she hadn't been paying attention to anything other than his body. She really needed to stop starring at him. When she lifted her head to look at his face she focussed on his lips to try and see what he was saying, but she was distracted again by how soft they looked.

She thought that they were definitely kissing lips and wondered how it would feel to kiss them. She managed to draw her eyes away from his lips and focus on his other features. His face. His jaw was defined and strong; he was clean-shaven that only accentuated his jawline, and his nose was a perfect feature to compliment the rest of his face. But what really stood out were his eyes. They were dark and mysterious and sparkled from the sunlight that was coming through the large glass windows.

As she looked at them closer there was something else, something much deeper to them, she wasn't sure what it was. Was it pain? Was it hurt? Annalise couldn't quite put her finger on it, but she knew that there was much more to this man who stood in front of her, and she wanted to find out more. As she was trying to figure them out, she was soon brought back to reality by the man waving his hand in front of her face. It was obvious by the look on his face that he wasn't impressed, and Annalise instantly became embarrassed and flustered.

"I am so sorry, I was miles away. I didn't mean to be rude, let me introduce myself, my name is Annalise Smith, and I am your new personal assistant. That is of course if you are Mr Maguire? If not, then I have just embarrassed myself."

Annalise knew that she was rambling but couldn't stop herself. She was nervous; he made her nervous, and they hadn't even had a conversation yet. It was the stern look that he gave her as she had just been told off at school. Well, this hadn't gone to plan, this wasn't the first impression she wanted to give herself, and she needed to start talking and try and bring the conversation back in her favour.

Monday, 8 June
Hunter

As Hunter walked down the hallway towards his office, he could see his new employee sitting at her desk. Candice had already informed him she had arrived and that she had been shown around the offices but had then left her to go over Charlotte's hand over notes. As he got closer to her, he noticed she was staring at him. No expression on her face other than a spark in her eyes. Like she was thinking about something that exhilarated her. He couldn't help but stare back.

Slowly noticing each and every one of her facial features, which gave him a feeling inside that he had never felt before. He noticed how her lips were round and soft with a slight pinkish tone to them, as though she had been chewing on them while deep in thought. Her cheeks were flushed that complimented her skin tone, and he wondered if his presence may have had something to do with that. Her nose was a petite button shape, which was perfectly in line with her other features and then there were her eyes.

He couldn't stop looking at them. They were dark brown with a slight glint of gold, and they were mesmerising to him. Eyes that he could imagine in the bedroom looking at him with nothing but desire and lust. He tried to shake the feeling. This was one of his employees, and he never had thoughts about employees like this, especially as he hadn't even met the women yet. This was inappropriate and his thoughts had to stop immediately. It was out of character for him. He had no idea what had just happened.

As he got closer to her she was still just sitting there starring at him and he wondered what she was thinking, he needed to break this situation and start off in a professional manner. He was her boss after all.

"I take it you must be my new personal assistant that the agency has arranged? I see that you have Charlottes handover notes, I'm sure that they will give you all the information that you need. Charlotte was very professional and knew exactly how I liked things done. I know that you are new to the company and working with me, but I am sure that you will pick it up quickly."

Hunter knew he his words may come across as more of an order than a welcoming tone. He was waiting for her to answer him, but she was just staring at him. Was she nervous, did he intimidate her? He had been told he had that effect on people. It was probably just her nerves, he thought. After all, her resume said she had only worked for smaller companies in Norfolk, nothing compared to London and Hunter recruitment. He was becoming more impatient as time went on.

Hunter stood there looking back at her waiting for her to answer him, but still nothing! Seriously what was wrong with this woman! What kind of person had the agency sent to him. This was all he needed, someone who was a stargazer and didn't have a lot going on in that head of hers. His impatience turned to anger, and he was about to tell her that maybe this wasn't the right company for her, when she finally spoke.

Hunter knew that whatever she had been thinking had made her flustered and embarrassed and now she was just mumbling. She had kept going until he had stopped her from continuing and confirmed who he was by a nod.

"Oh, thank god. I thought I was about to embarrass myself even more! Apologies again for staring at you, I sometimes do that when I am thinking about 101 things." She looked at him sheepishly. And he knew she was embarrassed by her foolish manner towards him.

"Not a problem. Just make sure that it doesn't happen again when you are at work. I need you to be focussed and on top of everything. Hunter recruitment is a fast-paced company, and I expect things to be done quickly and efficiently." He knew he was being demanding He needed to set the tone from the start. She needed to know her place in this company.

"Of course, Mr Maguire, I understand completely. You can rely on me. I am here to work hard and do an exceptional job for you." Her smile was broad yet innocent.

"Well, that's settled then. I will give you some time to go over Charlottes notes. You then have an orientation and work health and safety talk with human resources this morning. Once that is all done we will sit down together and go over how I like my day to be scheduled. I only expect to go over this with you once so make sure to take lots of notes, I'm not someone who likes to be interrupted a lot." He winced at his tone. Why was he trying so hard? He would scare the women away before they had even started.

"Of course, that sounds perfectly good with me." Her demeanour remained the same. His words seemed not to affect her.

"I have some urgent calls to make so please do not disturb me unless it's really urgent. You can always ask Candice if you need to know where anything is in the offices. And Mrs Smith, call me Hunter, everyone else does around here." His tone was now light. He was humouring her.

"Of course, Mr Maguire, I mean Hunter! And the same goes for you, call me Annalise. And It's Miss, not Mrs." Her eyes were glowing with a glint of mystery.

Hunter was intrigued, why had he thought that she was married; he had just presumed she was.

"Very well, Annalise, nice to meet you and welcome to Hunter recruitment."

And with that, he walked into his office and shut the door leaving Annalise starring after him.

As he sat down on the chair at his desk, he had a strange feeling he was unsure of. What had he felt out there with Annalise? It was a feeling that made him uneasy, and he didn't like it. Especially when it came to women and even more so when it came to women who worked for him.

She was pretty that was undeniable. But she looked tired. Like the whole world was on her shoulders. He wondered what had happened to her. It was obvious she hadn't slept well by the dark circles under her eyes. Maybe it was the move from Norfolk to London. Moving always was stressful and starting a job could put a lot of pressure on an individual. He would put it down to that.

As he sat at his desk, he thought back to how Annalise had been deep in thought when he approached her earlier and wondered if that's what she was really thinking about. He also remembered noticing that body of hers. She had a petite frame, but she was very lean, curvy and strong like she exercised frequently. He noticed that her breasts were perfectly sized, and it complimented her physique.

Her dress clung in all the right places showing off her curves, and he definitely liked that. Her hair was dark brown, straight and came just below her shoulders; she couldn't have been any more than 27/28 years of age and youth was definitely still on her side. He had noticed a small photograph of a girl on her desk and wondered who it could have been. Was it her daughter, her niece, a godchild? The girl did resemble her quite a bit, having the same dark hair and dark brown eyes.

But surely Annalise was too young to have a daughter of that age. He wondered if there was a father on the scene. Annalise had corrected him that she was Miss and not Mrs, which made him think that there wasn't. But nowadays a title didn't really mean much to people whether they were married or not. Hunter wondered why he wanted to know the answer to these questions, these things wouldn't normally bother him, so why did it with Annalise.

His thought was broken by the ringing of his mobile phone, and he felt relieved; he didn't want to start having thoughts like this and especially not today. Today he needed to focus on finalising deals. 'Maguire'. His tone was short and sharp.

"Hunter, how are you?"

It was Dave the Manager Director for the Australasia division of Hunter recruitment.

"Good thanks, Dave. How's the day been for you? We are just starting here." He eased back into his chair and felt himself relax.

"Good. Very well in fact. That's what I wanted to talk to you about, we have a large global investment bank that wants to do business with us. Solely!"

"That's excellent news, Dave. Well done! You guys must be working extremely hard over there to win business like that."

"Yes, we are! I have a good solid team. There is one deal though…. they want to meet you first before they sign anything. It's just how they do business. They like to know who the man is behind it all, the one who built it from the ground up."

Hunter thought about how much business this could potentially bring in for them, not just in Australasia but globally. This could be huge. He hadn't planned on doing any trips overseas until after the summer, as they had so much going on in the London office at the moment. But this would have to be an exception. He couldn't turn this down.

"Dave, when do they want to meet?" he waited in anticipation hoping that the timeframe would work with his current schedule.

"In a months' time—10 July, they have the MD of Australasia in town, and he is the one who wants to meet with you." Wow. That was soon—He thought.

"Talk about short notice! I hadn't planned on any business trips until after summertime, but I'll have to make this work. Schedule it in Dave and I'll get my

PA to book flights and accommodation. How long do you reckon you will need me there?"

"Probably a few days. It will give you time to have a few meetings with them, attend some dinners and then you can come and check out the Sydney office again. Finally, have a beer with me!"

"Sounds good, I'll get everything sorted. Sorry, Dave, I have to go. I have a few deals to confirm with Hong Kong before the offices close, so keep me posted with everything and I'll see you in July."

"See you then, Hunter."

Hunter finished up his phone call with Dave and hit his intercom to speak with Annalise about arranging all the details for his trip.

"Annalise, I have to go to Sydney, Australia on the 10 July for an important meeting. Can you please book my flights and accommodation? I prefer to fly with Emirates and make sure it's Business class. Oh, and try and get me a suite at the Intercontinental hotel, that's pretty central to where the offices are."

He could hear Annalise typing on her keyboard vigorously, trying to keep up with his demands.

"Of course, Hunter. How long will you be needing to stay there? Charlotte left me a list of the travel companies she used to book all your flights and accommodation, so I will get that all booked for you immediately."

"Four days. Thank you, Annalise. Just email me all the details and add it to my calendar when it's all done."

"No worries, Hunter. Leave it with me."

The morning had gone far too quickly, but Hunter had managed to speak with the Hong Kong office and confirm the deals he needed to which was a success. He still had a lot to do though and time was getting ahead of him. There was a knock on the door that interrupted his train of thought. He thought that he had made himself clear to Annalise that he wasn't to be disturbed until he told her so.

Pushing his frustration aside and giving her a bit of leeway as it was her first day; he walked over to the door and opened it. He had forgotten how pretty she was in the short period of time that he hadn't seen her. She was standing there smiling at him; however, the smile soon faded when she must have noticed the expression on his face. She started apologising profusely for interrupting him.

"Sorry, Hunter. I just wanted to let you know that everything is booked and confirmed for your Australia trip. Oh, and I thought that as you had been in here all morning that you must be thirsty, so I have also brought you a cup of coffee."

Hunter was a bit taken back by her gesture. Charlotte never brought him anything. Mainly because he had told her never to disturb him. Plus she knew how he liked to work. He had to make the same rules for Annalise, and make sure she abided by them. He didn't like to be disturbed while working.

"Thank you, Annalise. However, in future when I tell you not to disturb me please listen. I don't want to have to keep reminding you. And you could have just emailed me the confirmation to the flights and accommodation." He tried to hide his frustration and knew that his tone had scolded her. Which was not his intention. She seemed quite sensitive. Something that Hunter wasn't used to.

"Of course, Hunter. I am truly sorry; it won't happen again. But…. I'm sure once you taste my coffee you may have a different opinion."

He ignored her comment. Almost not wanting to engage her with his answer. He should make some kind of effort to settle her in. After all, it was her first day, and he should make her feel welcome with being the CEO.

"How did orientation go? Was it Sharon or Jo who took you through it all?"

"Jo and it went well. Fairly straightforward, once you have done one orientation, they all seem the same." She seemed pleased.

"That's good, glad it went OK. What do you have planned now?"

"I was just going to see what meetings you have in this week and if I was needed to take any minutes. I also have some invoicing to send over to the accounts department."

"OK, well, leave the diary for now. We can go through that together after lunch. Have you been shown where the main break out area is?"

"Yes, thank you."

"Well, if you fancy eating out for lunch there is a nice little café around the corner that does salads, sandwiches and soup. It's very popular, and I think most of the staff wages get spent there."

"I've brought food in today but may venture out for some fresh air as it's such a nice day. What about you, do you eat lunch? I can grab you something on my way back."

"Of course, I eat lunch, Annalise."

Hunter didn't mean to snap, but he was in unknown territory for him. Yes, he spoke to women every day. Engaged with them, took them out for dinner that would generally end with sex. But that was it. That was the end of it. But with Annalise, he felt something different that made him want to know more about her. This needed to stop he thought; he was just having an off day. Tyrell had put stupid thoughts into his head this morning, that's all it was. He needed to end the conversation before it carried on. He had way too much work to do, to stand here making small talk. There was nothing more to it. That was all.

"Now, if there isn't anything else Annalise. I must be getting on."

"Of course, let me know when you are ready to sit down together."

"I will."

Annalise stepped out of the office and Hunter was then left on his own, revelling in what just happened. He was going to give it to Tyrell the next time he saw him, tell him to stop with all the personal chat.

As he slowly turned his focus back to work, he was excited about the deals they had already done this morning. He had a few more follow up calls and emails to sort and then he would sit down with Annalise. Get her up to speed with how he liked his diary dealt with, then he didn't need to spend any more unnecessary time with her.

Monday, 8 June
Annalise

Annalise stepped out of Hunter's office feeling embarrassed. He had clearly told her earlier not to disturb him, but she had anyway. She just thought he may like a cup of coffee, especially as he had been locked away in his office for the past few hours. He did seem grateful in the end but maybe he did that only to be polite. No! Annalise had heard that Hunter Maguire never did things out of politeness.

If he didn't want something then he would say, so it must have meant that she did do something good, although maybe at the wrong time. As Annalise sat back down at her desk, she remembered seeing something in Hunter's eyes just before she was about to leave. He had stopped her and asked her some questions, although they were short and work-related, she couldn't help but think that he hadn't wanted her to leave. Why was that? Was he lonely? Maybe he was just sussing out what type of person he had just employed. Yes, that was it—she thought.

She couldn't quite figure him out yet, but then again it had only been one morning. She hoped that they would even build up a good working relationship. Annalise liked the thought of that. She had never really had many work colleagues in her previous role. She had worked for her auntie's plumbing company as their secretary and personal assistant.

Although that was a loose term for it. She was the only administrator for the whole company, which consisted of 20 people, and she dealt with everything from ordering the stationery to cleaning the toilets. Everyone had to help out, it was a family run business, and she took pride in her work no matter how big or small the job was. So, when it came to applying for the personal assistant role at Hunter recruitment, she knew that telling a few white lies wouldn't get her into trouble. After all, she had been a PA but maybe not in the capacity that they wanted someone to have worked in.

It seemed like they were in a difficult situation anyway and in a rush to find someone. So Annalise was pleased when the agency called her back to tell her that she had got the position on a contract basis for 3 months and that they would consider extending it if she did a good job. Annalise knew she would have to work hard but was more than capable. She had dealt with accounts, booking travel—even if it was to Europe, arranging and sitting in on meetings.

She knew how to run an office like the back of her hand, but then again Hunter recruitment wasn't anything like any other office. She was now reporting and working for Hunter Maguire, one of the most successful businessmen in London. That would take all her energy to show him and everyone else that they had chosen the right person for the role. She would show her family that she could make something of herself, and they would be proud of her again just like they once were.

Annalise had completed all her morning tasks and decided it was a good time to take a lunch break. It was such a nice day outside so she decided to take her homemade salad and go and sit in a park, soak up some sunshine and watch the world go by. She loved the summertime. How the air smelt different from the new flowers that were starting to bud, the birds tweeting around her. But most of all she loved how people changed.

They seemed happier like there was a purpose in life, and they could do anything. It's crazy how a bit of sunshine and the warmer weather on the skin can make everyone feel so different, it definitely did for her. She actually felt a pang of happiness, something she hadn't felt for a long time. It felt like she had made the right decision to move to London.

Penelope had been excited to go to school this morning and Annalise's day had gone pretty well so far, apart from embarrassing herself twice in front of her new boss already. Annalise thought about Penelope and hoped that she was getting on OK, she couldn't wait to pick her up and hear all about her day. She knew Penelope would do nothing but talk about it all the way home and then over dinner and probably until she went to sleep, but Annalise didn't care as long as she was happy, that's all that mattered to her. That's why she made the move to London, for Penelope.

She wanted to give her a better life, a life where she could be around people who cared for them both and wanted the best for them. That certainly wasn't the case back in Norfolk. When she had told her family that she had been accepted for a job in London and that they would be moving in less than a month, all her aunty did was moan about how she was leaving them in the lurch and that she had better help find them before she went. Otherwise, she would never forgive her especially after everything that she had done for her.

That was a lot more than what her parents had said to her. They had just replied with how busy they were and how they wouldn't have time to come and visit as it was too far for them on the train. Plus, they wouldn't drive as the traffic was terrible in London. Annalise had become accustomed to her parents' attitude towards her and Penelope, so didn't feel upset with their reply to her. She just simply changed the subject back to the garden, which was now her mum's pride and joy and all that she could talk about. At least her mum was talking to her, even if it was about the garden.

It was now 1:30 p.m. and Annalise thought she better start heading back to the office before Hunter started looking for her. She didn't want to give him another reason to be disappointed in her. As she arrived back at her desk, Annalise noticed that the door to his office was closed. She was thankful and relieved that he wasn't waiting for her but decided she would send him an email just to let him know that she was back from lunch and ready to go over the diary whenever he was.

While she waited for his reply, she decided to carry on looking over Charlotte's handover notes and highlight any areas that needed confirming with Hunter. That way, she could ask him later about them. As she was reading through the notes deep in thought, she didn't notice that Hunter had stepped out of his office and was now standing in front of her. When she looked up again, Annalise was surprised that he was staring at her with a look in his eyes that she hadn't seen before.

As she looked back at him, there was nothing but silence around them. Everything had become still, and time had stopped. Their eyes were communicating in their own language. She noticed that his breathing had slowed, and he had a light bead of sweat around his forehead. His face was slightly flushed and his gaze was intense.

Before she could work out what was happening between them. Something changed in him. A look of horror appeared on his face. His eyes became ice-cold. The moment was over.

Annalise didn't know quite what to do. How could the atmosphere change within a couple of seconds, from something so intimate to now feeling like she was standing in the middle of Hyde park alone and naked! She could tell Hunter didn't know what to do either. There was panic still in his eyes. She knew she had to be the one to get them out of this situation, by talking first.

"Sorry, I didn't see you come out of your office; I was just going over Charlotte's notes again."

She knew her voice had come out as a whisper. Her breathing was raspy and her heartbeat was slowly returning to normal. She was worried her voice wouldn't work altogether. He looked at her and was slowly realising that she had opened her mouth and words were coming out, yet he still looked like he wasn't present but managed to put an answer together.

"Sorry. I did call your name, but you seemed so focussed on what you were doing. I have some time now to go over my diary and the week ahead with you if you are ready?"

Annalise knew that whatever they had just shared was gone, Hunter was back to being her boss and focussed on work. In a way, she was relieved; she didn't know what she had been feeling or what had just happened, but work seemed like a better option for them both.

"OK, so I have mapped out your dairy for the week, month and year, I have colour coded them into different appointments/meetings. Blue is for client meetings, red for in house employee meetings, yellow for business trips, orange for personal and green for lunch. You did say that you ate lunch didn't you?"

Annalise knew that she was testing the waters, but she needed to keep things light. She decided to take a quick look at him and saw a slight glimmer of humour in his eyes, which made her relax again.

"Yes, Annalise, I eat lunch. But I don't always have time to take lunch breaks so you can just remove that from my diary and I'll just eat when I can."

"Of course, as long as you do. Food is important to fuel the body and the brain and will help you concentrate with work." He seemed to become frustrated.

"I don't need a lecture, Annalise, I know when I need to eat. I have been looking after myself for this long, and I haven't failed to die of starvation yet. I think I'm doing just fine."

"I'm sorry if I've overstepped the mark. I forget sometimes that I'm not talking to my daughter and I'm talking to another adult who can take care of themselves. I spend so much time just myself and her, that I forget what it's like to talk to an adult."

Annalise knew that she had already said too much. Why did she have to tell him that she didn't have any friends or social life? She knew that his life was so far from hers. She imagined him wining and dining clients, shopping in the most expensive shops, travelling overseas, staying in luxury villas and going out on dates with gorgeous women. She didn't know the last time that she even went on a date, let alone had sex.

Her life had been so busy with bringing up Penelope and working just to support them both, that she didn't have the time or money to socialise. She had forgotten what it was like to get dressed up and have a night out. Her nights out now mainly consisted of going to the supermarket with Penelope to decide what they were having for dinner that night. But that was going to change now they had moved to London.

She wanted to have more social life; she needed to for her own sanity. Maybe she could get to know some of the mums at Penelope's new school or even strike up some friendships with her work colleagues. Both Candice and Jo seemed nice and around her age. She would leave it a few days so she could settle in and then try and get to know them a bit better.

Annalise focussed back on Hunter, hoping that she wasn't deep in thought for too long and that he hadn't noticed. When she glanced at him she was relieved to see he was engrossed in the diary and moving some dates and times around. He was so close to her she could smell his aftershave; he smelt so good she felt herself breathe in deeply closing her eyes at the same time, taking him all in.

"OK, so apart from the lunch periods that I have now removed, everything else seems fine. For most of my meetings, I tend to go alone. If I need you in there with me to take notes then I will let you know beforehand. We have monthly board meetings, which you will need to attend. Take notes and then send them to all of the directors.

"Other than that, I will need you to work on proposals for me, handle my diary, take all incoming calls, schedule in house meetings, arrange company events that you can ask the receptionists to help you with. Actually, we have a company event happening on Friday, 19 June, it should all be sorted but can you just follow up with Candice to make sure. It's just to thank everyone for their hard work over the last few months. You should attend, it will be a good opportunity for you to meet everyone."

Annalise thought how amazing it would be to have a night out, get dressed up, put makeup on, mingle with people her actual age and have a few champagnes. But who would she get to look after Penelope? She didn't know anyone in London.

"I'm really sorry, but I think I have something already on that night. I would have loved to come, it sounds like it's going to be a really good night. Hopefully, I can make the next one."

She wasn't even sure when the next one would be or if she would still be working for the company. It was a real shame and Annalise felt a pang of sadness. She wanted so badly to have a social life again and be able to attend fun things like the company party, but how could she when she didn't have anyone to lean on for help. She felt like she was constantly hitting brick walls every turn she took; she just wanted someone to look out for her once in a while. She knew that it was her choice to have Penelope, and she took full responsibility for that, but for once she just wanted to act her age, be a woman. Not a mother. Even if it just lasted a few hours.

Hunter was looking at her with an intense look like he was trying to figure something out.

"Oh. I thought that you had just moved here, you must be popular to have plans already and on a Friday night. What is it a hot date with one of your neighbours?"

Annalise was surprised by his question, and she thought that she even heard a hint of jealously. Why was he being so curious and interested in her life?

"Ha! You must be joking, right? The last time I had a date was over 7 years ago!"

As soon as she said it, she regretted her words. Why couldn't she have just said that she was going on a date and leave it at that?

"I mean, no I don't have a date."

She thought about lying but then thought it was just easier to tell the truth.

"I have to look after my daughter, I mentioned that I had a daughter, didn't I?"

"Yes. You did."

"Well, as we have just moved down here, we don't really know anyone else so I wouldn't have anyone to ask to look after her."

Hunter's face was hard to read; she had just literally told him her life story in 2 minutes except she left out the part about the real reason why she moved to London.

"I know someone who could look after her for you. Candice has a sister who is a nanny and also does babysitting jobs, I can give you her number if you like?"

Annalise didn't quite know what to say; she was excited at the prospect that she could have a night out, but then she also had a doubt. She couldn't leave Penelope with a stranger. Yes, Candice's sister may be a nanny, but they didn't know her, and it didn't feel right with Annalise. How could she just leave Penelope with someone just so she could go out and have a few drinks? No, she couldn't do it.

She would just make up some excuse that Penelope is funny with people she doesn't know and that would be the end of it. Knowing deep down that Penelope loves meeting new people and would jump at the chance to have someone look after her for a night, Annalise just didn't feel right about it.

"Thank you so much for the suggestion, but I'm not sure it's fair on Penelope to leave her after only being here a short time. Maybe once we have settled in more, I might feel a bit better about leaving her." She thought she saw the disappointment in his eyes but chose to ignore it.

"Just a suggestion. I just thought that it might be nice for you to meet some of the other staff members. I probably wouldn't have seen much of you anyway. I always have to mingle with everyone especially the directors, and then I tend to leave early. These things tend to bore me half the time."

"Don't you have to stay until the end of the night with you owning the company and all?"

"Definitely not! I tend to leave before everyone gets too drunk and starts making fools of themselves. I definitely don't need to be around to see that. It's bad enough the next day when HR comes to see me about some bad behaviour. Plus, I have to be up early for my training sessions and need all the energy I can get for those!"

Annalise's eyes moved to his body, she noticed how his suit clung to his muscles and knew how good his body would be underneath all of the clothes.

"Oh! what kind of training do you do?"

"Boxing."

"I've never tried boxing; I can imagine it's a very physical sport! But you look like you can manage it with that body."

Annalise couldn't believe that she had just said that to her boss. What was she doing saying things like that? She was definitely heading for the way out if she kept being unprofessional. Annalise felt her whole face flush with heat, and she knew that her face was starting to go red with embarrassment. When she finally looked up, Hunter was looking at her again, and it looked like he was deciding on his reply. She wondered how he would take a comment like that from her.

"Well, I think that's everything we have to go over, do you have enough work to be getting on with for the rest of the day? From tomorrow it will be much busier for you, so hopefully, you can keep on top of things. As you know, I am a very busy man, but I am here to assist you if you need anything. Just make sure not to disturb me unless I tell you to."

Annalise was taken back; he had just completely shut down on her. The conversation was over, and he seemed like he couldn't get back to his office quick enough. He was already standing up and walking back to his office door; she wanted to apologise for what she had said, but then she thought that if he had washed over it then so should she. The comment was history and didn't exist anymore; she just had to remember to think before she spoke next time.

"Yes, I have enough to be getting on with. Will I see you again before I leave tonight?"

"I doubt it, I have a lot of work to do, and I probably won't be leaving my office until after dark has well and truly settled."

"Well, if I don't, enjoy your night, and I will see you bright and early tomorrow."

And with that Hunter closed his door and shut Annalise and their conversation out.

Monday, 8 June
Hunter

Hunter was pacing his office unsure of what had just happened out there with Annalise. Why had he acted so strangely? Asking her about having a hot date was so inappropriate! What had he been thinking? This was way out of his territory. He was normally professional with his employees. This had never happened with Charlotte, but Hunter knew that there was more than just being attracted to Annalise, there was something deeper, something that he couldn't quite put his finger on.

He had to maintain professionalism with her; after all, he was her boss. She was just on a 3-month contract, and then after, he would make up some excuse that she wasn't fulfilling the job role and that they were not going to renew her contract. He could do 3 months. He would avoid her when he could and only have physical interactions when necessary. That would work out just fine.

Monday, 8 June
Annalise

Annalise's afternoon went quickly. She felt organised for tomorrow by the time it reached late afternoon, and she had to leave the office to go and pick up Penelope from after school care. She hadn't seen Hunter for the rest of the afternoon, and she made it her priority not to disturb him this time. She didn't want to end the day the same way she started, feeling embarrassed.

Come to think of it; she had embarrassed herself every time she was around him today. It was surprising that he wanted her to come back tomorrow. As she finished off what she was doing, she was tempted to quickly knock on his door and say goodbye, but instead settled on sending him a quick email.

[EMAIL] 5:30 pm

Hi Hunter,

I didn't want to disturb you, but I am now leaving the office for the day. I hope you have a good evening, and I'll see you bright and early tomorrow.

Annalise.

Rush hour traffic was a nightmare in London. It was bad enough in Norfolk, but nothing compared to this. She hoped that Penelope was OK in the after school care. She hated leaving her for so long and most of the other parents more than likely picked their children up at the normal time, but then again most of them wouldn't be single parents.

Anyway, she knew that Penelope wouldn't mind at all, they would no doubt be doing fun things like painting and colouring that were all the things Penelope loved doing. As she pulled into the gates of the school, she could see Penelope in the window of one of the classrooms. By the time she was outside the classroom door Penelope was heading straight towards her and embraced her into a big cuddle spreading Annalise with nothing but love and warmth.

"Mummy I had the most special day ever. Look what we have been doing.... PAINTING!"

Annalise looked at her with admiration.

"I can see my darling girl and you have it all on your fingers and in your hair. How on earth did that happen?" she let out a hint of laughter.

"I just got creative, I like the feel of the paint on my fingers. It's all slippery."

As Penelope was finishing off her sentence, a lady was heading over to them and Annalise presumed that it must be Penelope's teacher.

"I'm Mrs Green the aftercare teacher. Penelope has been a joy to have in our class today, she is so talented and nothing has fazed her, especially with it being her first day. Most children tend to hide in the back or be a bit shy, but not Penelope. She was talking to everyone. You made lots of new friends didn't you?"

Mrs Green seemed to be in her early 50s. She had short dark/greyish hair, was fairly tall and slender. She had a warming presence to her and could see why she was a primary school teacher.

"I can't wait to play with everyone again, it was so much fun."

Penelope was jumping around full of excitement, and it made Annalise's day just knowing that she had settled in at the school.

"Well, you will be able to see them all again tomorrow and Mrs Green too."

Mrs Green confirmed this with a nod and smiled back her contently.

"Yay, I can't wait!"

"OK, little one, let's get you home. You need to be fed, bathed and into bed at a reasonable time tonight. You have had a long and exciting day, and I think that we need to give you some rest before the day starts all over again tomorrow. Say goodbye to Mrs Green."

"Bye, Mrs Green, see you tomorrow."

"Bye, Penelope, I'll look forward to it."

By the time Annalise had put Penelope to bed, she was exhausted. All the feelings and events from today came crashing down on her, and she could barely keep her eyes open. It had been a good day, actually a great day. Penelope had loved her new school and even made some new friends. Annalise's first day at work had gone well, even though there were a few slippery slopes along the way, but she did a good enough job that they wanted her back tomorrow.

She was excited to go back to Hunter recruitment, everyone seemed lovely who she had met so far. As Annalise sat in her living room looking out onto her quiet road, she thought about her first interaction with Hunter. She had been mesmerised by him. His face, his body, his persona. She had never met a man before who had so much power and confidence in the way he walked.

He made you feel like there was nothing else around you, but him. There had been moments in the day where they had both been caught off guard, but she was glad that it wasn't just her. She wasn't sure what had happened or what he had felt, but for her, it was something deep. A connection between them that Annalise had never had before, and she didn't know what to do about it.

The best plan would be to just try and focus on her work and stay professional, this was her job at the end of the day, and she needed it to support Penelope. She needed to pay the rent, and take care of them both. There was no way that she was going back to Norfolk, she had made this move and this was their home now. So anything that she felt today with Hunter had to be forgotten, it was already history in her mind.

It was now dark outside and Annalise could just see the lights from the street lamps shining through her curtains. It was getting late, and she thought rather than sitting up pretending to watch mindless television, it was time to go to bed. She had a long week ahead of her, and she wanted to be on top form. She thought about the company party on Friday and how it was a shame that she wouldn't be able to go; she would love nothing more than to get all dressed up for a change, put on a little black dress, high heels, have her hair styled, make-up on and feel like a woman again.

The more she thought about it, the more she was coming to terms with having a babysitter for Penelope. After all, if she was going to start living her life again there were going to be more times when she would need one for Penelope. She would speak to Candice tomorrow and ask for her sister's number.

As long as Penelope was OK with it, then she might consider going even If it was for just a few hours. She needed to get out and start having a life and maybe this could be the start of it. Annalise stood up, stretching out her limbs and muscles, tiredness washing through her whole body; she felt exhausted so decided to descend up the stairs, get changed and get into her bed waiting for sleep to take her.

Monday, 8 June
Hunter

The rest of the afternoon went quickly for Hunter; he was finalising contracts for a big company deal in London that had to go to the in-house lawyers by the end of the day. Once they had checked them over, the contracts could go out and be signed by both parties. When he looked up from his computer screen he noticed that the time displayed 8:00 p.m. He hadn't even eaten lunch today he had been that busy.

Mondays were always busy for him and today had been no different. He stood up, stretched out his legs and started walking to the door; he could see that most of the lights were off in the main hallway, meaning that he was the last one left in the office again. As he exited his office, he looked over at Annalise's desk and remembered the encounters that they had shared today. She had sent him an email saying that she was leaving for the day and that she would see him in the morning.

He liked the thought of seeing her again tomorrow and wondered why. He had to stop these thoughts immediately, it was so out of character for him, and he wasn't sure where it was coming from. It had been a while since he had gotten laid, maybe he just had sex on his mind and as Annalise was new and attractive that he had taken a shine to her. He walked over to her desk and noticed that she had added a few more of her belongings.

It was the picture of her daughter he noticed again; he picked it up examining it in detail and remembered Annalise telling him that she hadn't had a date in over 7 years, which must mean that her daughter was around this age. The girl in the photo looked so similar to Annalise, and he thought back to earlier. They had a connection that was for sure; he felt it when looking into her eyes. They had communicated without even saying anything. He could see the pain and hurt in her eyes, and he wondered who had caused it.

He had also noticed lust, the same lust that he had felt. He felt like he connected with her on some kind of level, whether it was the same pain that he had felt all these years and hope that one day it would be replaced with happiness. But for him, he knew that was never going to happen, and he had come to terms with it; he hoped that for Annalise' sake that she could find happiness if that even existed.

Putting the photo frame back in its place, his stomach started to grumble, and he thought he better go get some food before he headed home. Just as he was leaving the office his mobile phone started to ring. Looking at the caller ID, it was Rosie calling him.

Rosie was a woman who he had met at a yearly social networking event. She also worked in recruitment so they hit it off straight away by talking about companies that they were working with. After that night, he had been on a few dates with her, and he used that term lightly. They both had busy schedules and had agreed on just casual sex, which suited Hunter fine.

But now she had started to call him a lot more, and he was starting to feel concerned. He only did dinner and casual sex, nothing more. He couldn't cope with anything else. He looked at the phone deciding on whether to answer it or not; he needed something to take his mind off today, it had been an extra intense day for him especially with everything that had happened with Annalise, and it had been a while since he had seen her.

"Maguire."

"Well, hello to you too, Hunter! Why do you always have to answer the phone so bluntly? You could answer it. Hello lovely Rosie, how nice of you to call." He sighed with frustration.

"Rosie, that's how I answer the phone to everyone, I'm not going to change it just for you." Anger tipped into his tone; he tried to calm himself, but he was tired and hungry.

"Well, I'm not just anyone. I'm sure I have seen more of you than most people who call you!"

"You probably have Rosie, but that has nothing to do with it. I suppose you are calling to meet up?"

She was starting to annoy him now, Rosie had always been a bit of a princess, but Hunter has previously just ignored it as most of the time she was tolerable.

"Well, if you are going to be like that, then no. I wasn't calling to meet up!" He rubbed his forehead and blinked away his frustration.

"Come on Rosie, don't take offence, this is me. You know what I'm like. Where did you want to meet? I need to eat first so do you want to head to mine in an hour?"

"Oh, how romantic! Do I not even get an invite for dinner? You know what Hunter, it would be nice for just once for us to have a proper date and not just sex."

"Rosie, this was our agreement. Casual sex that's all! I told you that I can't do any more than that. You said that was fine, so why are you changing your tune now? We can just leave it if you want, I have to be up early tomorrow anyway."

"Wait! I know we agreed, I'm sorry. I just wouldn't mind a bit of the romance stuff now and again, that's all a girl wants sometimes."

"I can't do romance, It's not in my genetics! No flowers, no romantic dinners, no spooning and definitely no L-word."

"Maybe one day, Hunter!" He heard hope in her tone and worry took over.

"Never Rosie! I'll see you in an hour at mine."

Hunter hung up and headed to get food; he was feeling cranky and knew his favourite restaurant around the corner from his apartment would get him back on track.

Hunter lay in bed looking up at the ceiling with the events of the day twirling around in his head like a mini-tornado about to swallow everything up until nothing, but debris was left. It was now nearly midnight and Rosie had just left. She always wanted to stay the night, but Hunter didn't do sleepovers. He can remember her face when he told her to leave, her eyes were sad like he had just told a puppy to go and sleep outside in the rain.

Rosie knew what Hunter was like; he didn't do romance or commitment. They had agreed from the start that it was just a casual thing, but it felt like she wanted more; he had to break it off with her before it became too serious. Of course, he would miss the sex, but that's a sacrifice he was willing to make. She was a nice person and deserved better than him; he couldn't give her happy endings and that was that.

He felt like his life was starting to become complicated and out of his safe zone and not just with Rosie. He knew it had only been one day with Annalise, but that didn't matter; he had felt more of a connection with her than he had with any other woman he had met. He just didn't know what to do about it or whether he should act on it. He had no idea what was happening to him; he barely knew the woman, so how could she have this effect on him? He never felt like this with anyone.

There was something about Annalise though, something that connected them as if they had been through a similar event in their lives that had caused them heartache and pain. He could see it in her eyes earlier today. Hunter knew that he had to push whatever this feeling was away. For one, she was his employee and two she had a daughter and that was always going to end badly when children are involved. If he did then it could open up a whole new set of feelings that he wasn't quite sure whether he was ready for yet, let alone how HR would have a field day with this.

How could he promote a safe sexual harassment-free workspace for his employees when he wanted to do things to his PA that would get him into more trouble than he knew of? Nothing good could come of this; he couldn't pursue it anymore. It was unprofessional of him to have these thoughts and feelings especially when he knew that all it would be was casual for him. He couldn't offer her anymore, and he knew that Annalise was someone who wanted a full romantic fairy tale ending.

As his thoughts grew duller and the weight of the day started to hit him, his body started to relax; his eyes became heavier; and it wasn't long before he had fallen asleep with nothing but visions of Annalise in his mind.

Tuesday, 9 June
Annalise

OMG she had overslept. What time was it? How had this happened? Annalise was sure that she had set her alarm, or was she too tired to do that last night. She was exhausted and had crashed into bed. She glanced at the clock and realised that it was 8:00 a.m. already. She still had to drop Penelope off at school at 8:30 a.m. and then be at work by 9:00 a.m., if she was late after everything that happened yesterday then she was sure that Hunter would fire her. Annalise quickly got out of bed and ran towards Penelope's room trying not to trip over shoes that had been left in the hallway.

"Penelope, you have to get up, Mummy overslept and now we are running late! We don't have much time so can you quickly get dressed while Mummy has a shower."

Annalise nearly jumped out of her skin when she heard a noise behind her.

"Mummy, I'm already up and dressed, I didn't want to wake you from your dreams of Prince charming."

Annalise chuckled to herself at Penelope's comment; she had been dreaming of Hunter when she woke up but was sure that he was no prince charming.

"What are you laughing about Mummy?"

"Oh, nothing darling, Mummy's still not awake properly. Penelope if Mummy is sleeping next time and you know that we are running late could you please come and wake me."

"I never like it when you wake me from my dreams."

"I'll quickly get ready and then we will have to grab some toast on our way out. Your lunchbox is already packed in the fridge, do you reckon you could get all your school things together and wait on the sofa for me? You can watch cartoons if you like."

Annalise saw Penelope's face fill with happiness and knew that would keep her entertained while she got dressed.

"Yay cartoons!"

Annalise managed to get showered and dressed all by 8:20 a.m. Thank god Penelope's school was only a 5-minute drive, which meant by the time they got sorted, into the car and set on their way that they would actually be running on time. Relief washed over her; she couldn't believe she had slept in like that it never happened, and she was angry at herself for doing it. She put it down to it being a big day yesterday, and it must have taken its toll on her more than she thought.

As they pulled up to Penelope's school, it was a quick goodbye and Annalise watched as Penelope skipped her way to the school gates and entered the building. She thought back to being a child and how happy she was, just like Penelope. But that seemed a lifetime ago now and so much had happened since then. She just hoped that Penelope would stay a child as long as she could before having to deal with the life of being an adult and the responsibilities that came with it.

Trying to tackle the London traffic again, especially at rush hour was a nightmare. Car horns beeping with angry faces filling the cars, everyone looking like all they wanted to do was get to work before they were late, just like her. As the traffic started to clear she noticed that apart from the noise and ugliness of London rush hour, London was beautiful and especially on a spring morning like today. The sun glistened on the buildings mirroring the scenery that had all colours of the rainbow, the trees lightly swaying in the wind like they were dancing to a slow song and the birds singing to each other to entertain the people around them.

She knew that she wasn't the only one who was admiring it and how something so small could improve everyone's mood instantly. As she continued her journey into work, she was excited to see what today was going to bring. She would speak to Candice and ask for her sister's number, and she would also see if she fancied going for a coffee one lunchtime this week. It would be nice to have some girl time and talk about things other than Barbie's, fairy tales and cartoons, which were currently daily conversations for her.

By the time Annalise had parked up and got into the office, it was 9:02 a.m., surely Hunter wouldn't mind her being 2 minutes late. She would just blame it on the lift being busy if he did ask. The lift had actually been busy, but she didn't have to wait; hopefully, Hunter was already in his office or wasn't in yet; either way, hopefully, he wouldn't notice her being slightly late. It was more than likely that he wouldn't even notice anyway. As she sat down at her desk and started planning her day, Candice came walking in looking rather happy.

"Morning, Annalise. I have some post for Hunter, could I leave it with you to give to him? He asked not to be disturbed."

"Of course. When did he get in the office?"

"I'm not sure, long before I got in. He just sent me an email to say that he wasn't to be disturbed, you probably have one as well." Annalise wondered if Hunter was like this with everyone.

"I'll check when I get into my emails. Candice, Hunter mentioned that your sister is a nanny and also does some babysitting."

"Yeah, she is currently working for this really rich family in Chelsea, gets paid a fortune and gets to meet all the rich men. So lucky!"

"I was wondering, would it be possible to have her number? I may need to use her services." She looked at her anxiously and was nervous about her reply.

"Of course. I didn't know you had kids." Her smile was intriguing.

"Kid. Just one. Her name is Penelope. Hunter mentioned that there is a company party a week on Friday, I wasn't sure I could make it and then he suggested asking your sister to babysit. I've never left Penelope alone with anyone other than family before so was a bit nervous. To be honest, I'm new to the city and would love a night out."

"I can't imagine what it must be like having a child. Your freedom is taken away from you. Oh, sorry! I didn't mean it like that."

"That's OK. It has been tough, I'm not going to lie about that, but I love Penelope, and I wouldn't change my situation for anything."

"That's sweet. I bet she is a cutey, how old?"

"Seven." Annalise didn't want to discuss Penelope too much. It always opened up to more questions about her life, and she wasn't ready for that just yet.

"Oh, wow, you must have been young? That must have been tough for you. At least you had family around to help you that must have made it easier for you."

Annalise thought about her family and how she had felt more alone with them being around than she did moving to London.

"Yeah, I suppose so."

Annalise kept treading carefully; she didn't really know Candice, and she didn't want to be office gossip.

"Here is my sister's number, give her a call and tell her that you work with me. I'm sure she will be free the night of the party; she generally gets all weekends off from her Nanning job so should be able to help you out."

"Perfect! Thanks, so much Candice."

"No problem. So do you know what you are going to wear to the party? I have this amazing little red cocktail dress, comes just above the knee and falls off the shoulders!"

Annalise looked at her in envy. Her dress sounded amazing. And she knew that Candice would look gorgeous in it.

"It sounds lovely. I'm not sure what I'll wear yet, I haven't really thought about it. Plus I don't go out much so only have one black dress, I'm sure that will do."

"Well, we could always pop to the shops one lunchtime, and I could help you pick something if you like?"

Annalise thought about money and how she was supposed to be saving especially after the recent move and the deposit she had to pay for the rental house, but she would love to have a girly shopping trip, and she did need some new clothes.

"Only if you're sure Candice? I don't want to take up your lunch break."

"I love shopping so it's no problem for me. It will be fun! We can grab some lunch on the way back. I'm sure Hunter won't mind you taking a little longer than an hour, just say it's important and for work, which technically it is. Shall we say Tuesday next week?"

Annalise thought to herself that she was starting to like Candice. She had this friendly and fun persona about her, and she was being so kind taking her to find a dress.

"I'm sure he won't notice anyway he spent most of yesterday in his office."

"Yeah, he doesn't like to be disturbed a lot, says he needs to concentrate on the business."

At that moment, they were interrupted by a man's voice, Annalise was so deep in conversation with Candice that she hadn't even noticed the door to Hunter's office open and him exit it. He was now standing in the doorway looking at them both with an intriguing look in his eyes.

"Yes, Candice, if I didn't then there might not be any business. So I think it's best you get back to work and do the job that I pay you to do."

Candice was obviously taken back by the way Hunter had spoken to her. Maybe he was in a bad mood this morning, but he didn't need to take it out on Candice; she was just being nice.

"Yes, of course, Hunter. I was just bringing your post to Annalise, that's all."

Candice headed back to reception leaving Hunter and Annalise in the room. When Annalise looked up at him, he had that same look in his eyes as yesterday, but this time it was more intense. It was like he couldn't look away and something was pulling him deeper and deeper. She didn't want to repeat what had happened yesterday; she needed to stay professional, this was her boss, and she needed this job. She didn't need a man complicating things; she needed to change the atmosphere quickly.

"Sorry, Hunter, Candice really was just dropping off your post. I also asked for her sister's number, so you can blame me for the extra conversation. Hopefully, her sister can look after Penelope for me so I can come to the company party."

As she waited for Hunter to say something, she noticed that he looked slightly uncomfortable. How could this strong successful man get uncomfortable in her presence?

"It will be good for you to come and get to know your colleagues. Just make sure you behave yourself, you will still be representing the company."

She didn't quite know how to take his comment. It was verging on rudeness, and she was shocked by it.

"I can assure you that I will be on my best behaviour."

"Good to know, Annalise."

This time he said her name slowly and more intimately, letting each letter roll off his tongue, making her crumble in front of him. Was he trying to flirt with her? She would have no idea if he was, it had been so long since she had flirted with a man. As the tension in the room started to build, she wondered how he could have so much effect on her.

She always felt like she was fumbling around him or saying the wrong thing. If he wasn't flirting with her then she was just making a massive fool of herself. It was like he could read her mind because when he spoke again, he was back to being his professional self, and she was relieved.

"I have a busy day and need to get on, unless there was anything else?"

As she was about to answer him, he was already halfway to his door. It was at that moment that he turned around and looked straight at her like he was about to say something else. She waited for him to speak, but instead, he just turned back around, walked into his office and shut the door behind him.

Thursday, 11 June
Hunter

The last couple of days had been intense for Hunter and nothing was going to plan. Come to think about it nothing this week had gone to plan, and it was now Thursday. It seemed like ever since Annalise had started working for Hunter recruitment, his mind had been preoccupied. Yesterday had been OK as he had been out at meetings for most of the day so didn't really see her, but the way he was reacting wasn't normal for him; he only ever focussed on work with the rest of his life taking a back seat.

But since Annalise had been around his thoughts were all over the place. She was all he could think of, especially her body! He wanted her in ways that he had never wanted another woman. Trying to set his thoughts aside and get back to business; he needed to get prepared for his meeting, which started in half an hour.

He tried to think of a reason to stop her from attending the meeting, but deep down, he knew that she was needed. He needed her for the business, and he would just have to keep focussing on what he was doing and not her. Deciding he better let her know now so she could get prepared for it; he thought it was best to intercom her rather than going to see her. He needed to keep his head clear, at least until the meeting.

"Hi, Hunter, anything you need me to do?"

Hunter thought that there were a lot of things that he needed her to do and work wasn't one of them.

"I will need you to attend the meeting today with me. It's just to take some minutes and then you will need to send it out to the rest of the directors in our other offices. It starts in half an hour."

"I'll make sure I'm ready. Who is the meeting with?"

"It's with all the managers of each division. It's the start of a new quarter for us, and I need to let them all know what their team targets are, and I also want to hear from them how they are all going to achieve it. Just make sure you are ready to go and have everything with you."

"Will do. See you shortly."

The start of the quarter was always exciting for Hunter with new targets to hit for him and the company; he loved seeing the new drive and determination locked into the eyes of the managers and consultants. The office was always buzzing. As he exited his office, Annalise was already waiting for him and was smiling at him as he approached her.

"Ready?"

"Sure am. I'll just do shorthand on the writing pad if that's OK and then type it up later?"

"As long as the directors get the accurate minutes I don't care how you do it. Charlotte never bothered me with the details." His tone came out harsher than he had meant it to. He looked at her searching for any kind of emotion for a response.

"Um sorry Hunter, I'm just trying to learn how you like things done. I didn't want to do it my way and then you preferred it a different way. That's all."

"It's fine. Just don't bother me with the small stuff. We better get a move on, I don't like to be late to my own meeting."

The meeting had gone well; all the managers were clear with their direction and knew what had to be done to achieve their set targets. Everyone seemed happy about the figures and confirmed to Hunter that it was all achievable. As they all started to stand and proceed back to their offices, Hunter soon realised that he was just left in the room alone with Annalise. The room was silent apart from the sound of their breathing.

The air started to become thicker and the atmosphere soon changed. He was unsure whether to look at her, knowing that if they locked eyes again then he wouldn't be able to stop himself from climbing over the table that separated them and taking her right then and there. He didn't care who walked in; he just had to have her. He decided to keep the conversation brief to avoid any of that from happening. He didn't need to complicate things any more than they were.

"Thoughts on your first meeting?"

"It was exciting! I could feel the energy coming from every manager. They all seemed really impressed with how the business is doing and what's to come this quarter."

"Yes. It was a positive meeting and I'm happy with the way it turned out. Sometimes some of them can become quite negative and blame other teams for stealing clients or interfering with a relationship that they have built, but this one was good. The party on Friday should be a success with everyone being in good spirits. The last one we had didn't end so well. There was a bust-up happening between two senior consultants, they both got warnings, but have been fine ever since. I blame it on the alcohol!"

"Yes, alcohol can definitely get you into trouble; we've all had our moments."

Annalise's tone was obviously meant in a light way, but Hunter couldn't help noticing that it had a deeper meaning to it. He could tell by the way her posture changed, how her eyes went darker and her pupils dilated. He didn't know whether to push her on the subject but was unsure of how she may take it.

"Well, let's hope that it doesn't cause too much trouble this time unless it's the good kind of trouble. If you know what I mean."

Oh, god, did he really just say that. Was he actually trying to flirt with her but epically failing. Hunter knew if the conversation carried on like this, then Annalise would not only think that he was abrupt but also a sleaze who tried to sleep with his staff members after a couple of days.

"Well, anyway, it should be a good night. So do you reckon you will be able to make it?"

"It depends if Candice's sister can babysit. I left her a message at lunch to ask her, so hopefully, she will call me back today. I know I haven't given her much notice, so I might be out of luck, which would be a shame. I've actually started to look forward to it. It's just been a while since I have been out and interacted with adults, It would be nice to have a few wines and get to know some of the others."

"Everyone deserves a night out. Did I tell you that it's a cocktail party? Do you have something suitable to wear?"

"Candice did mention it and has kindly offered to take me shopping next Tuesday in our lunch break. I've got a few dresses in my wardrobe, but probably nothing suitable for a cocktail event."

"I'm glad you have it covered. I'm sure you will look gorgeous in whatever dress you decide on." Hunter's eyes grew darker just thinking about her in a tight-fitting cocktail dress and knew his comment was inappropriate, but he didn't care.

"Thank you that's very kind of you, but I don't think my budget will stretch to a gorgeous dress. Just getting dressed up will make me happy."

"When was the last time you got dressed up and went out? Surely it wasn't 7 years ago like you mentioned?"

"Pretty much. I had Penelope when I was young. Much younger than I thought I would have children and Penelope became my life. I worked and when I wasn't working I was bringing her up."

"And what about your family, were they not there to help you?"

Hunter knew that he was pushing into unknown territory and wasn't sure if it was safe or not; he just waited for her reply, which seemed to come much quicker than he thought.

"My family didn't want to be involved much, they had their own lives to deal with and anyway, Penelope is my daughter and my responsibility, so I shouldn't have to ask anyone else to help. I was more than capable to do it on my own."

"I'm sorry if I've overstepped the mark, I didn't mean to. I know what it's like not having family around."

Why was he telling this stuff to her? He never opened up to anyone about his family, Hunter was going into personal information that he wanted to leave as history.

"Anyway, enough of personal talk, we should be getting back to work, I'm sure it's nearly time for you to leave. Do you have to collect your daughter after work?"

"Yes, from aftercare school. Oh, god it's nearly 5:00 p.m., I should be leaving soon otherwise I'll get stuck in traffic, and she might have to wait outside."

They both stood up and headed to the door. As Hunter went to grab the door handle Annalise did the same. Her hand overlapped his sending shockwaves through the whole of his body. He didn't know how to react. The touch had been so intimate. It would have looked normal to anyone else.

But with Annalise, it felt different. He could see that she felt it too. They both just stood there not letting go, scared that the feeling would go away and not return. They looked at each other, communicating through their eyes, letting each other know that it wasn't just them feeling this, that it was mutual.

They stood like this for a while not knowing what else to do, Hunter just wanted to reach up with his other hand and softly touch her face and brush her lips with his fingers, but he had to take this slowly, for her sake as well as his.

Her hand was still on his when he released the door handle and felt her shift awkwardly. He then proceeded to open the door and exited the meeting room leaving Annalise still standing there looking at her hand.

Thursday, 11 June
Annalise

What the hell had just happened, she was now driving through rush hour traffic to collect Penelope from school on time and couldn't get that touch out of her head. How could a small touch have such a huge effect on her? She knew that he had felt it too by the way his whole body had changed in the space of a few seconds, but why did he leave and not say anything? They could have talked about what had just happened, the feeling that they both felt, but she knew that Hunter wasn't probably the type of person to open up about his feelings.

Annalise could remember the warmth of his hand, how her heart rate had increased by the touch of his skin, her breathing had become deeper and all she wanted to do was to lean up and kiss him, closing the distance between them. It had taken all her willpower not to in case she had misread the signs, and he rejected her. He had just left her standing there in the meeting room, and she wasn't sure whether he had done it because he wasn't sure of his feelings or whether he knew that it was unprofessional. She never thought that she would come to London and feel like this about a man, especially her boss and so soon.

She was still unsure of what those feelings were but knew that they were more than just friendly or professional ones. Annalise had to remember though that Hunter was her boss, and she shouldn't be having feelings about him, full stop. How would it look to her colleagues and the agency who got her the job if she was seen throwing herself at him? Imagine if his feelings weren't mutual, and this was all in her head; she made a fool of herself over it all.

It would be unlikely for the agency to use her again, then what would she do? Annalise had to make sure that this all stopped. No more dreamy eyes, no more fumbling over him or embarrassing herself. She needed to make it clear to him that she only wanted a professional relationship, but how would she do that without knowing if he even had feelings for her.

Maybe she would just mention how she is enjoying working at the company and is glad that it's working out as far as she needs the job and can't let anything jeopardise it for her. That would surely give an underlying message to him. Yes, that's what she will do first thing tomorrow morning when she saw him, then it would ease her mind, and she would be able to actually start doing the job that she came to do rather than being distracted by Hunter all the time.

Friday, 12 June
Annalise

Annalise woke early the next morning. The sun hadn't even come up yet and her room was pitch black. Normally it was the light from outside that woke Annalise up naturally, but not today. She had been tossing and turning all night thinking about Hunter. She was feeling nervous about speaking to him, especially after what had happened yesterday.

She didn't know if he would bring it up or if he would just ignore it; she had to speak to him first and clear the air. After she had collected Penelope from school last night, Candice's sister Katherine had called her back to say that she was free to babysit Penelope on Friday night. Annalise was so excited at the news that she had to try and hide her excitement in her voice. She definitely didn't want Katherine to tell Candice how excited she had been on the phone as Candice may ask her why and that could open up a whole can of worms.

Penelope was also excited at the fact that she got to meet someone new and play with them. As Annalise brought her thoughts back to the present day and tried to calm her nerves, she thought about how excited she was to go shopping with Candice at lunch today. She didn't have much money to spend, but she was sure that Candice would know some good places.

She was trying to think about what kind of dress she wanted; she knew it had to be a cocktail dress, but what colour? Black would make her look sophisticated and sexy, but then red always made her stand out especially with her dark features. Oh, but Candice had mentioned that she was wearing a red dress and Annalise didn't want to seem like she was trying to copy her. She was sure that something would stand out when they were shopping.

After laying there thinking about the day ahead before it had even started, the sun had started to rise to bring beautiful colours of reds, pinks and ambers into her room and to light the whole room up. It was going to be a beautiful day with the sun and warm weather looking like it was going to make an appearance. Annalise decided to get out of bed and go and make some breakfast for herself and Penelope, it was nearly time she woke Penelope so that they had enough time to get ready before they both had to leave. She gave herself a little inspirational talking about how today was going to be a good day, everything will work out with Hunter, and she was going dress shopping, and then made her way down to the kitchen.

Annalise had enjoyed her morning so far with Penelope; she had managed to make herself and Penelope a nice healthy breakfast, then they had both gotten ready for work and school. Penelope had been singing and dancing around the house to Beyoncé that made Annalise smile; she had even had a quick dance herself. Then it was dropping off time for Penelope at school and then had headed straight into work. She was pleased, as for the first time this week the traffic had been fairly pleasant.

Maybe it was the weather and more people wanted to walk to work; she would have done the same if she didn't live so far away. Annalise hadn't really thought about locations when she agreed on the house, but it was in an area that she could afford and close to schools, so her commute to work would just have to be part of it. She would make sure that she got out for a walk this weekend; she and Penelope could discover the sights of London. Go see Tower Bridge and then go up in the millennium dome or go visit the London history museum.

Annalise had been to London as a child and visited a few places, but everything had changed so much since then. It would be a new experience for her as well as Penelope, and she felt excited. As she exited the lift into the reception area Candice was approaching her with a broad smile.

"I hear Cinderella can attend the ball after all! Maybe you will meet your prince charming!"

She was chuckling as she said it.

"Well, if you mean the party then yes, your sister is going to babysit Penelope. And I doubt very much prince charming even exists."

"I know right. The closest we are going to get to prince charming is if we watch Cinderella on DVD."

"Well, I have to say that I have watched that film maybe 50 times now, Penelope absolutely loves it! She thinks she will meet her prince charming when she is older, I can't bear to tell her the real truth about men and how they will do nothing but let you down. Are you still on for shopping on Tuesday? I mentioned to Hunter that I will be heading out, and he seemed fine about me taking a little longer for lunch."

"Yes, definitely. It's in my diary! I'll come and get you from your office at midday on that day if that works."

"Perfect!"

Annalise headed to her office wondering whether Hunter was already in. She started to get all nervous at the thought of seeing him and how she was going to casually start this conversation. She didn't want to embarrass herself. She just hoped that he got what she was trying to say without her actually having to say it, then they could forget that touch and carry on as employer and employee.

The office was clear when she entered it, and there was no sign of him yet; she needed to keep calm and keep herself busy until he arrived, but all she could think about was that conversation. She knew she was now mumbling to herself and probably not making any sense to herself let alone anyone who may be listening. What if Hunter was in his office, and he could hear all of this; she couldn't see any shadows in his office from the frosted glass, but maybe she would just knock to see if he was there any way that way she could casually mention what she needed to say and then they could go back to normal.

As she approached his office door she still couldn't hear or see anyone inside, she decided to knock and waited for a response. Nobody answered the first time so she decided to knock one more time just to make sure, but when there was still no answer she decided to walk in just to have a quick look while he wasn't there. Annalise had never been in Hunter's office before, well not long enough to have a proper look. As she looked around the space she noticed that his office was quite casual and not as professionally styled as the rest of the offices.

He had a nice long dark wooden desk with a big black leather seat that looked so comfy you could fall asleep in it. There was a couch in the corner with a low coffee table and a flat-screen TV and then a small fridge just big enough to fit some drinks in it. No wonder he never left his office with a space like this. As she looked around, she noticed there were no photos other than professional ones of scenery or quotes.

It surprised her considering his office was so casual and almost homely; she thought he may at least have a photo of his parents or friends somewhere in there, but nothing. As she was casually walking around his office she noticed a black shadow in the corner of her right eye and knew it was Hunter just by the presence that he brought with him. She wondered how long he had been standing there, what was she going to say to him about why she was in his office? She could say that she was dropping some papers off, but she didn't have any papers on her; she had to think quickly.

"Oh, hi, Hunter."

Annalise knew that she was fumbling over her words and had to put on her professional persona quickly before she caved into a mess under his intense stare.

"I didn't see you there, I was just popping in to see if you needed anything and then this view caught my eye. You must find it hard to concentrate on work with a view like this, I know I would."

He was still looking at her, and she was unsure of what he was thinking. He started walking towards her, and she caught the smell of his aftershave, it made her close her eyes and take him all in.

"The view caught your eye did it, Annalise?"

When she opened her eyes again, he was looking at her with an intense look and held his gaze on her. She wondered if he was trying to make her feel uncomfortable.

"Yes. You must get distracted by it every day, I don't know how you get any work done."

"I suppose you get used to it after a while, and it just becomes part of the background."

"Well, it's beautiful, especially on a day like today. Anyway, I'll leave you to it, I didn't mean to come in here when you weren't here, it won't happen again."

"Make sure it doesn't. I should have locked the door like I usually do, it's unlike me to forget."

Annalise looked at him noticing his posture change; he did remember what had happened last night; she knew it even if he hadn't brought the subject up. This was Annalise's time to get the conversation out of the way before it was too late.

"Umm, Hunter, while I have you alone could I talk to you about something for a moment?"

She started to blush and become hot and uncomfortable; she needed to remain calm and not to panic, just get it out quickly and clearly.

"I um, I… I just wanted to say that I am really grateful for the opportunity to work at Hunter recruitment. I like it here already. Plus it's more than just a job for me, it's giving me a life I have always dreamed of ever since I had Penelope and it's giving her a life that she deserves. I can't or won't have anything jeopardising that. I hope you understand that I'm here to do a job and maintain a professional working relationship with my colleagues. Anyway, that's all I wanted to say, I won't take up any more of your time."

Annalise automatically felt relieved, but she was also anxious to hear his response, or maybe she should just exit the office quickly before he could.

"Annalise, that's the way I expect all my employees to act and present themselves, if it was any different then they wouldn't be working at Hunter recruitment."

They were both just looking at each other unsure of what to do, Hunter wasn't giving anything away, but Annalise knew that something else needed to be said about yesterday before they could move on. As Annalise was thinking about this it's almost like Hunter read her mind.

"Annalise, I feel I need to clear the air about what happened yesterday after the meeting ...."

He stopped talking and looked like he was contemplating what to say.

"Nothing happened Hunter. We talked for a bit and that was it."

"Look, Annalise. Something happened that I can't explain, I've never had a feeling like that before, but after what you have just said about your daughter, it's confirmed to me that this is wrong and we shouldn't act on it. We are two responsible adults who can work together in a professional manner."

Annalise didn't quite know what to say; she had no idea how to respond to him. should she be professional about it and just say thank him and leave the office or should she tell him how she had felt it too and that she had tossed and turned all night thinking about that touch.

"Hunter, I'm not going to lie and say that I didn't feel anything from the touch. It's stupid really because it was only a touch. I don't know why it was different with you. But, I still stick to what I said before, I can't jeopardise this job. I need it, Hunter, more than you know. I can't fail London or go back to my old life."

Annalise knew that she was starting to get choked up and water was filling her eyes, but she didn't care, for some reason she didn't feel embarrassed because he was looking at her like he knew how she felt.

"Annalise. I promise you that whatever happened last night and any feelings that may have been woken up, I will close the book on them."

"Thank you, Hunter. This isn't easy for me, but I have to be strong for Penelope's sake, thank you for being so understanding."

"All good."

"Well, I best be getting back to work, I have a lot to do before lunch."

"Just make sure those meeting notes get typed up and emailed to all of the directors before you go to lunch."

Hunter was back to his normal stand-offish self again and Annalise started to think if he had a guard up to protect himself, but from what. As she stepped out of his office and back to her desk, she felt relieved with how he had reacted but also disappointed. She had to forget everything that had happened up until now, this was the start of their new working relationship together.

Friday, 12 June
Hunter

Hunter hadn't slept great again last night, his mind had been racing with thoughts of Annalise. He had woken up more tired than he had been before going to bed. His training was off and Tyrell had started to notice, which meant that Hunter was getting more crap from him. Today marked the end of the first week of Annalise working for him, and it had been an emotional roller coaster. His brain had been filled with thoughts and feelings that he didn't know existed.

It was also very unprofessional of him, which unnerved him even more; he had never let personal and professional mix especially when it came to his company. He was going to be out of the office for most of the day today so it was another day that he didn't have to see Annalise, which pleased him and disappointed him at the same time. There was a charity day event happening in the office, which he had said to Candice that he would attend. It was an event that the company held every year to raise money for the children's hospital.

They put on a business development day and all the recruiters put in for a raffle, wore casual clothes with a donation and did a bake sale. All money raised went to Great Ormond Street. Hunter only had to show his face at the end of the day to present an award to the person who picked up the most jobs during the day. It would be a quick well done and then he could leave before he got asked to go to the pub with them all to celebrate.

As he entered his office to grab a few things he needed before his meeting, he was surprised to see Annelise by the window looking out as if she had the whole world's problems on her shoulders. She didn't move at first, and as he watched her he couldn't quite believe how beautiful she was.

It must have been a few minutes before her eyes registered him and he wondered what she had been thinking about. After a few seconds he noticed her demeanour change and her face became flushed. She started to look uncomfortable and Hunter knew what was coming before she had even said anything to him.

He had phoned James at Sweeney and Co and had informed him he would be 30 minutes late; he was fine about it knowing Hunter wouldn't be late if it wasn't for a valid reason. As Hunter arrived at the offices he headed straight to level 18 and into the suites of Sweeney and Co. He had been coming here ever since he had started Hunter recruitment, mainly to talk about the stresses of building and running the business. But over time James had managed to bring Hunter's guard down, and they had spoken about Hunter's childhood and his parents.

Hunter hadn't given in easy, but over the years, he had started to feel comfortable with James and knew that all their sessions were completely confidential; he had even had a special contract drawn up. James probably knew him the best, Tyrell knew some stuff, but Hunter had never really opened up to him; he didn't want to seem vulnerable to him even though he knew that Tyrell would never judge him.

The receptionist Jenny knew Hunter and nodded to confirm that James was waiting for him and to enter his office; he knocked on the door first to be polite and heard James call for him to enter. As he proceeded through James was sitting at his desk typing on his computer but looked up with a warm smile when he saw Hunter.

"Hunter, long time… how are you?"

James was in his late 40s; he was shorter than Hunter, but that wasn't hard to be. He was medium built with dark hair. He was a charming man, very confident, and he held himself well. Most of all Hunter respected him and his profession. James was very good at what he did; he had a PHD in psychology and had even written research papers and lectured at one of the top universities in Cambridge before relocating to London when he was offered at the opportunity to run his own practice.

Hunter hadn't even been looking to see a psychologist, but he had met James at a business event one year and got talking to him. Hunter found his brain mesmerising and James had explained his work in a totally different way to what Hunter had originally thought would be involved when seeing a psychologist. It had taken Hunter a few months before he reached out to James, and at first, he felt unnerved about opening up to a total stranger, but at the end of the day it was about business, and he knew that if he stayed to the professional stuff, that he would be fine.

He never thought that James would be able to open him up to talk about his family and had actually helped him deal with the emotions that he had been holding on to. It had actually lifted some weight that Hunter had been carrying around and improved his focus at work, that's when he started to see a change in the business for the better.

"Hey, James! Works been crazy busy." He took his usual seat and tried to relax.

"All good Hunter, as long as you are OK?" He could see James reviewing him and his body language.

"Yeah, I'm good."

"You don't seem your usual self, a bit tired and drained. Is it all from work?"

"Yeah."

James was looking at him like he knew Hunter wasn't telling him the whole truth; he had this way of getting the truth out of him.

"OK well… it works… but not at the same time."

"OK, well, sit down, and we can discuss it, that's if you want to?"

"It's nothing really."

Hunter sat down and pinched his nose trying to release the tension, which had been building up all week.

"It doesn't look like nothing… has something happened with the business?"

"No, we are doing extremely well. Big deals are coming our way, and it looks like we will be in the running this year for the number one recruiting agency."

"That's great news, Hunter; well done."

"It's not done yet James, let's not get ahead of ourselves. Still, a lot more hard work to put in."

"Yes, but remember what we discussed about you celebrating the wins and not just keep fixating on what else needs to be done. Enjoy the ride at the same time."

This has been a problem for Hunter ever since he started the business; he was always working towards something. Putting all his determination and effort into making the company a success, and he didn't care what it took. Early mornings, late nights, no sleep, working through the weekend, not socialising. It was his life.

"There is something else though Hunter, what is it?"

Hunter didn't know where to start; he had no idea what he was feeling as he had never felt like this before. If he couldn't understand them, then how could James.

"It's just one of my employees."

James just sat there giving Hunter all the time he needed. This is what he appreciates about James. He never rushed him. Never pushed him.

"She just started this week actually… my new PA."

"Yes, you did mention that Charlotte was going on Maternity leave."

"Well, I'm not sure what I think of her." James was looking quizzically at Hunter, unsure of what he meant.

"Well, if she isn't the right fit for you or the business then simply end her contract and get someone new in."

"It's not that……she is settling in well."

Hunter removed himself from the chair and started to walk towards the window, which overlooked Hyde Park. It was a nice spring day and the sun had brought everybody outside.

"Am I correct in thinking that you are unsure of your feelings towards her?"

"You are."

"Can you describe the feelings to me?"

"James, I've never felt these feelings before. Why am I getting them now, I'm not this type of person. These feelings don't come into my equation."

James gestured for Hunter to sit back down so he could gain eye contact with him again.

"Hunter, it is understandable that you don't know how to react to these feelings, you have had your guard up for so long now. Can you describe the feelings to me?"

"I can't focus, James! That's the most frustrating thing. She is all I've thought about this week. It's irresponsible of me…. I've not even known her a week, and she is an employee."

"Before you start giving yourself a hard time, let's try and work out what these feelings are first. It may just be a physical attraction, nothing more."

"Trust me, James it's definitely physical… but there is something else, something more."

"OK, let's focus on the more part. Why do you think that there is more?"

"It's like we have a connection. I can't explain it!"

Hunter's mind was going a thousand miles an hour, and he felt drained from just talking about it.

"OK, Hunter, this is what we are going to do. Between now and our next session, I want you to have a think about your feelings towards this new employee. Write any feelings that you have down on paper, this could be physical, mental or emotional. That way we can talk through them the next time you are here. I can see that you are not yourself, and I think you are being too hard on yourself. It's OK to develop new feelings, Hunter; sometimes, it's best to just go with the flow rather than fight them, see how they turn out. You could just be overthinking and trying to control the situation like you normally do. Sometimes, our emotions can't be controlled."

Hunter got up from the chair and James did the same; he shook his hand and headed for the door.

"Thanks, James."

"I know that you might feel more confused than before you came here, but just enjoy the new emotions, you never know what could happen. And I'm not condoling an employer–employee relationship, but I do have my patient's best interest at heart."

Hunter just nodded to James and exited his office and the building, glad of the fresh air. He decided that he would walk back to the offices; he needed to clear his head, and he wasn't ready to see anyone yet especially Annalise. Hopefully, she would be at lunch by the time he got back and then he had another internal meeting to attend before the end of day rewards event.

Monday, 15 June
Annalise

It had been a funny few days for Annalise. She thought back to Friday and how she had survived one week at her new job. She had really enjoyed it, it was a great company to work for. Everyone that she had met so far was really friendly, and she liked the fast pace of it all. There was one thing in particular that she liked about it though and that was Hunter.

When taking this role, she never thought that she would be attracted to her boss, it was so unprofessional and how she had been acting was irresponsible, it was like she was a teenager again with a crush. She was glad that it wasn't one-sided though, even though Hunter hadn't really said that he had feelings for her she knew deep down that there was a connection between them both. He had been acting strange ever since she had spoken to him last week, and then on Friday, it was like he had been avoiding her.

She had seen him come back to the offices after his important meeting, but he went straight into his office and asked her not to disturb him. Annalise had been contemplating on knocking on his door before she left for the day but had decided not to.

It was now Monday again, and she was heading into the office. Penelope had been dropped off at school, and she was so excited after having such a good week last week. She had already made lots of friends and had been invited over to one of the girl's houses one afternoon next week.

As Annalise entered the reception of Hunter recruitment, she couldn't see Candice anywhere. It seemed strange as she had been the first person in the offices all of last week. Maybe she had an appointment or something. Anyway, Annalise would find her later and see how she was. As she headed to her office she wondered if Hunter would be in yet, and she became nervous just thinking about it.

How would she react with him after Friday, should she just be normal and skip right over it, she was sure that he would? She was relieved when she entered and saw that his office door was closed; she knew that he was in there as she could see a shadow moving and hear his voice; he must be on the phone with someone so knew that she could just settle at her desk and start the work that she needed to do today. As she opened her emails she noticed that she had one sitting there from this morning from Hunter.

[EMAIL] 07:05 am

From: Hunter Maguire
Subject: See me
Date: 15 June
To: Annalise Smith

Annalise,
Could you please come and see me when you get in this morning?

Hunter
Hunter Maguire
CEO, Hunter Recruitment

She wondered what he wanted to see her about, maybe it was about any meetings this week or his trip to Australia. Whatever it was, her heart rate had increased, and her hands became clammy just thinking about seeing him again. It had only been 2 days, but she had missed seeing his face. She couldn't hear him talking anymore so thought that she would bite the bullet and go and knock on his door.

She knocked once and waited; when there was no response, she knocked again but harder this time.

"Yes!"

She heard Hunter shout, and she proceeded to enter. As she stepped into his office she noticed that he was sitting at his desk, his head resting in his hands, and she wondered if everything was OK. He looked up at her, and she instantly had a flush of emotions run through her body. How could one look make her whole entire body fall under his spell? She was sure that he felt it too, his pupils had dilated and his gaze became an intense stare.

"Did I disturb you? I just received your email."

He was looking at her while pinching the bridge of his nose. Obviously, something was on his mind.

"I can come back."

As she started to head back to the door, he answered her.

"Wait! …. A major deal is hanging on by a thread and I'm the one having to sort it out. You caught me at a bad time."

"What did you want to see me about?"

She knew that she was being standoffish, but he always acted this way with her, and she didn't have time to play games from now on.

He removed his hands from his nose and adjusted his position to make him look more confident in his chair, then adjusted his tie and cleared his throat.

"I wanted to check you were ok after our conversation on Friday?"

"It's fine, Hunter. I 'm glad we cleared the air and we are now both on the same page."

She was unsure of what her last comment meant, was she bringing up emotions from earlier on last week.

"OK, well, as long as you are OK."

"I'm fine. I really must be getting on. I have a lot of work to do today. Have you seen Candice this morning?"

"Yes, why?"

"No reason, I'll go and find her at lunch."

"Everything OK?"

"All good."

Annalise exited his office quickly, proud that she stood her ground and didn't cave into her feelings. She was strong and if she could maintain that then she would be fine to work with him and stay at Hunter recruitment. She just needed to keep her distance.

Tuesday, 16 June
Annalise

Yesterday hadn't been so bad in the end; she barely saw Hunter, but when they did interact, they both stayed professional and kept it brief. She had gone looking for Candice at lunch to check that she was OK and all was reassured when Candice said that she had just had to run some errands for Hunter that morning. Annalise had wondered why he hadn't asked her to do them seeing as she was his PA, but then again, she never got into the office until after Candice. She has confirmed their shopping trip for today and Annalise was excited to try and find a dress for Friday's event; she just hoped that she could find something within her budget.

Candice came to get Annalise just after midday, and she was glad of the break, it had been non-stop all morning with arranging meetings for Hunter.

"Ready to go?"

"Sure am!"

"Busy morning? You looked completely focussed when I came in, working on something important for Hunter?"

"I've just been finalising some meetings, all last minute of course. Just had to juggle a few things around for him."

"Right let's go and spend some of your money on a fabulous dress."

"Sounds good to me, although that fabulous dress will need to be no more than £70, that's all my budget can stretch to right now."

"I know of a few good shops that have some sales on at the moment, I'm sure we can find you something within your budget."

So far, they had been to Top Shop, H&M, Marks and Spencer's and French Connection but after trying on several dresses Annalise still hadn't found one that she liked. They were now in Zara and already she felt happier with the styles in here, and it was still within her budget. She had picked up a few dresses to try on, but the one that really caught her eye was a thin silk emerald green dress.

It had capped sleeves that fell slightly off the shoulder, a straight neckline that ran from one shoulder to the other, and it was tightly fitted, which she knew would suit her body shape. The main thing that she loved about it though was the sweeping lowered backline, which just made the dress. She had to try it on and hoped that it would suit her let alone fit her. Candice approached her with several dresses for herself.

"Ooh I like that one, are you going to try it on?"

"Yes. It's the only one that has really stood out for me, let's hope it fits!"

"It definitely will! And that colour will compliment your dark features really well."

"I'll just go and try it on then, shall I come out and show you?"

"Of course. I need to see it on so I can give you my approval."

As Annalise looked in the mirror, she almost didn't recognise herself. The material of the dress clung to her body showing off all her curves. The emerald green really did make her features stand out and the back of the dress was revealing but in a sexy way. She instantly felt confident in it and got excited about wearing it to the party. She would quickly show Candice, but she knew that this was the dress to wear!

"So what do you think?"

"Oh, my god, you look hot! All the men will definitely be looking at you. You might even show me up!"

Annalise knew that Candice was only joking about her last comment and that no one could outshine her; she was beautiful.

"Right, well this is definitely the dress, I'll just get changed and pay and then shall we grab some food before heading back to the office. Do we have time?"

"Sounds good to me, and we definitely have time. I said that I was taking a slightly longer lunch break today, so I'm covered, what about you? Will Hunter be looking for you?"

"I doubt it, anyway I told him I was coming shopping with you so he knows that I might be longer than normal."

They got back to the office around 2:00 p.m., taking a little bit longer than she had anticipated. Annalise had thanked Candice for taking her out and said that she would buy her coffee next week to make up for it, which Candice kindly accepted. Annalise felt that she was going to make a friend out of Candice, they both were roughly the same age and had things in common. She also seemed fun and Annalise definitely needed a fun friend.

She placed her bag under her desk and started to go through her job list; when she opened her emails, she had one sitting there from Hunter and in the subject, it read, "I hope you found a dress." Annalise didn't know how to take the message, was he asking her, or was he saying it as she had taken too long out of her lunch break. How should she respond to him? She decided to keep it brief.

[EMAIL] 01:05 pm

From: Annalise Smith
Subject: Dress
Date: 16 June
To: Hunter Maguire

Yes, I did thank you. Sorry, if I took too long, you know how females get when it comes to shopping!

Annalise
Personal Assistant to Hunter Maguire, Hunter Recruitment

Obviously, he didn't know how females got when they went shopping unless he had taken his previous girlfriends shopping, but she wasn't sure whether he was that type of man or not to do that. She waited for a reply, not knowing if he would or not.

[EMAIL] 01:07 PM

From: Hunter Maguire
Subject: Dress
Date: 16 June
To: Annalise Smith

I can't stand shopping. Glad you found a dress. I look forward to seeing you on Friday night.

Hunter
Hunter Maguire
CEO, Hunter Recruitment

Annalise's heart rate started to increase; she forgot that he was going to be there and see her in the dress. She wondered whether he would like her in it; she hoped that he did. That's all that was going through her mind when buying it. Maybe she should show him now so the pressure was off on Friday, that way there would be no awkward moments.

[EMAIL] 01:08 pm

From: Annalise Smith
Subject: Dress
Date: 16 June
To: Hunter Maguire

Well, I can show you now if you like? It would be nice to get a male's opinion.

Annalise
Annalise Smith
Personal Assistant to Hunter Maguire, Hunter recruitment

She waited for his response in anticipation not knowing if this was overstepping the mark.

[EMAIL] 01:09 pm

From: Hunter Maguire
Subject: Dress
Date: 16 June
To: Annalise Smith

You want to show me your dress?

Hunter
Hunter Maguire
CEO, Hunter Recruitment

Oh, god, why had she suggested showing him of course he didn't want to see her in the dress now. She was stupid to think that.

[EMAIL] 01:10 pm

From: Annalise Smith
Subject: Dress
Date: 16 June
To: Hunter Maguire

Well, not on, of course, I was just going to show you it on the hanger. Get a male's opinion.

Hunter
Hunter Maguire
CEO, Hunter Recruitment

His reply was quick and short.

[EMAIL] 01:11 pm

From: Hunter Maguire
Subject: Dress
Date: 16 June
To: Annalise Smith

Bring it into my office and show me then.

Hunter
Hunter Maguire
CEO, Hunter Recruitment

Annalise didn't know what to think; she was nervous to see him after how they had been with each other the last few days and why was he now being nice to her. Maybe she should just email him back and say that she had an urgent email come through that she had to deal with and that he could just see it on Friday. Before she could say anything, another email came through from him.

[EMAIL] 01:12 pm

From: Hunter Maguire
Subject: Dress
Date: 16 June
To: Annalise Smith

Annalise,
I don't have all day, either come and show me the dress or don't.

Hunter
Hunter Maguire
CEO, Hunter Recruitment

She decided to just be brave and picked up the bag with the dress in and headed into his office, stopping just outside his door to build up her courage before knocking and entering. As she walked in he had his head down and was typing something on his computer.

"Give me a moment, I just need to send this email. Take a seat rather than just standing there."

Once he was finished on his computer he looked up and straight into her eyes.

"Right, so where is this dress?"

"Um…."

"Come on Annalise, I don't have all day. You wanted a male opinion, and I can also let you know if it is suitable for the party."

"Of course."

She took the dress out of the bag with it still on the hanger and held it up against her body, feeling slightly embarrassed at what he may say. He was studying it looking between her and the dress, and she thought she saw a darkness change in his eyes.

"What do you think?"

His eyes grew darker and his look became more intense. She waited for his reply that seemed to take forever. Maybe he didn't like it and was working out how to tell her.

"Annalise, I think it's just as beautiful as the person who will be wearing it."

She was taken aback by his comment and started to feel embarrassed. She was unsure of how to respond. He had just told her that she was beautiful. She couldn't even remember the last time someone had called her beautiful, it almost brought tears to her eyes. She stood there looking at him, their eyes connecting again when she finally managed to get some words out.

"Thank you, Hunter. That's very kind of you."

"I'm sure you will turn plenty of heads on Friday, just don't believe everything the consultants tell you. They are full of bullshit half the time!"

"I'm sure there will be much nicer looking dresses and females there than me to keep them occupied."

Hunter stood up from his chair and started to walk around his desk closing the distance between them.

"I doubt it."

He was now standing in front of her looking directly into her eyes and Annalise was unable to move, it was like her limbs had frozen up. She was unsure of what he was going to say or do next.

"Don't put yourself down like that Annalise. You are beautiful."

She looked down at the floor, unsure of what to say to his comment.

"I know that you can feel it too Annalise, this connection between us."

He rubbed his forehead like something was causing him a headache, and she knew the feeling all too well.

"But I promised you last week that I wouldn't take it any further, and I meant it."

He walked back around his desk and sat down in his chair, breaking the atmosphere that had been building up. Annalise just stood there, her brain rattling around trying to think of what to say.

"Annalise?"

"Yes"

"Was there anything else? I have to get on with some work."

It had happened again; he had put his guard back up before she could even respond to him. How could he just turn it off and on like a switch.

"No, sorry. Thank you for your opinion on the dress."

By this point, Hunter was already typing on his computer and acted like she wasn't even there; she headed for the door and back to her desk.

Tuesday, 16 June
Hunter

Hunter knew he had overstepped the boundaries again, especially after their chat last week, but he couldn't help it. He didn't know what was wrong with him; he was never like this. He was taken by surprise by these new feelings, and it was making him act differently. When he was with Annalise, he just had the urge to take her in his arms and kiss her.

He wanted to get to know her and knew they shared something, but he wasn't sure what it was. He knew it was more than just a physical attraction. He had been attracted to many women before, and it would usually always go the same way, dinner and sex, nothing more. He never wanted to know about their personal lives or what they wanted for the future; he couldn't care less to be honest.

But, with Annalise, he wanted to know everything there was to know about her. And the one time when he actually wanted to get to know someone, he couldn't do anything about it. She needed this job for her and her daughter, and he wasn't going to be the one to take it away from her, especially as he was still unsure of what he was feeling. He couldn't offer her a future, that wasn't in his plan; he certainly wasn't going to start changing that all now just because of some small connection with a woman.

He said that he would be professional, and he had to keep his promise. He would see how he felt again when it was the end of Annalise's 3-month contract and if he still had these feelings at that point, then he would have to speak with her about getting a new job. He couldn't be distracted from work and the easiest option for him would be to remove the distraction.

The afternoon had been tough for Hunter knowing that Annalise was just in the next room. He felt his sexual tension build, and he needed to do something about it; he needed a distraction. He took out his phone, scrolling through it until he came to the name he wanted. Rosie. He hit dial.

"Well, hello, Hunter. Isn't this a surprise! You calling me!"

"Very funny Rosie, I've called you plenty of times before."

"Only to return my phone calls. Anyway, why are you calling me?"

"I thought that we could meet up?"

Is this really what he wanted? No, it wasn't, but he just needed a distraction for the night and Rosie could definitely do that.

"Well, let me think about this. I may have plans already and I'm not sure if I can change them. I suppose I could if we were to go somewhere really nice and romantic for dinner!"

"Rosie, you know I don't do romance."

"OK. Well, don't worry about it then. I'll see you around."

"Don't mess with me Rosie, I could end this right now."

"God Hunter, I was only joking! Can't you take a joke?"

"Yes, when it's a funny joke! So, do you want to go for dinner or not?"

"Yes. What time and where?"

"I have a few things to tie up here, so let's say 8:00 p.m. at Balthazar in Covent Garden?"

"Ooh, I love that place! Perfect, see you then!"

Hunter put his phone down and put his head in his hands, what was he doing? He knew he was just using Rosie and normally it didn't bother him because they had an agreement, but it felt different this time. He was basically using her as a distraction and that was wrong. He would make sure tonight was the last time. He would take her for dinner and tell her that he couldn't see her anymore, that she needed to move on and meet someone who could offer her more than he could.

It had been fun while it lasted, but he didn't need any more drama in his life now that he had Annalise to deal with. It was only Tuesday and his life had gone from maintaining control to almost falling apart in the space of 3 days. How a woman could do that to a man, let alone him. He didn't know. Even though he still had a lot to do, he needed to get out of the office so he decided to text Tyrell to see if he could fit him in for a quick training session. Tyrell's reply came quickly and simply said 'yes'. Hunter grabbed his things and headed out of his office.

"I'm leaving early, Annalise. I have a few things to do, enjoy your evening."

He kept it brief; he didn't want any more moments with her. He noticed that her facial expression seemed slightly concerned but simply replied that she would see him in the morning.

He entered the gym and felt the familiarity of it release some tension that he had been carrying. Tyrell was heading towards him and Hunter could tell that he was going to be in one of his annoying moods.

"Well well well, look who it is! You must be frustrated if you need to come and train twice in one day. What happened, a deal goes south?"

"Yeah, something like that. I just need to clear my head before tonight."

"Why what's happening tonight?"

"I'm seeing Rosie for dinner. I need a distraction, and she always manages to take my mind off things."

"I'm sure she does!"

"I think I'm also going to call it a day with her. I'm losing focus on work, and I can't have that happening, it's too important to me. She is just a distraction that I don't need right now."

"Hunter, it is OK to have a life outside of work you know. Stop fighting these things. Rosie's a nice woman. She's hot; she has a good job and good connections. She's a catch!"

"Yes, but a woman like Rosie also comes with demands. Plus, it's not just her, it's my new PA, Annalise. She is distracting me all the time."

"Well, fire her then, if she isn't doing a good job."

"It's not that she is doing a great job. It's… god what is wrong with me!"

Tyrell was looking at him unsure of where this conversation was heading.

"Oh, you have a thing for her, don't you?"

"Tyrell, I don't know what I have for her. I've never felt a connection like this before, and I don't even know her very well! Plus she has a daughter!"

Hunter was now pacing around the gym feeling more stressed out just by mentioning her to Tyrell.

"Well, get to know her then and so what if she has a daughter. Maybe that will help you get over your fear of a family."

"Tyrell that's not going to happen. I have to put whatever feelings I have to one side and be professional. She can't jeopardise her job either, and so nothing could ever happen. I'm her boss!"

"Hunter, calm down! I can see why you wanted to train. Let's get started, and we can talk about this afterwards."

"There's nothing to talk about, Tyrell. I've got it covered. I'm gaining control back, and it starts tonight with Rosie."

"Yeah, sounds like you have!"

Hunter instantly felt better after his workout. He felt energised again and more focussed; he still had emotions going on in his head, but he had a clearer picture now. He needed to end things with Rosie tonight, maintain some kind of distance from Annalise and focus on the business. Tyrell was approaching him with a smug look on his face.

"What you are thinking about Hunt?"

Only Tyrell got away calling him by that name; he had started calling him it when they first started to train, and it had just stuck.

"Just the trip to Australia that I have soon. It could be a big deal for us, so I have to be on top form."

"So no more women on the brain?"

"No. Your workout has given me some clarity."

"Well, I hope that's a good thing, I don't want you going and breaking anyone's heart now!"

Tyrell was laughing, making a joke at Hunter's situation, which riled Hunter up again.

"Tyrell shut it or I'll be dragging you back in that ring. I better get going, I've got to meet Rosie soon, and I doubt she will like what I have to say."

"Good luck with that one!"

It was now 7:30 p.m., and Hunter had to leave to meet Rosie in Convent Garden. He had called his driver to collect him and hoped London traffic wasn't too bad. He wanted to be there before Rosie so that he could control the situation. As the concierge called him to inform him his driver was waiting outside, he grabbed his jacket and headed downstairs to meet him.

"Good evening, Mr Maguire, how have you been?"

"Very well thanks Tony, how about you?"

"All good from my end! So you are off to Covent Garden tonight?"

"Yes, that's correct. Balthazar to be precise."

"Very nice indeed. Traffic isn't too bad so I should get you there just before 8:00 p.m."

As Tony drove Hunter to the restaurant, he noticed all the hustle and bustle of the busy London streets, wondering where people were off to tonight. Were they about to be put into an uncomfortable situation like him. Even though Rosie

83

and he had agreed on a casual thing; he knew that she felt more for him. He had just been ignoring it, more so because their situation suited him.

He was always the one in control and that's the way he liked it. He thought back to Annalise and how every time he had been around her; he was never in control. His emotions always took over and that scared him because he didn't want to do something that he may regret.

The car stopped, and he hadn't realised they were so close to Covent Garden. His thoughts must have taken over.

"Here you are, Mr Maguire. I hope you have a lovely evening. Will you need collecting as well?"

"More than likely Tony. Can I give you a text in a little while to let you know?"

"Of course. I have a few errands to run tonight, so I'll wait for your text."

As Hunter approached the restaurant, he was greeted by the maître d' who welcomed him with a warm smile.

"Do you have a reservation for tonight, sir?"

"Yes. Maguire. I am also waiting on a guest, has she arrived yet?"

"No, sir, not yet. I will let them know that you have been seated when they arrive."

As the maître d showed Hunter to his table, he looked around and noticed the restaurant was filled with couples. They were holding hands, laughing, and genuinely having a good time. Doubt started to kick in, and he wondered whether he had chosen the wrong place to bring Rosie to. Maybe it would have been best to of just phoned Rosie to let her down, but that would have been the coward's way out, and he wasn't a coward.

He would treat it like a business meeting, professional and polite. As he looked up, he noticed Rosie heading towards him; she looked amazing although maybe a little overdressed for the occasion. She obviously thought this was a romantic dinner for them or hoped at least. As she approached the table, Hunter stood up and gave her a kiss on the cheek.

"You didn't have to go to all this effort for me."

He instantly knew he had said the wrong thing, as her smile had faded, and she looked disappointed.

"Well, sometimes Hunter, women like to get dressed up for dinner, even if it's just to feel good about themselves, and it's not appreciated by their date. Have you been waiting long? London traffic was a bit of a nightmare and the cab driver I had was useless. He kept taking me the wrong way; he must be new to the area."

"No, not long. Wine?"

"Of course. You decide, but I prefer red."

Hunter ordered them a bottle of Shiraz and reviewed the menu, deciding to have the duck confit.

"Do you know what you want to order, Rosie?"

"I'll have the grilled fillet of salmon, please. It sounds amazing, and not full of calories. Have to watch my figure to be able to wear a dress like this."

They gave their order to the waitress, and she poured their wine before leaving them both alone. Hunter decided that it was best to wait until they had finished their main meals before he brought up the main topic of conversation.

"So how's business going?"

"Oh, Hunter do we really have to talk about business tonight?"

"We share a common interest in the business. It's what we normally talk about."

"Yes, but can we have one night where it's less business and more personal. I want to get to know the real Hunter Maguire."

"I don't do personal, Rosie."

There was a long pause, and she just looked at him trying to work him out.

"I don't get you, Hunter. What happened to you as a child, why don't you ever open up to anyone. I mean we have known each other for a while now, and I still don't know anything about you, other than work. Do you have siblings?"

"Rosie, I like it this way. It's how I am, and it's easier for me. You knew the deal from the start, why are you saying all this stuff now?"

"I just want to get to know you more, that's all."

"Why? Why is this not enough for you?!"

Hunter knew what the answer was but kept pushing, maybe this was a way out for him. He wanted to wait till after the main course, but it looked like it wasn't going that way.

"Surely, you must know, Hunter?"

"No, I don't Rosie. We go for dinner and have sex, that's it. Well, that's all it is for me, isn't that the case for you? We had an agreement."

"Dinner and casual sex, is that all I am to you?"

"Rosie! We agreed on this from day one. You knew I don't do relationships or feelings. I can't."

"Yes, but I thought it may change. That you may change and start to get feelings for me as I have for you. I thought you would like the person I am and want to spend more time getting to know me."

Her whole demeanour had changed, and she now seemed like a vulnerable little girl. Her eyes had started to tear up, and she was fiddling with the stem of her wine glass. The waitress at that point came over to deliver their main meals and Hunter didn't know whether he was pleased for the break or annoyed that it had caused a delay in their conversation.

"Rosie, can we just enjoy this meal and then talk about it afterwards?"

She didn't answer but simply picked up her knife and fork and started to cut into her salmon.

They finished their mains, although Rosie had barely touched hers. There had been a minimum conversation, it had mainly been Hunter talking and Rosie nodding.

"Rosie, I didn't mean to upset you. I just thought that you knew the situation and this was all it was going to be."

"I had hoped Hunter like every woman does that this might become something more. That I would be the woman who you want to open up to."

"No. You thought that you could be the one to change me."

"No, not at all. I just thought the more time you spent with me, the more you would open up, but that hasn't been the case. You only ever call me when you want some company or need some distraction. I have feelings for you Hunter. I have tried to stop them, but I can't."

"Rosie. I'm sorry, I truly am, but I don't get involved like that. I never meant to hurt you, I honestly thought we were on the same page. I have never led you to believe that it was something more. You know I am not capable of anything more. I'm doing you a favour really Rosie."

The look on her face was like thunder and Hunter knew the conversation wasn't going down well.

"You use people Hunter. It's that simple, and I have only just realised it. God, I have been so pathetic. Always being at your beck and call, dropping anything I had planned just to meet you for a few hours and then it's back to waiting again until the next time you call."

Hunter just sat there not knowing what else to say; he didn't want to hurt Rosie, but it had obviously turned out that way.

"Are you not going to say anything, Hunter?"

"Rosie, I think it's best if we end this now. You have feelings that are not reciprocated, and they never will be. It's best if you go and find someone who can give you the happy ending that you want, as that will never be me."

"So that's it then? Just see you later Rosie, thanks for being my sex buddy, but I'm done now! Well, Hunter, I'm done! You are not using me anymore! I deserve better than this."

Rosie had increased her volume and a few tables had started to look their way. Hunter didn't care about the other people; they could stare all they liked. Rosie then proceeded to down the rest of her wine and storm out of the restaurant telling the other tables that the show was over.

He wanted to end it on a nice tone with them being civilised, so as not to make it awkward if they bumped into each other in the future, but that hadn't been the case. He didn't mean to hurt Rosie. It was hard for him to see it from her perspective, as he had never felt that way about someone before, and he hoped he never did. If it looked like that, he was glad of the way he was.

He finished his wine and asked for the bill and then decided to text Tony to come and get him. It was only 9:30 p.m., which meant that he could finish some work when he got home before going to bed. Hunter sometimes wished he didn't always think about work, but he had always been that way ever since he started the business. He knew most people would be at home with their families now or out for dinner with friends or loved ones. He then wondered what Annalise would be doing but instantly pushed that thought aside; he couldn't be thinking about her right now. He headed outside after he had received a text from Tony informing him that he was waiting in the car outside the restaurant.

"I didn't expect you to call me so quickly. Is everything OK Mr Maguire?"

"Just a meeting that didn't go as well as I had hoped. Actually, today hasn't been a very good day at all. I'll be glad when it's over."

"Sorry, to hear that. Hopefully, tomorrow will be a better day for you."

"Yes, me too."

When Hunter got back to his apartment, he decided he wasn't in the mood to do work. The day and evening he just had, had taken their toll on him, and he needed some quiet time. He poured himself a glass of red wine and decided to just sit and watch the people of London go by, hoping tiredness would hit him soon and today would be over.

Wednesday, 17 June
Annalise

It was now 2:00 a.m., and Annalise had been up with Penelope for a few hours. Penelope hadn't been herself when Annalise had picked her up from after school care; she had looked very pale and had a temperature coming on. She had asked one of Penelope's teachers if she was OK, and they had said that she only started feeling unwell just before she had arrived. Annalise had asked Penelope what was wrong, but all she said was that she had a stomach-ache and had felt sick.

When they got home, Annalise had put Penelope to bed and that's when the throwing up started. It had been quite aggressive to start with but was now slowing down, and she had just been giving Penelope water to drink to try and keep her hydrated. She hated seeing her little girl like this, knowing that there was nothing that she could do but give her lots of cuddles and take care of her. She would have to call work and let them know that she wasn't able to come in tomorrow as Penelope wouldn't be going to school after the afternoon/evening that they had had.

She may have to take her to the doctors if this carried on, Annalise just hoped that it was just a 24-hour bug and nothing more serious. Penelope seemed like she was over the worst of it and had now managed to fall asleep in Annalise's bed. Knowing that she was unable to attend work tomorrow she thought she should email Hunter and let him know now in case he needed her to attend any meetings, then she would let HR know in the morning.

Annalise knew he would probably be asleep, but he would get it when he woke up giving him enough notice if he had to reschedule anything. She hated she had to have a day off so soon in to her employment, but she could do some work from home; hopefully, he wouldn't mind. She took out her laptop hoping not to disturb Penelope and started to type the email.

[EMAIL] 02:30 am

From: Annalise Smith
Subject: Work from home
Date: 17 June
To: Hunter Maguire

Hi Hunter,

I thought I better let you know as soon as possible, but I will have to work from home tomorrow. My daughter has been unwell, which means she won't be able to go to school tomorrow. I don't think it will be fair to get someone else to look after her when she is like this and at such short notice. I am really sorry to let you down on my second week of work. Please still send me any work that you need doing, and I will make sure to get it done here.

Thanks, Annalise.
Annalise Smith
Personal Assistant to Hunter Maguire, Hunter Recruitment

She put her laptop to one side and went to go and get some more water for Penelope in case she woke up again. On her return, she was surprised when her email was flashing saying that she had one new message. Thinking it was probably a spam email she clicked it open only to realise that it was a reply from Hunter. What was he doing up she thought, had she woke him? Surely he wouldn't be working at 2:30 a.m. She opened his email up and read it.

[EMAIL] 02:35 am

From: Hunter Maguire
Subject: Work from home
Date: 17 June
To: Annalise Smith

Annalise,
I will check what work I need you to do when I'm in the office.

Hunter
Hunter Maguire
CEO, Hunter Recruitment

She noticed at the bottom of his email that it had been sent from his phone rather than his laptop. Maybe he was in bed, maybe she had woke him up. She would feel terrible if she had.

[EMAIL] 02:45 am

From: Annalise Smith
Subject: Work from home
Date: 17 June
To: Annalise Smith

Hunter,
Thank you for the reply and sorry if I woke you?
I'm sure Penelope will be fine after some rest. Keep me posted on the workload.

Thanks, Annalise
Annalise Smith
Personal Assistant to Hunter Maguire, Hunter Recruitment

[EMAIL] 02:46 am

From: Hunter Maguire
Subject: Work from home
Date: 17 June
To: Annalise Smith

You didn't wake me; I was already up. I haven't been to sleep yet. Long day.

Hunter Maguire
CEO, Hunter Recruitment

He hasn't been to bed yet? Annalise wondered what he had been up to and her mind started thinking of everything possible that a single hot wealthy man could be doing.

[EMAIL] 02:47 am

From: Annalise Smith
Subject: Work from home
Date: 17 June
To: Hunter Maguire

Well, I'm sorry if I disturbed you, I hope you had a good evening.

Annalise Smith
Personal Assistant to Hunter Maguire, Hunter Recruitment

[EMAIL] 02:48 am

From: Hunter Maguire
Subject: Work from home
Date: 17 June
To: Annalise Smith

You didn't disturb me. I was just finalising some paperwork.

Hunter Maguire
CEO, Hunter Recruitment

[EMAIL] 02:49 am

From: Annalise Smith
Subject: Work from home
Date: 17 June
To: Hunter Maguire

You are dedicated working at this hour.

Annalise Smith

Personal Assistant to Hunter Maguire, Hunter Recruitment

[EMAIL] 02:50 am

From: Hunter Maguire
Subject: Work from home
Date: 17 June
To: Annalise Smith

Well, it is my business Annalise; I have to be.

Hunter Maguire

CEO, Hunter Recruitment

[EMAIL] 02:51 am

From: Annalise Smith
Subject: Work from home
Date: 17 June
To: Hunter Maguire

Sorry. It must be very stressful running a business and here I am emailing you in the early hours of the morning when we should both be asleep. Although I forget that some adults are out partying till the early hours of the morning having a life. I'm sure most of your evenings are spent out at fancy restaurants, nightclubs and having intellectual conversations. How I wish to have some of those events in my life.

Annalise Smith

Personal Assistant to Hunter Maguire, Hunter Recruitment

She waited for his reply that was taking longer than recent ones.

[EMAIL] 02:53 am

From: Hunter Maguire
Subject: Work from home

Date: 17 June
To: Annalise Smith

I don't have time to socialise much. Generally, my meals out are for client meetings, and I can't remember the last time that I went to a nightclub. You must have a very different opinion of my life that I don't lead, Annalise.

Hunter Maguire
CEO, Hunter Recruitment

Annalise was starting to think that he was different to how everyone else perceived him. Maybe he wasn't this flashy rich businessman who charmed all the ladies. Annalise wanted to know more about him and decided to ask him how he started the business. She had tried to read about it on the internet, but there wasn't really anything on there. Everyone else had just said that he had started it when he was young and had worked his way up. She was feeling braver behind her computer and not having his gaze on her.

[EMAIL] 02:55 am

From: Annalise Smith
Subject: Work from home
Date: 17 June
To: Hunter Maguire

Can I ask you a question?

Annalise Smith
Personal Assistant to Hunter Maguire, Hunter Recruitment

[EMAIL] 02:56 am

From: Hunter Maguire
Subject: Work from home
Date: 17 June
To: Annalise Smith

It depends, is it business or personal?

Hunter Maguire
CEO, Hunter Recruitment

[EMAIL] 02:57 am

From: Annalise Smith
Subject: Work from home
Date: 17 June
To: Hunter Maguire

Both.

Annalise Smith
Personal Assistant to Hunter Maguire, Hunter Recruitment

[EMAIL] 02:58 am

From: Hunter Maguire
Subject: Work from home
Date: 17 June
To: Annalise Smith

I don't talk about my personal life, Annalise.

Hunter Maguire
CEO, Hunter Recruitment

From: Annalise Smith
Subject: Work from home
Date: 17 June
To: Hunter Maguire

Well, I just wanted to know how you started the company. Was it something that you had always wanted to do?

Annalise Smith
Personal Assistant to Hunter Maguire, Hunter Recruitment

[EMAIL] 03:01 am

From: Hunter Maguire
Subject: Work from home
Date: 17 June
To: Annalise Smith

I knew I always wanted to be successful and just kept pushing until I got here. The business still has a long way to go.

Hunter Maguire
CEO, Hunter Recruitment

Well, that didn't really answer her question. She thought that he might have said that it was his family who helped him or he inherited the money to start it, but nothing. Maybe she should push further to see how far she could go with him.

[EMAIL] 03:02 am

From: Annalise Smith
Subject: Work from home
Date: 17 June

To: Hunter Recruitment

So did your family help you set it up?

Annalise Smith
Personal Assistant to Hunter Maguire, Hunter Recruitment

She waited for his reply, but it had been 5 minutes now and still nothing. Maybe she had pushed too far; he said that he didn't talk about his personal life. Unless he had fallen asleep. She was getting a bit anxious that she had irritated her boss, especially in the early hours of the morning. She was about to turn off her laptop when she got another reply.

[EMAIL] 03:03 am

> **From:** Hunter Maguire
> **Subject:** Work from home
> **Date**: 17 June
> **To**: Annalise Smith

No. Family doesn't come into my equation. I achieved it from pure determination and wanting a better life for myself.

Hunter Maguire
CEO, Hunter Recruitment

Annalise knew there was more to his comment; she knew the feeling too well. It was best she didn't push any further.

[EMAIL] 03:05 am

> **From:** Annalise Smith
> **Subject:** Work from home
> **Date**: 17 June
> **To**: Hunter Maguire

You have done exceptionally well for yourself. I am sure everyone is very proud of you. Well, it's going to be light soon and Penelope will no doubt wake up shortly so I'm going to try and get a few hours' sleep before she does. I will touch base with you again in the morning to see if there is anything that you need me to do. Good night Hunter.

Annalise Smith
Personal Assistant to Hunter Maguire, Hunter Recruitment

She turned her laptop off still thinking about Hunter's comment about his family. She felt sadness for him wondering what had happened to him during his childhood. She didn't want to ask anymore knowing what it was like when people probe about situations in your life that you would rather not talk about. As she lay there thinking about what had happened between her and her parents, her eyelids became heavy and sleep started to take over her.

Wednesday, 17 June
Annalise

Penelope woke Annalise at 8:00 a.m. As she stretched out her body feeling exhausted from the lack of sleep she had got the night before, she turned to look at her little girl who was still slightly pale but definitely had more colour in her than yesterday.

"How are you feeling today my little princess, is your tummy better?"

"My stomach hurts still, but I don't feel sick anymore. Do I have to go to school today? I don't think I'm well enough."

"It's a good job you are staying at home, otherwise you would be late already. I'll call the school shortly to let them know you won't be coming in today. Do you feel like you could eat something?"

"Maybe some toast. I don't want to be sick again Mummy, it hurt."

"I know darling, let's try some plain toast and see how you feel after that."

"Can I have some water as well? I'm super thirsty."

"Of course. Right, you stay in bed under these warm covers. I will make you some toast and bring you some water. How about we watch a Disney movie?"

Penelope just smiled and nodded at Annalise and then snuggled back under the duvet.

Annalise phoned the school and informed them that Penelope was still unwell and that she was going to rest at home today. The school seemed thankful in case it was a bug, they didn't want it spreading to other kids. She then made some toast and took it up to Penelope along with some water.

Penelope had insisted on watching frozen again and Annalise knew that she must be feeling better as she only chose that film so she could sing along to the songs. Then she decided to get her laptop and snuggle up in bed with Penelope. She thought she better log on and email Hunter to see if he needed her to do anything, at least she could do some work from home that way she wouldn't feel as bad for not going into the office today, even though it wasn't technically her fault.

[EMAIL] 08:30 am

> **From:** Annalise Smith
> **Subject:** Work from home
> **Date**: 17 June
> **To**: Hunter Maguire
>
> Morning Hunter,
> I hope you slept well?
> I've logged in online so if there is anything that you need me to do, then just say.
>
> Thanks,
> Annalise.
> **Annalise Smith**
> **Personal Assistant to Hunter Maguire, Hunter Recruitment**

While she waited for his reply, she decided to enter his name again into Google to see what came up. As she pressed enter her screen became one big image of Hunter's face and body, things that she had started to become acquainted with over the past few days. All the images though seemed like they were from business events or functions. He was always pictured with other high powered businessmen, a few with women but no family photos that she could see.

She wondered for a moment who the women were but put them in the bank of either business or friends; she couldn't think of Hunter with other women right now. She clicked on one of the photos of him in a suit; he looked extremely smart and handsome and was smiling, which she hadn't seen him do very often, but it suited him in this photo. It made his whole face light up and a warm glimmer in his eye.

She wondered what had made him so happy or whether it was just fake for the cameras. She wanted to see more of that smile and hear his laugh. As she was deep in thought thinking about his features she heard a ping from her emails, one new message from Hunter.

[EMAIL] 08:35 am

From: Hunter Maguire
Subject: Work from home
Date: 17 June
To: Annalise Smith

Annalise,

Can you please arrange a couple of meetings for next week? I need to see these clients before my Australia trip and don't have much time before I go. Coordinate with Tanya the team assistant for Jason, she will let you know who needs to attend them. I also need you to reply to a few of these urgent emails and can you please confirm with Candice that everything is ready for Friday evening. I could do with your help.

Hunter
Hunter Maguire
CEO, Hunter Recruitment

He was straight to business, nothing more about their conversation last night. Maybe he was just busy; she would try and get it all done by early afternoon.

[EMAIL] 08:37 am

From: Annalise Smith
Subject: Work from home
Date: 17 June
To: Hunter Maguire

Of course, Hunter. I will let you know once it is all done.

I hope the rest of your day is less busy and that you managed to get some sleep last night.

Annalise.

Annalise Smith

Personal Assistant to Hunter Maguire, Hunter Recruitment

She checked Penelope was OK and then proceeded to complete the tasks that Hunter had given her. First emailing Candice about Friday night. She wasn't sure what she needed to finalise as she hadn't been involved in organising it but knew that Charlotte had been, that must be why Hunter had asked her to check everything. As she thought about Friday night, she hoped Penelope was OK by then, there was no way that she would leave her with a stranger.

Her dress could be stored in the wardrobe until another opportunity came up. She felt a pang of disappointment at the thought of not having a night out, but this is what she had to do as a mother. This always came first and her personal life came second, which was the deal she had made with herself when having Penelope.

By mid-afternoon, Penelope was feeling much better; she had watched two Disney films, had slept for a few hours and managed to eat some toast and was now proceeding to tell Annalise that she was bored and wanted some fresh air. As Annalise had nearly finished the tasks that Hunter had given her, she decided that it might be nice to go for a walk to the local park. It looked nice outside, still cooler, but when the sun hit you, it felt like a warm summer's day.

"Right Penelope let's get our coats on and go for a walk. I think some fresh air will do us both good!"

"Yay, can we go and play on the swings?"

"I'm not sure you are up for that Penelope; you haven't been very well. Maybe we will just walk today, but I promise I will take you on the swings on at the weekend, sound good?"

"OK."

They both grabbed their coats, put their boots on and headed out of the house. It was such a beautiful day, still a bit crisp, but you could tell that it was the start of summer; she couldn't wait until the weather started to warm up and Summer being in full swing.

"Mummy, what are you smiling at?"

"I'm just thinking about all the things we can do when the weather gets warmer."

"Like going to the beach? I would love to go to the beach, build sandcastles, splash in the sea, and go crab hunting."

Penelope's face lit up just talking about it and Annalise knew how excited she was. They used to go to the beaches in Norfolk, and they loved them. Although it did make Annalise sad at times watching all the families play together with their brothers, sisters, grandparents, aunties and uncles, and for Annalise, it was always just her and Penelope. It didn't bother her that much, but she didn't want Penelope to feel like she was missing out.

Her parents had never wanted to come to the beach with them, even though she would always offer every time that they went on the off chance that they might change their minds but no, never. As Annalise focussed back on the present day, she just enjoyed spending time with her daughter. The little things, like now walking around their local neighbourhood holding hands and taking in the sights, the sounds, the people, it was all so interesting and new to them both This is what made her happy.

"I'm tired and my legs are aching Mummy."

"Right missy, let's head back; we have been walking for a while now, and I don't want to use all your energy up. Shall we get you tucked back up in bed and you have a rest before I make some dinner?"

"Yes. I want to dream some more about prince charming."

"And what is prince charming doing in your dreams? Has he met his princess yet?"

"Nearly, he is looking for her, and she is waiting for him to come and rescue her."

"Well, I'm sure they will find each other."

Annalise didn't always like Penelope thinking that there were prince charmings in the world, but then again, she was only 7, and why should she spoil her dreams? Penelope would soon find out when she was older that there were no fairy tale endings, but for now, Annalise wanted Penelope to have hope. As they arrived back home, took their coats and shoes off, Annalise tucked Penelope in bed and then decided to check her emails before starting dinner for them both.

It was now 4:30 p.m., and she doubted that there would be any work for her to do, especially as she would be back in the office tomorrow as Penelope was feeling better. As she logged on she noticed that she had several emails from Hunter and wondered what it could be.

[EMAIL] 03:05 pm

From: Hunter Maguire
Subject: Australia trip
Date: 17 June
To: Annalise Smith

Annalise the meeting in Australia has been brought forward, I need you to rearrange my flights for this coming Monday.

Hunter
Hunter Maguire
CEO, Hunter Recruitment

[EMAIL] 03:10 pm

From: Hunter Maguire
Subject: Australia trip
Date: 17 June
To: Annalise Smith

Also, contact the hotel and change the booking.

Hunter
Hunter Maguire
CEO, Hunter Recruitment

[EMAIL] 03:20 pm

From: Hunter Maguire
Subject: Australia trip
Date: 17 June
To: Annalise Smith

Can you also email Dave in the Sydney office and ask for my itinerary? I want to be prepared as this is a very important deal.

Hunter
Hunter Maguire
CEO, Hunter Recruitment

[EMAIL] 03:45 pm

From: Hunter Maguire
Subject: Company event—Friday
Date: 17 June
To: Annalise Smith

Did you also manage to finalise everything for Friday night?

Hunter
Hunter Maguire
CEO, Hunter Recruitment

[EMAIL] 03:55 pm

From: Hunter Maguire
Subject: Company event—Friday
Date: 17 June
To: Annalise Smith

Annalise?

Hunter Maguire
CEO, Hunter Recruitment

[EMAIL] 04:05 pm

From: Hunter Maguire
Subject: Please respond!
Date: 17 June
To: Annalise Smith

Annalise, I've tried calling your mobile but no answer. Can you please contact me when you get these emails as I need the Australia trip sorted ASAP!

Hunter Maguire
CEO, Hunter Recruitment

[EMAIL] 04:15 pm

From: Hunter Maguire
Subject: Please respond!
Date: 17 June
To: Annalise Smith

I have tried calling you a few times now. I know you are not in the office because your daughter is unwell, but I need you to still answer me! This is what I need from my PA, I don't need to stress that work isn't getting completed.

Hunter Maguire
CEO, Hunter Recruitment

Annalise arrived back home and checked her phone, which she had left on silent on her bedside table and noticed that she had 5 missed calls from Hunter and a few voicemails. She quickly checked her laptop, and he had sent her quite a few emails. Should she email him back or just call.

She hadn't been gone for too long, and she had sorted everything else out that he had asked her for. She could easily change his flights and email the Sydney office; they would be in the office in a few hours anyway. As she picked up the phone and clicked redial on Hunter's missed call, she waited for him to answer feeling nervous at how he was going to react to her.

"Maquire!"

"Hi, Hunter. It's Annalise. I am so sorry for not answering your emails and missing your calls. I was just out with Penelope."

"I thought she was unwell."

"She was. I mean she is. Well, she is feeling better, so I wanted to get her out and have some fresh air."

"Right, why didn't you answer your phone? I tried calling you several times."

She could hear the anger in his voice.

"Sorry, I left it in the house. I have read your emails and will get on to everything ASAP, I promise to get it sorted by this evening."

"In future, Annalise, don't leave your phone at home. I need you to be available, even if you are working from home. I know you have other responsibilities, but this is your job, and I need you to start doing it."

Annalise felt stupid for not taking her phone with her, but then again, she was only gone for a short time. It would just be like her having a lunch break.

"Will do Hunter, and I apologise again. I'm just trying to juggle work and a sick child."

"Well, that's not my problem Annalise. I pay you to work, and I expect it to get done."

He was definitely angry, maybe something had annoyed him or maybe it was just her. She hadn't been the best this week, and she knew she could do better. She was just trying to settle in, but he didn't need to be so mean to her, surely he could understand that she was trying her hardest.

"Hunter, I am sorry; I was only gone a short while, and I said that I would get this all sorted by this evening. I have completed all the other work that you asked me to do so I don't know why you are being so horrible about it all."

Annalise knew that she sounded upset and frustrated. Had she had said too much and overstepped the line; he was her employer at the end of the day. She should have just apologised again and simple said bye and let it be in the past. As she waited for him to answer all she could hear was his breath and the sound of his feet moving across the floor.

It was like he was trying to calm himself down. She wondered what had got into him. Had the Australia trip been brought forward really disrupted his schedule or was he stressed about it? He did say that it was a very important deal.

"Annalise."

His tone was much calmer now, but there was no warmth to it.

"I expect you will finalise everything and email me once it's all done?"

"Of course, Hunter, I will get on to it all now."

"OK then. I'll wait to hear from you this evening."

The phone went dead. No, goodbye. He had simply hung up the phone. Annalise was left feeling unsure of Hunter's mood. Was he really that angry with her for not being by her phone or emails? Annalise knew deep down that there was something else making Hunter react like that. All she could do was to act normal the next time she saw him, and hope that he would do the same.

Wednesday, 17 June
Hunter

Hunter was pacing around his office after speaking with Annalise. Why had he been so angry with her? He knew she was at home with her daughter who was unwell, but she also had a job to do. He needed her to do that job. He hated the fact that he couldn't get hold of her; he liked things to be done when he wanted them done.

Maybe with her being a single parent and having this responsibility wasn't right for his PA. He never had this problem with Charlotte, well he might in the future once she comes back from maternity leave, although she has Tim her husband to help. Annalise didn't have a partner; it was just her and her daughter. Hunter had been feeling angry all day, actually ever since last night after his email conversation with Annalise.

She had tried to ask him a personal question and asked about his family; he didn't talk about his personal life to anyone. His mood was also from a lack of sleep and to top everything off, his Australia trip had been brought forward, which meant that the pressure was on for him to be on top form. He didn't want to go in the first place and now it was messing with his schedule, but he couldn't cancel the trip, it was too important and this deal was huge for the company and for Hunter. He was now starting to play with the big players this was going to get him to be number one in the industry.

So these were just the sacrifices that he had to make to get there. He knew deep down that even though all of that had happened, it was the fact that he hadn't seen Annalise today that had really got to him. He hadn't realised any of this until he was just speaking with her. Even in the space of nearly 2 weeks, he enjoyed seeing her face and talking to her, even if it was about work.

But when he had come in this morning, he knew she wouldn't be there, yet he still felt disappointed. He had been in a bad mood ever since, and he had been taking it out on his other employees, as well as Annalise. Hunter knew he should apologise to Annalise for the way he spoke to her, maybe he would wait until later when she had emailed him about completing the work that way; he could casually drop it in and still maintain his authority.

As he looked at his watch, he realised that it was now 6:00 p.m.; he still had a lot of work to do but just didn't feel in the right headspace for it. Maybe he would go for a workout with Tyrell again, but then he remembered that Tyrell had a date tonight with a girl that he had been training recently. Maybe he would just go home and chill out, but then he would be thinking of Annalise no doubt. He was stuck.

Normally, when he felt like this, he would call Rosie, but that had all ended now. He needed to find an alternative, maybe he would go shopping. It was late night shopping after all, and he could do with a new suit for Friday night's party. He was going to wear one of his normal ones, but as it was a cocktail party, he could invest in a new black-tie suit.

Hunter got home from buying his suit and felt it had shifted his mood slightly. The lady in the store was actually really helpful and after trying on a couple of suits he had decided on one from that store, not needing to go to any others. He hung the suit in his wardrobe and decided to check his emails. He poured himself a glass of whiskey, turned on his laptop and noticed he had an email from Annalise. As he hit the open button, he was anxious to see if she would mention anything about their conversation earlier.

[EMAIL] 06:20 pm

From: Annalise Smith
Subject: Australia trip
Date: 18 June
To: Annalise Smith

Hunter,

I have rescheduled your flights and accommodation, please find attached the new documents. I have also contacted Dave in the Sydney office and spoke with his PA Tash, who is going to send your itinerary over to me shortly, which I will then forward to you. Also, just to let you know that I spoke with Candice and everything is finalised for the party on Friday evening and all of your other meetings have been rescheduled and all emails replied to.

Thanks,
Annalise.
Annalise Smith
Personal Assistant to Hunter Maguire, Hunter Recruitment

Hunter suddenly felt a pang of guilt hit him. He knew that she would have spent the last few hours finalising everything, and she was supposed to be looking after her unwell daughter plus it was working into her evening. He was unsure of how to reply; she might not even get the email until the morning anyway.

[EMAIL] 09:10 pm

From: Hunter Maguire
Subject: Australia Trip
Date: 17 June
To: Annalise Smith

Annalise,

Thank you for letting me know and for sending over the documents. It was very proficient of you. I hope that your daughter is much better. Will you be back in the office tomorrow?

Hunter
Hunter Maguire
CEO, Hunter Recruitment

As he waited for her reply, he hoped she would be in tomorrow. It also meant she might still be able to attend the party unless she didn't feel happy to leave her daughter when she hadn't been very well. Maybe he would ask her if she does respond tonight; after all, it's just a company question, and he could say that he just needs to know numbers. As he was thinking this all through an email came pinging back.

[EMAIL] 09:20 pm

From: Hunter Maguire
Subject: Australia trip
Date: 17 June
To: Annalise Smith

Hunter,

Not a problem at all. I had taken time throughout the day for personal duties, so it was expected that I should work a little later tonight. Penelope is much better now, so she is going to school tomorrow, and I will be in at my normal time.

Thanks,
Annalise
Annalise Smith
Personal Assistant to Hunter Maguire, Hunter Recruitment

She was being extremely blunt, and he wondered if he had upset her earlier. This was all new to him; he didn't normally get feelings for a woman, especially a work colleague.

[EMAIL] 09:22 pm

From: Hunter Maguire
Subject: Australia Trip
Date: 17 June
To: Annalise Smith

I am glad to hear your daughter is feeling much better and you will be back in the office tomorrow. It was very busy today, and I think that it was harder with you not being in the office. I apologise for my tone earlier, please forgive me. As your daughter is much better, does that mean you will still be attending the party on Friday night? I just need to know for numbers, that's all.

Hunter
Hunter Maguire
CEO, Hunter Recruitment

There he did it; he apologised to her. He wanted to have a fresh start tomorrow, and she had sounded slightly upset when he had put the phone down on her. He didn't want her to leave he needed her for work reasons, and maybe personal as he was starting to find out.

[EMAIL] 09:25 pm

From: Annalise Smith
Subject: Australia trip
Date: 17 June
To: Hunter Maguire

I'm unsure yet, I will see how Penelope is in the morning. I feel bad for palming her off on someone else after she has been unwell. If she is OK at school then I may just come for a few hours.
    PS: Thank you for apologising; it means a lot. You are forgiven ;)

Annalise
Annalise Smith
Personal Assistant to Hunter Maguire, Hunter Recruitment

A winky face? He was confused. What did that mean? He never did understand when people ended their text messages or emails with an emoji.

[EMAIL] 09:27 pm

From: Hunter Maguire
Subject: Australia Trip
Date: 17 June

To: Annalise Smith

That would be a shame if you didn't come.

Hunter
Hunter Maguire
CEO, Hunter Recruitment

He didn't know what had come over him, was he really that sexually frustrated that he had to flirt over an email. He was treading in deep waters, especially if HR ever found out that he was acting like this with his employees. He remembered Annalise also asking him to keep their relationship professional, but a little bit of flirting never hurt anyone. He waited for her reply, eager to see how the conversation would go.

[EMAIL] 09:30 pm

From: Annalise Smith
Subject: Australia trip
Date: 17 June
To: Hunter Maguire

Well, I was looking forward to seeing you in your tux and possibly a smile!

Annalise
Annalise Smith
Personal Assistant to Hunter Maguire, Hunter Recruitment

[EMAIL] 09:32 pm

From: Hunter Maguire
Subject: Australia Trip
Date: 17 June
To: Annalise Smith

Oh, really? Do you not think I smile, Annalise? I can tell you know my smile does make an appearance when I'm around beautiful women, I'm surprised that you haven't seen it yet!

Hunter
Hunter Maguire
CEO, Hunter Recruitment

He was definitely heavily flirting with her now, and he didn't care. It had made him relax, and it's the best that he had felt all day.

[EMAIL] 09:35 pm

From: Annalise Smith
Subject: Australia trip
Date: 17 June
To: Hunter Maguire

Hunter, I'm not sure if that was supposed to be a compliment towards me, but I can tell you one thing, I am definitely not beautiful. Well, compared to the women you must have dated previously.

Annalise
Annalise Smith
Personal Assistant to Hunter Maguire, Hunter Recruitment

What was she talking about, why would she not think that she was intelligent or beautiful? She was the most beautiful and interesting woman that he had met in a long time. He didn't feel like this for just anyone.

[EMAIL] 09:37 pm

From: Hunter Maguire
Subject: Take a compliment
Date: 17 June
To: Annalise Smith

Annalise, you should think more of yourself. You are an intelligent and beautiful woman, don't put yourself down like that.

H
Hunter Maguire
CEO, Hunter Recruitment

[EMAIL] 09:40 pm

From: Annalise Smith
Subject: Take a compliment
Date: 17 June
To: Hunter Maguire

I've never been told I am so I never think it. But thank you for the compliment.

Annalise
Annalise Smith
Personal Assistant to Hunter Maguire, Hunter Recruitment

[EMAIL] 09:42 pm

From: Hunter Maguire
Subject: Take a compliment
Date: 17 June
To: Annalise Smith

So what are you up to now?

H
Hunter Maguire
CEO, Hunter Recruitment

[EMAIL] 09:45 pm

From: Annalise Smith
Subject: Take a compliment
Date: 17 June
To: Hunter Maguire

Well, I could lie and say that I am doing something lavish and fun, but to be honest I am just sitting here in my PJ's watching TV. Penelope is asleep so I can't really head out for a night on the town! What about you? How's your evening been?

Annalise
Annalise Smith
Personal Assistant to Hunter Maguire, Hunter Recruitment

[EMAIL] 09:47 pm

From: Hunter Maguire
Subject: Take a compliment
Date: 17 June
To: Annalise Smith

Noneventful too. I went suit shopping after work and now I'm currently chilling with a whiskey, looking out at London and all the people around. I'll probably try and do some work before bed.

H
Hunter Maguire
CEO, Hunter Recruitment

[EMAIL] 09:52 pm

From: Annalise Smith
Subject: Take a compliment
Date: 17 June

To: Hunter Maguire

I bet you have an amazing view! Do you ever just switch off, you always seem to be working. What do you do for fun?

A

Annalise Smith
Personal Assistant to Hunter Maguire, Hunter Recruitment

Hunter thought about that question. Work and training were his fun, it always had been. Going out for dinners were more business events, and he didn't really do much else.

[EMAIL] 09:53 pm

From: Hunter Maguire
Subject: Take a compliment
Date: 17 June
To: Annalise Smith

Of course, I switch off Annalise, but when you run your own business, that's what comes first. It's always a priority.

H

Hunter Maguire
CEO, Hunter Recruitment

[EMAIL] 09:55 pm

From: Annalise Smith
Subject: Take a compliment
Date: 17 June
To: Hunter Maguire

I would have thought with you running a successful business that you could delegate more. And then go off driving in fast cars, going to premiers, going for dinners, holidays. I just presumed that you lived this fast-paced exotic life.

A
Annalise Smith
Personal Assistant to Hunter Maguire, Hunter Recruitment

[EMAIL] 09:57 pm

From: Hunter Maguire
Subject: Take a compliment
Date: 17 June
To: Annalise Smith

No, Annalise, you have a very different opinion of who I am. I like the simple things in life. Work, training and home. That's it. I can't even remember the last time I had a holiday. What about you, what do you do for fun?

H
Hunter Maguire
CEO, Hunter Recruitment

[EMAIL] 09:58 pm

From: Annalise Smith
Subject: Take a compliment
Date: 17 June
To: Hunter Maguire

Well, I don't know whether you realise, but I'm a single mum, we don't have much time for ourselves. But I suppose Penelope is my fun. We go for days out to the beach, watch films, and we like trying new recipes. It might sound boring to you. I wish I could do more, but that's just how it is at the moment. I have made a promise to myself since moving that I would have more of social life, and hopefully, that will start tomorrow night.

A

Annalise Smith

Personal Assistant to Hunter Maguire, Hunter Recruitment

[EMAIL] 09:59 pm

From: Hunter Maguire
Subject: Take a compliment
Date: 17 June
To: Annalise Smith

Let's hope it does. I'm still keen to see you in that dress of yours!

H

Hunter Maguire

CEO, Hunter Recruitment

[EMAIL] 10:00 pm

From: Annalise Smith
Subject: Take a compliment
Date: 17 June
To: Hunter Maguire

Hmmm, I'm sure you are! Well, I better be getting off to bed, but I'll see you tomorrow. Good night Hunter.

A

Annalise Smith

Personal Assistant to Hunter Maguire, Hunter Recruitment

Hunter instantly felt happy at the thought of seeing Annalise tomorrow and seeing her in that dress! He remembered when she showed him on the hanger and knew that it would cling to her body in all the right places. Showing off her amazing curves. He had to shake the image out of his head otherwise he wouldn't be able to think about anything else until tomorrow night.

From: Hunter Maguire
Subject: Take a compliment
Date: 17 June
To: Annalise Smith

Goodnight Annalise.

H
Hunter Maguire
CEO, Hunter Recruitment

He felt like he was starting to get to know bits of Annalise just by her tone and how she communicated. She seemed very loving and caring of other people, maybe it was the mother in her. He hadn't really met many women like her before and maybe that's what had attracted him to her in a different way. Of course, she was stunning in his eyes, but he had felt other feelings that had never been there before.

It scared him especially as he had promised her that he wouldn't act on them. The one time that he wanted something more than anything else, and he couldn't do anything about it because she worked for him. He thought he had this under control, but his body was obviously disobeying his head, and he was unsure of whether to just let it be or fight for it.

Friday, 19 June
Hunter

Hunter was up bright and early that morning. He didn't sleep much again last night with having Annalise on his mind, but he had woken up feeling in a good mood and excited for the day ahead. Yesterday was a good day; he had surprisingly been in a positive mood, but he knew deep down that it had been due to a certain someone being in the office. He hadn't seen Annalise much as he was in and out of meetings all day again, but he managed to speak with her before he left for the day.

Hunter grabbed his bag and headed out the door, it was training time, and he felt like he had a lot of excess energy to burn off. He needed to keep his cool when he was around Annalise, and for him to be able to do that, he needed to channel that energy into something else. As he pulled up to the gym, he saw Tyrell with a girl; he didn't think that he had met her before. She was definitely attractive but in a posh Chelsea kind of way.

She was in designer sports gear, face full of make-up and driving a black Porsche and other than Hunter, no one else drove an expensive car in this neighbourhood. He wondered who the woman was, maybe she was just here to train with Tyrell or maybe she had been recommended to him by someone, but it looked more than that. As they said goodbye, Hunter saw the spark in both of their eyes it was the same spark that he saw when he looked at Annalise. He got out of the car and headed towards Tyrell as the girl drove off.

"So who is your lady friend, she doesn't look from around here?"

"That's Katie, she's been training with me for a few weeks now. She's off on a gap year around Australia and her parents wanted her to do some boxing before she went. You know, so she can defend herself."

"Well, you two looked like you had some chemistry; anything else going on other than boxing?"

"Nope. I take my business seriously Hunter. I don't get involved with the clients, it causes too much trouble and especially with her parents. No way!"

"Ha, yeah we will see about that, the way you two were looking at each other, something is bound to happen!"

"Leave it, Hunter! Anyway, why are you so happy this morning? You have never been interested in my love life."

"I'm not. I was just observing the situation that's all!" He was smirking at Tyrell, knowing all too well that his gesture would annoy him more.

"Well, you can keep observing, but the view will still remain the same. Talking of women, what's going on with you and that PA of yours?"

"Nothing. It's purely professional. I thought there was something, but then I changed my mind. I'm her boss at the end of the day, what example would that be?"

"If you feel something for her though, you should act on it. I haven't heard you speak about a woman like this before. OK, well, maybe you mention Rosie, but you never acted like this. So what if she works for you? She is only a temp, surely if it goes further then she can just get another job."

"No, she can't. She has a daughter. What kind of person would I be if I slept with her and then told her that she had to leave? No, it's simple, I'm just going to push whatever feelings I have aside and get on with work. I just have to get through tonight and then I'm off to Australia for work. A bit of distance will be good."

"Oh yeah, the party is tonight, do you think you are going to get too drunk and then hit on her or something? And I'm telling you Hunt if you have feelings for this woman just going to Australia for a few days will make it worse. All you will want to do is see her, trust me I've been there."

"No, you know I don't stay long at these work parties. I just have to show my face and then leave. I'll see her at work today but keep my distance and then tonight I'll probably barely see her and then I'm off. It's fine, Tyrell, I've got this. You know me, I don't do emotions. I can easily forget about a woman, that's what I have always done."

"Well, if that's what you think, let's just wait and see. Come on, let's do some training, I think we both need to burn off some extra energy."

As Hunter walked into the office, he could see Annalise was already at her desk. Normally he would be in before anyone else, but he and Tyrell decided to do an extra-long session today. As he reached the office, she looked up at him, starring directly into his eyes. It sent a bolt of lightning straight through his body.

"Morning Hunter. I thought that you might be in already, but I didn't want to disturb you if you were. Let me know if there is anything you need me to do for you today."

"Morning Annalise. My training ran over this morning that's why I wasn't in beforehand. Right, well I'll be in my office if you need me. I have a few things to sort out for Australia. I'm also letting everyone go an hour earlier today so they can get ready for tonight so that applies to you too."

"Thanks, Hunter, I'll see how I go later. I still have to pick Penelope up from school so I may just stay until then."

"OK, see you later."

Hunter headed into his office trying to calm his heart rate down after seeing Annalise again. Seriously, what was going on with him?

Friday, 19 June
Annalise

Annalise didn't realise she would feel nervous seeing Hunter again, the electricity that was charging through her body was unknown to her. She had felt herself start to blush, her heart rate rise and her skin prickling with beads of sweat, how could he have this effect on her. Just his smile had increased her heart rate dramatically. She knew that she had told him that nothing could happen, but that's all she could think about.

Hunter had started to be flirtier over the past couple of days, and even though she had returned with various comments, she was still being cautious. Annalise needed this job and had to keep reminding herself of that.

It was alright for Hunter; he owned the company and nothing would change in his life. But for Annalise, she would lose her job, and what if she couldn't find another job. She and Penelope would have to move back to Norfolk, and it meant that they would have failed. She couldn't let that happen; she wouldn't let it happen; she would be strong.

Tonight she would have to steer clear of Hunter for both their sakes; she knew if she saw him in his tux and alcohol was involved, then it would more than likely end in a scenario where she wouldn't be able to control herself. She tried to focus back on her work even though she knew that Hunter was just in the room next to her. Annalise couldn't help but wonder what he was thinking, was he having battles with himself just like she was or was this just natural to him, maybe he has been in this situation before, but then again, she hadn't heard any gossip around the office and Candice hadn't mentioned anything. Annalise thought back to her first day and how Candice had spoken about Hunter in a very familiar way, maybe they had had a thing. Anyway, even if they had, it was none of Annalise's business.

It was late afternoon and Annalise hadn't seen Hunter all day; he hadn't even come out of his office or sent an email to her. The more she thought about it, the thought that he may be avoiding her popped into her head. She had told him that she wanted a professional relationship and maybe this was him respecting her boundaries.

Annalise wondered how men could just flip a switch, one minute he was flirting with her and then nothing at all, it was confusing her head and her heart. She noticed people were starting to leave the office, obviously going home to get ready for the party tonight. They were all laughing and chatting as they walked out of the office doors. Annalise thought to herself that she would try tonight to get to know some of the consultants; she had been here nearly 2 weeks now and had only really met 3 people, one of those being Hunter.

She was nervous about tonight though. She hadn't been in a social situation like this since she was much younger, and she wondered if she would be able to hold a conversation with anyone. At least she got on well with Candice, and they had arranged to share a cab together tonight, which eased her mind. Annalise decided that she would see if Hunter needed anything before; she left the office for the day.

As she stood up from her desk and approached his office door, she hesitated before knocking. She instantly became nervous again; she knew what he did to her, and she just hoped that she could be strong. As she knocked, she waited for his reply, which seemed to take much longer than she anticipated.

"Come in."

Annalise entered the office and walked towards Hunter; however, he didn't look up from his computer; he seemed focussed on something else. Maybe that's why he hadn't been out to see her; she instantly felt bad for interrupting him.

"Sorry, to disturb you, Hunter, I just wanted to see if there was anything you needed before I left for the day."

She stood there waiting for his reply, it was like he was trying to make her feel uncomfortable, and she wondered why. She straightened her dress and smoothed her hair down, playing with her fingers to stop her nerves from exploding. As she looked back at him, he was looking straight at her, right into her dark brown eyes. There was a smirk on his face again like he was enjoying himself.

"Do I make you nervous, Annalise?"

He knew that he did, he was teasing her. Annalise shifted her stance and cleared her throat trying to make it look like she wasn't affected by him, but who was she kidding. He made her so nervous, especially with that look that he had given her.

"No, of course, not Hunter, why would you say that?"

He then proceeded to get up from his desk and walk around to where Annalise was standing, not taking his eyes off of hers the whole time.

"Well, you keep playing with your dress and twiddling with your hands, those are signs of someone who is nervous."

She instantly stopped moving.

"I've just got things on my mind."

He walked closer to her and reached out to touch her face, it caught her by surprise. Her body became mesmerised by his affection, and she just stood there, not being able to move. She instantly had a desire deep inside and her breath started to deepen. What was he doing to her? It was the smallest of touches, but it was like he had some kind of control over her.

"Annalise, I know I make you nervous. I can tell by the way your whole-body changes when you are around me."

She leant into his touch and closed her eyes. It was so nice to be touched by a man, it had been so long, and she had forgotten what it had felt like. His hands were strong and masculine but soft at the same time. The heat that was generated from his hand to her face could have caused a fire to start.

She just stood there with her eyes closed, until she felt him pull away all of a sudden and the connection was lost. When she opened her eyes, he was now walking back to his desk. When she looked at his face it was like something had changed, the atmosphere had become cold again and the Hunter that was just there standing in front of her was gone. She felt confused, why did he keep changing all of a sudden.

It was like something had been triggered in his mind and had pulled him out of whatever he had been feeling. She saw the coldness return in his eyes, and it made her angry. How could he make her feel like that and then just stop it without any explanation? Did he get off on winding women up, was he just a tease. She kept standing there thinking this over in her head when he spoke.

"There is nothing I want from you Annalise; you can go home."

His tone was cold and direct like it was an order. She looked at him hard trying to work out what had changed.

"Hunter, do you get off on doing that to women?"

He looked at her, nothing changing in his expression.

"I don't know what you mean Annalise, I simply touched your cheek. I admit that I shouldn't have touched you, but at the end of the day, it was just a touch. Why do women always think too much into things?"

She was seething from his comment.

"Just a touch! Just a touch!"

She felt her anger increase, how could he just dismiss it like that. He was just like every other male, why hadn't she seen it from the start.

"Is this what you do Hunter, you play with people's emotions? Flirt with them, tell them there is a connection, give them compliments and then go hot and cold on them. You get your fix and know that you are the alpha male and you can control women whenever you want?"

He wasn't saying anything, just looking at her.

"What's the matter Hunter, cat got your tongue? Or is it because I have figured you out. Well, screw you, I won't let you do the same to me, I am here to do a job and that doesn't involve doing you!"

Annalise couldn't believe that she just said all of that and let alone to her boss, but she felt alive and loved that she was standing up for herself for once in her life. Before Hunter could reply, Annalise turned on her foot and headed for the door, slamming it on her way out.

Well, tonight might be awkward; actually, the whole working together might be awkward now, but hopefully, he had got the message. She decided she would go and pick Penelope up; she was only a little bit early and was sure that the teacher wouldn't mind. That way she could get home, cook some dinner and then get ready before Katherine came around.

Annalise could see Penelope from the classroom window as she walked up to the main doors of the school. She was chatting away to another little girl, and they were giggling at something and then continued to get back to whatever they were doing. Annalise loved that it hadn't even been 2 weeks and Penelope was really enjoying school and had even made some new friends.

They would lock some play dates in soon, especially as the weather was starting to get warmer so they could venture outside a bit more. Annalise knocked on the classroom door and a different teacher to who she normally saw came across the room and opened it to greet Annalise. Everyone in the after-school care team was ever so friendly, and it made Annalise feel more at ease knowing that they were looking after her daughter.

"Hi, I'm Penelope's mum, Annalise. I know that you normally don't finish until 5:30 p.m., but I have an event on tonight and was hoping to pick Penelope up slightly earlier today so that she is ready for the babysitter tonight."

"Very nice to meet you, Annalise. I'm Mrs Finch one of Penelope's teachers. I can't see that being a problem today. Normally we ask you to let us know beforehand so that we can organise the schedule, but everyone is just drawing today so it will be fine. I'll just go and get her."

As Mrs Finch headed over to Penelope, Annalise could see her look over at her while listening to what Mrs Finch was saying. She watched as Penelope said goodbye to her friends and came walking over to where she was standing.

"Mummy, I've had so much fun today, look at what I drew, do you like it?"

Annalise looked at the drawing, it was of a park with lots of children playing in it and a rainbow in the sky.

"It's amazing Penelope! What a clever girl you are, I particularly like the rainbow."

"Me too! This is me, and this is Jenny, my friend; we are playing tag."

"Is Jenny your friend sitting over there?"

"No, that's Ashley, Jenny doesn't come to after school care, and her older sister picks her up and looks after her until her parents get home."

"Would you like to have a play date soon with all your friends?"

"Really? I can invite Jenny… and Sophie, Hannah, Rachel oh and Teagan."

"That's a long list of friends…. I'll speak with the other mums next week about it. Shall we head home? Mummy has to get ready and make you some food before Katherine comes around to look after you."

"I can't wait to play with Katherine, we are going to have so much fun."

Annalise felt a sudden sadness that another adult would be having fun with Penelope when she should be, but she had to let those feelings go if she wanted to start having a social life again. This was a good thing for both Penelope and her.

Annalise had cooked dinner, had a shower, washed and dried her hair, and was now applying her makeup before putting her dress on. Penelope had been fed and was now watching a film in the lounge. Katherine was due shortly and was arriving with Candice, so Annalise had to make sure that she was ready to leave by then. She was starting to feel nervous.

What if she didn't look good enough or what if she didn't know what to say to everyone? Deep down she knew that she was more worried and nervous about seeing Hunter again after what had happened in his office earlier. Would he avoid her all night or would he just be polite and say hello? Well, she would just make sure to try and get to know the rest of her colleagues and have a good time. As she slipped the dress on, she had forgotten how good of a fit it was, showing off her curves.

She loved the low back and now that she had styled her hair into a loose side bun with some fallen curls and her makeup was subtle but sexy, it all complimented the dress really well. She was actually shocked at how good she looked and felt. It had been so long since she wore anything like this. Annalise heard the doorbell ring and Penelope shout that she would get it.

"It should be Katherine and Candice; I'll be down in a moment."

Annalise heard the door open and some talking, which was mainly from Penelope who was informing one of them that she was going to plait her hair and then they could paint each other's nails. Katherine seemed OK with this by replying that she would let Penelope plait her hair first. As Annalise looked at herself in the mirror one last time, she put her black heels on, straightened her dress and headed downstairs, feeling nervous at what Candice would think of her. Annalise hadn't met Katherine before, but she could instantly see the resemblance between herself and Candice. Candice was standing there in her red cocktail dress; her hair was curled and down, and she had matching red lipstick.

"Oh, wow, you look incredible Candice!"

"Thanks, Annalise. You also look amazing! That dress really suits you; the green is amazing with your skin tone."

Katherine stepped forward and introduced herself.

"Nice to meet you, Annalise. I've already met Penelope, and it seems that we have a lot planned for tonight."

"Ah yes, did she tell you what she has planned for you both tonight?"

"Ha yes she did, I love a girls night!"

"Glad to hear it! I've said that she can stay up later tonight as it's not a school night, but if she could be in bed by 9:00 p.m. at the latest and if there are any problems just give me a call. Also, help yourself to any food or drink in the cupboards and fridge."

"Will do. I'm sure everything will be fine, go and enjoy yourself. I hear these parties can get a bit wild!"

Katherine looked at Candice as she made her comment, and Annalise thought that there must be a story there.

"Well, I won't be too late home. Penelope, come and say bye; Mummy is now leaving."

Penelope came running and leapt at her.

"Wow, you look like a princess, Mummy, are you going to meet your prince?"

"Hmmm, I doubt that Penelope, it's a work event. Right don't be any trouble to Katherine and I'll see you in the morning ready for our day out together."

Annalise kissed Penelope said goodbye to Katherine and headed out to grab a taxi with Candice.

It was one of the busiest nights for cab drivers and the city was swamped with black taxis on the roads, but it didn't take for them to be on the way to the event.

"So are you excited for tonight? These parties are always good, everyone makes a real effort dressing up and there is always some drama or gossip in the offices on Monday morning."

"It's just nice to have a night out and get dressed up! I'm a bit nervous to be honest; it's been a while."

"You will be fine, you look amazing. Once you have a drink your nerves will ease."

"Thanks for sharing a lift with me, I would have felt uncomfortable turning up on my own when I don't know anyone."

"Anytime! And you know Hunter as well as me. I promise that everyone is really friendly so don't worry. You will fit right in."

Annalise thought about Hunter as soon as Candice mentioned his name, her heartbeat rising just at the sound of it. As the taxi pulled up to the hotel where they were holding the party, Annalise's palms started to sweat, and her nerves tripled instantly. She didn't think that she could move her legs; she just sat there until Candice nudged her to get out of the car first.

"Come on Annalise, we don't have all night, there's champagne with our name on it!"

Annalise had no choice but to open the door and step out. The cold air instantly brought a chill to her body. Candice joined her on the pavement, and they both headed into the hotel. As they entered the master ballroom, Annalise looked around in excitement, it was amazing. There was an elegant long white bar with chandeliers hanging from the ceiling, waiters/waitresses walking around serving champagne in crystal glass wear, there was a dance floor with a DJ, and the décor was just on point for the cocktail attire.

Very elegant. Annalise felt like she was at a red-carpet event, somewhere that she didn't really belong, everyone looked so stylish. The ladies wore elegant and expensive dresses, with most of them wearing black, and the men in tuxes. Everyone was beautiful. Annalise felt nothing in comparison to them all.

Here, she was feeling like Cinderella all dressed up and knowing that she would have to go back to being a single mum after tonight, back to wearing her jeans and t-shirts again But, tonight, she would make sure she had a good time and enjoy herself. Candice was next to her and handed her a glass of champagne; she took a sip, and it tasted amazing with the bubbles hitting her tongue and the alcohol helping her to relax. As she carried on sipping her drink, she looked around the room wondering if Hunter was here yet; she couldn't see him, but maybe he would come later once it had properly started, it was still early.

"Let me introduce you to some people, Annalise."

They walked over to a group of people who were fully in conversation. There was one person in particular who was talking to everyone about a deal that he had just put through. Apparently, it was going to bring in a lot of money for the company. She noticed that the guy was very good looking; he had short blonde hair and bright blue eyes, and he obviously was a hit with the rest of his colleagues.

They were all falling over every word he said. At that moment, he stopped talking and looked directly at her, a glint of humour in his eyes and his smile broaden. Annalise didn't know what to do, her cheeks instantly flushed pink unsure of why she got like this in front of attractive men. It was nothing compared to how she was in front of Hunter, but she seriously needed to get a grip. Candice whispered to her that his name was Andy, and he was the heartthrob of the office, all the girls wanted to be his girlfriend, even she and Annalise could see the attraction. He then stepped past everyone else and was standing in front of her.

"And who must you be?"

Annalise was almost taken aback by his confidence and nearly stuttered her words out.

"Umm… I'm Annalise. I'm Hunter's new PA."

"Well, lucky Hunter, he has definitely won the gold prize with you."

Annalise found Andy to be extremely confident, and she didn't like how he had referenced her as a prize. If he was trying to flirt with her, then this kind of flirting wasn't working.

"I'm not a prize, Andy! Please don't reference me in that way."

Andy didn't look shocked at her comment; he was still smiling like he was trying to humour her.

"Can you not take a compliment, Annalise? I meant it in a nice way. I think you are beautiful, and Hunter is lucky that he gets to see your face every day. That's all."

Annalise instantly felt embarrassed again; she didn't know how to take a compliment let alone from a man.

"I'm sorry I responded the way I did, that's very kind of you to say those words. I didn't mean to snap at you, I must have taken it the wrong way."

"Don't be sorry, I like a woman who stands up for herself."

Annalise noticed that it was just the two left standing there, Candice had now started talking to another group of people, and Annalise felt nervous again; she didn't really know what to say to Andy.

"So how long have you worked for Hunter?"

"Not long, I only started last Monday."

"That isn't long at all. Where were you before? Another recruitment agency?"

"I've actually just moved down here from Norfolk; I was working for a smaller organisation so this is all very different for me, but I'm enjoying it so far. Everyone seems extremely nice and welcoming."

"Oh, so you are new in town, I must take you out next week. I know all the best bars and restaurants, and generally, they know me, so we wouldn't have to wait for a table."

She knew he was trying to be nice, but his confidence was on the verge of arrogance, and it was putting her off Andy's charm. Annalise could imagine that this might work on other women, but not her. She didn't need the fancy restaurants or expensive bars; she was simple at heart.

"Yeah, maybe sometime, I'll have to see when I'm free. I'm still settling in at the moment."

"Are you playing hard to get Annalise? Or do you have a boyfriend?"

"No, of course, not and no I don't have a boyfriend. I'm single."

"Well, that's good then. I can show you my apartment later if you like. It's right near Hyde Park and has an awesome view. You know there are also some very high-profile people who live in my building as well. I had to go on the waiting list for nearly a year, but it's worth it. Just by mentioning where I live, I get into all the hot spots and mingle with some celebs."

"Oh, wow, that sounds amazing. Lucky you."

Annalise tried to sound genuine, but Andy was boring her; she didn't care about hanging with celebrities or fancy apartments. He just seemed all about that lifestyle, which was very different to hers.

"So what about tonight, fancy a nightcap at mine later?"

Annalise didn't know quite what to say, there was no way that she was going back to his after the party, and she couldn't quite believe that he had asked her after only just meeting her.

"That's very nice of you to offer, but I actually have to get home to my daughter."

She saw the instant shock on Andy's face and him trying to register the information in his brain. Annalise knew by telling him that she had a daughter, that it would take him back down.

"You have a child? Aren't you too young?"

"Yes and no. I had her when I was young, and she is now 7."

It seemed like he was trying to finish an argument that was going on in his head.

"Err well…. Maybe…. sorry Annalise there's John over there who is the director of the Marketing team, and I really need to speak to him. Catch up with you soon though, yeah?"

And with that, he took off heading towards another group of people, relief on his face like he had nearly cheated death. Annalise understood that she came with baggage, and it would take a certain type of man to take her and Penelope into their life, but she still had hope that it would happen. It just wouldn't be with someone like Andy.

The waitress walked past Annalise, and she took another glass of Champagne, it was only her second, but she could feel the bubbles going to her head. It had been so long since she had drunk champagne that she would have to pace herself. She felt the atmosphere change around her and felt an instant presence, knowing it was Hunter even before he spoke.

"Annalise."

He said her name with desire and her heart started to race. He looked gorgeous.

"Hunter. Nice to see you."

"Having fun? You looked like you were with Andy just then?"

"Ha, well, that was until I told him I had a child. If you ever need to turn off a guy or girl in your instance, that's one thing you just add into the conversation, and it brings everything to a halt."

She tried to make light of the situation, but it had affected her the way Andy had acted after she had told him about Penelope. Hunter was examining her face trying to work out what she was thinking.

"Well, no loss there, all the women in the office seem to like him, but I honestly think that he is too confident for his own good."

"But doesn't he make you a lot of money?"

"Yes, but he also ruins a lot of relationships with our clients."

"So why do you keep him on?"

"Because he still makes the company a lot of money, Annalise."

"Fair enough."

She was looking around the room twiddling her fingers trying to calm her nerves; she could feel Hunter's gaze on her face.

"Am I making you nervous again, Annalise?"

Why did he always have to go straight to the point? He knew he made her nervous, but he just had to hear it from her, just to please him.

"No, Hunter, I am just looking at all the beautiful females in the room, surely you have noticed them."

"Annalise, the only female I find beautiful in this room is you, so why would I be looking at any others when I'm standing here talking to you."

She didn't know what to say; he had just called her beautiful. The words kept twirling around in her head and his gaze still on hers. They were just looking into each other's eyes with the tension building between them, fire deep inside her burning, and she had this longing to kiss him. Annalise hadn't wanted anything more in her life than to feel his lips on hers, for him to kiss her deeply and passionately, letting everything around them fade away. She was then reminded of what had happened earlier in the day and how he had dismissed her. He had made her feel stupid, and she wasn't going to let him this time. Not twice in one day.

"Hunter, I don't know what you are playing at?"

"I don't know what you mean, Annalise?"

"Don't play dumb with me Hunter. You dismissed me earlier making me feel stupid, saying that it was just a touch and nothing more!"

He looked away rubbing his forehead like he was trying to calm a headache.

"Annalise. This is driving me mad."

He looked like he was in pain.

"What's driving you mad?"

"I don't know what you are doing to me."

"Don't you mean, what you are doing to me?"

"Annalise, you are driving me mad. I can't stop thinking about you. You are all I have thought about since you started working for me last week, and it's disrupting my work and routine."

Annalise was confused, Hunter had been the one who had dismissed it early that day, but she had been the one who had told him that nothing could happen. Maybe he was just doing what she had asked him to do, so why was she annoyed with him so much.

"So why did you react the way you did early?"

"I wanted to kiss you so badly Annalise, but then I kept thinking about what you said, about how you couldn't jeopardise the job for your daughter. Then I remembered that you had a daughter…. AND I don't do families, Annalise."

Annalise could only focus on the part about kissing her. He did feel the same as her, but he just couldn't act on it; he was doing this because of what she had said.

"Hunter, I know that you are respecting my wishes because I told you not to do anything, but right now all I can think about is how I want to feel your lips on mine and to lose myself in that kiss."

She felt slightly embarrassed from her comment, but all she could see in Hunter's eyes was desire. He was feeling the exact same thing as she was.

"Annalise."

Her name came out as a whisper and something in his eyes changed.

"I can't do this! You have a daughter, and I don't want a family. I know for you that this wouldn't be a one-off and that you would want more and I'm not that kind of guy. Never have been and never will be."

As she thought about what he had said, she knew that he was right. She wouldn't want it to be a one-off thing; she wanted more from the next man that she invited into her life. Ever since Penelope's father had been off the scene, she had stepped up to become both parents, but time had taken its toll, and she had been longing for a man. Not only for her but to be a father to Penelope as well.

Hunter couldn't give more, and he had been upfront and honest about that, which she admired, but it didn't stop her from feeling disappointed that nothing could happen. For the first time in forever, she had felt an attraction to someone, and it couldn't go any further than a friendship.

"You're right. I could say that I wouldn't want more, but I would be lying. I need to be serious about the next man I get involved with, and I want someone who not only wants me but Penelope as well."

"And I'm afraid I'm not that man Annalise. A part of me wishes that I was, but it's just how I am."

He looked upset and angry at the same time like he wanted to give more, but he couldn't. She wondered what had happened for him to not want to have a family or be part of one. Annalise didn't like to think of Hunter alone with nothing but his work, but how he had been speaking made her think that that was all he had known.

As she looked at him, he was now looking around the room almost like he needed to make an escape plan and an awkwardness started to build between them. They had both agreed not to take it any further and now that there was nothing left to say. She was about to change the subject and start talking about the party and how great it was when he interrupted her thoughts.

"Well, if that's all, I better go talk to a few of the other employees before heading home."

Moments ago, he was saying how he wanted more and now he was back to his cold persona. Annalise wasn't fooled by his words; she had started to notice how if Hunter didn't know what to do or was unsure of something, especially with her; he would make it a professional situation again like he needed that control. Annalise was about to say something when Hunter just walked off leaving her standing there on her own. She looked around feeling uncomfortable and slightly embarrassed; she needed to start making an effort; she came here to meet people and have a good time and so far, that hadn't happened.

She saw Candice across the room talking to a few people so decided to head over there. On her way, she walked past Hunter in mid-conversation with a group of men in their late 40s who looked like they were in management, one of them made a joke and everyone roared with laughter, even Hunter. As she walked past him, she noticed that he glanced at her but quickly returned his eyes back to the people he was talking to. His face had been blank with no emotion.

She approached Candice who was smiling at her broadly; obviously, she had had a few champagnes by now and was all giggly and flirting with a few of the men, but they didn't seem to mind at all. Actually, they were giving each other daggers, like Candice was a hen, and they were all having a cock fight as to who was going to win over her affection. Annalise could tell that Candice was interested in just one of them; she seemed to be spending more time talking to him as well as touching his arm constantly and laughing at everything he said.

"Annalise, you have to listen to Dan; he is soooo funny!"

Dan seemed to feel proud of Candice's comment and adjusted his posture to stand up straight and raise his head looking down at the other men in the group.

"Anyway, you don't seem to have a drink in your hand, you need to keep up, Annalise! And what were you and Hunter talking about? I saw the way you were around each other."

She said the last bit like she was a detective trying to solve a crime by interrogating an innocent woman, although Annalise wasn't that innocent when it came to Hunter.

"Just work stuff. He needs me to sort something out before he travels to Australia on Monday, that's all."

Another guy who was in the group butted in on their conversation, which annoyed Annalise.

"He is so boring. I know he owns the company and all, but he doesn't do anything else. What kind of life is that? If I was him, and I earned the money he did then I would be out driving nice cars, going to fancy restaurants, having lavish holidays."

Who was this guy and who did he think he was, Annalise was about to defend Hunter when Candice jumped in before she could defend him.

"Well, I can honestly say that he is less boring than you. Maybe you should watch what you say about your employer in front of two people who work closely with him. We wouldn't want him to hear any of this, now would we?"

The guy looked at Candice unsure of his next action.

"Whatever! You two just fancy him, that's why you are defending him. Trust me, I could give you a better time than he could."

The guy headed off towards the bar, not before winking at them both as he made his last comment.

137

"God, I hate that guy! He walks around the office acting like he owns the place, and he isn't even very good at his job. I may just casually mention to Hunter about what he said, and hopefully, he will fire him."

Candice was now laughing at her comment like she was brewing up a plan.

"Maybe let's just keep it to ourselves, I'm sure karma will get to him one of these days."

"You are too nice, Annalise. You could never be a consultant like these lot, they are so cutthroat. Everyone has to watch their backs. Thank god you are a PA."

"I don't think I could ever do sales; I just don't like all that pushiness."

"Right let's get a drink and then hit the dance floor, I need to burn off some calories while consuming them!"

"Maybe a drink, but I'm not dancing, I'm not drunk enough yet!"

"Well, we will soon change that."

Candice grabbed 4 drinks off the waiter's tray and passed two to Annalise and kept two for herself. "Wow, Candice. I only need one drink at a time, I do have a daughter to get home to."

"Oh, shit, sorry, I forgot about that. I couldn't imagine having a hangover the next day and having to look after anyone else other than myself."

"Well, I haven't had to do it yet and I'm not sure I'm ready to start now."

"Hmmm, we will see about that! Come on let's go dance, I love this song."

And before Annalise could do anything, Candice had grabbed her hand pulling her towards the dance floor spilling her champagne on the way. She was about to protest but stopped herself; she needed to let herself be young for once. Plus no one really knew her there anyway.

They had been dancing for a few songs now and Annalise was getting tired, the champagne had kicked in, and she felt slightly woozy. Her feet were starting to ache from the high heels, Candice looked like she could dance all night and had a small group of males surrounding her, which she seemed to love. Annalise decided that she was ready to go home; she had had a good time and met a few people, had some alcohol and danced. In her mind, it was a great start to her social life. "Candice."

She had to shout as the music was so loud.

"Candice! I'm going to head home."

Candice's face had a slight glow to it, and she was wiggling her hips in line with the beat of the music.

"What, no! Don't go yet we still have more dancing to do."

"I'm tired and have to get back to let your sister go home. Plus, I have to be up early for Penelope tomorrow."

"Fair enough, but let's do a girl's night soon."

Annalise loved the thought of that; she hadn't had a girl's night in forever. Candice was a lot of fun to be around and even made her relax, which didn't happen a lot.

"Sounds good, see you Monday."

Candice carried on dancing as Annalise headed to get her coat and wait for a taxi. She didn't know how long it would take at this time of night. In Norfolk, they were very few and far between, but this was London. It was a Friday night so she was sure that she wouldn't have to wait long. As she grabbed her coat from the cloakroom, she headed outside.

She was going to ask the girl on the reception desk to call her one, but she looked busy with an unhappy customer. She looked for a cab on the road, but none were there. She would just wait until one came past, there was no one else waiting at the moment, which was good as she could get the next one.

Annalise hugged her coat tighter around her body blocking the cooler air and rubbed her hands together she couldn't wait to get back home and into her comfy warm bed. She heard footsteps behind her, which made her jump and a man's voice; she thought she recognised it and when she turned around; it was exactly who she thought it was.

"You shouldn't be out here on your own, Annalise."

"I'm waiting for a cab."

"Why didn't you ask the girl at reception to book you one?"

"She looked busy, and I didn't want to hassle her. It doesn't matter I'm happy to wait."

Secretly she was shivering under her coat, trying not to let Hunter know how cold she was.

"Annalise, you look freezing, you can't wait out here. I was about to head off myself, so let me give you a lift home."

She was unsure whether to accept, wondering how it would be sitting next to Hunter in a small confined space. Her feet were starting to go numb from the cold, and she decided that she would prefer the warmth of his car than standing on the pavement in the cold.

"Only if you are sure? It's not going out of your way?"

"It's fine. I have a driver for tonight so he can do a detour to your house first, where do you live?"

"Islington."

Hunter headed to a black Range Rover and opened the door for Annalise.

"Come on; it's freezing."

She quickly walked to the car and went to get into it. She was having difficulties getting into a larger car, her dress was fairly tight-fitting not giving her much room to move.

"I'm having a bit of trouble getting in with this dress on."

She looked at Hunter feeling embarrassed to find that he had a glint of humour in his eyes.

"Just pull your dress up slightly and hop in."

She didn't want him to see her legs, but she also wanted to get out of the cold. She grabbed the bottom of her dress and pulled it up to her knees holding it with one hand; she then used the other hand to hold on to the car to pull herself in.

"OK, I'm in finally."

As she looked at Hunter, she noticed that his eyes were on her legs, they then proceeded to slowly move up her body until they were looking straight into her eyes.

"Hunter?"

"Yes?"

"I said I'm in and ready. Don't you want to get in the car?"

"Yes."

He shut the door and headed to the other side of the car to sit next to her. She had never sat so close to him before, and she could instantly feel the heat from his body.

"James's we are just going to take Annalise home first. She lives in Islington."

"Of course, Hunter, and then back to yours?"

Hunter looked at Annalise before answering like he was contemplating his answer.

"Yes."

They sat there in silence for the first 5 minutes, Annalise wondered whether she should say anything about their conversation earlier. It had ended so awkwardly, but the tension was still there and also the attraction. She decided that it would be less uncomfortable if she just chatted to him like they were friends and try to defuse any tension.

"It was a good party; did you have fun?"

He was still looking out of the window and took a few moments until he replied to her.

"It was OK. All these things are the same, but I have to show my face because it's my company."

"But I thought you shared the same interests, with you all doing a similar job?"

"Just because I run a successful recruitment company doesn't mean that I have the same things in common with the people I employ. Yes, I enjoy sales and making relationships with clients, but that's all professional. They all just want to get drunk and enjoy the rewards without putting in the hard work. They are just lucky that we aren't in a recession at the moment. Jobs come in easily compared to when I was first starting out. It was cutthroat. Working 12-hour days just to possibly get one job on your books."

"Well, why don't you employ people like you then? People who want to work hard."

"It's not the simple Annalise. It's very rare to find people like that in this industry nowadays, everyone just wants a free ride."

"I'm sure if you got to know a few of them that they wouldn't all be like that. Maybe it would be good for you to hang out with some of them?"

"Annalise, I don't need you telling me what I should be doing."

His voice had risen, and she had obviously gone too far. He got so defensive, so quickly. He must be in a bad mood, and she wasn't obviously helping matters.

"OK, well, I was only making a suggestion; you don't need to raise your voice at me."

Yep, the champagne was definitely giving her confidence to talk to him that way. Why should he be allowed to get angry at her when she was only suggesting? He turned his head away from the window and looked straight at her.

"Is that the champagne talking now?"

"I don't know what you mean, I'm not drunk if that's what you are getting at."

"Well, you are a lot more confident than usual."

"I'm just standing up for myself, I don't need to be spoken to the way that you talk to me. You get so defensive when I ask you a simple question."

"It's because it was irrelevant. I don't like when people tell me what I should and shouldn't do."

"Well, you don't need to be mean about it. I don't understand why you put your guard up and become cold. I was only making conversation with you. I wish I hadn't spoken now."

"Cold? You think I'm cold?"

He almost looked offended.

"Yes, cold. But I know that you have a warm side to you as well, you just don't show it very often."

"And how would you know that? You have not even known me for 2 weeks."

"I've seen it in your eyes and in your smile. Not that you smile very often."

She was being cheeky, but she didn't care; he seemed to be relaxing a bit more as well.

"Oh, really, you have been admiring me."

"I don't know why you don't smile more often; it suits you."

"I smile when I have something to smile about Annalise, and it doesn't happen too often."

"That's a shame. Maybe you will meet someone who can make you smile; everyone should have someone who does that to them who makes them happy."

He looked away for a brief moment and then returned his gaze to hers. This time there was sadness in them, and it made Annalise's heart ache for him. She wanted to hug him and take the sadness away like she did when Penelope was upset. She didn't know what came over her but the next thing she knew she had turned towards him and embraced him in a hug.

It was a slightly awkward hug because Hunter was just sitting in the same position not moving. Annalise knew that this was foreign to him and so she just kept hugging him and until she felt his body relax. As she slowly pulled away their faces were inches away from each other, and she looked him in the eyes. Her body just froze in that position; she could feel the heat rising and her breathing become deeper.

She instantly felt desire take over her body, and she wanted him. Their bodies were touching, and she could feel his breath on her skin, the heat from his body seeping through their touch. She was looking in his eyes searching for something, pleading with him to release the tension building up inside of her. It felt like hours that she was just sitting there with the sound of the London traffic in the background unaware of Hunter's driver in the car with them. Just as she was about to pull away from him, breaking their connection and almost feeling defeated; he slowly and gently touched her jaw forcing her to look at him.

"Hunter, I don't know what you…."

Before she could finish her sentence, his lips were on hers, his hands in her hair, and it was like he was trying to breathe her all in. His lips were smooth but hard, and he definitely knew how to kiss. His tongue started exploring her mouth, and she returned the movement, wanting to take every part of him in; she couldn't get enough of him. Her hands were in his hair, then on his arms, then on his face.

She didn't know what she wanted or how to control herself, but he seemed to respond exactly the same. The tension had built up so much that it was now all being released and there was so much of it. So much passion and desire. She didn't want it to stop; she could just keep kissing him like this forever. She felt like he had opened up to her, let her in and this kiss was his way of showing her that.

He seemed like he needed her; he needed affection for once in his life. She was now pinned up against the car window with her seatbelt in an uncomfortable position. He had undone her coat and his hands were now caressing her whole body, working down to her breasts and then back up to her face. His strong body was pressing onto hers, and she could feel his heartbeat through his jacket and knew that he was turned on just as much as she was.

She felt brave and decided to undo his jacket and a few buttons of his shirt, so she could gain access to his chest. She just wanted to feel his body. He seemed to respond well to it and started pulling her down, almost to a lying position. He moved his hands slowly down to the lower half of her body and Annalise could feel the heat rising from deep within. She pushed her hips up to him, feeling his response in his trousers, and they became uncontrollable.

They just wanted to touch every part of each other, and for Annalise, it had been such a long time; she could almost feel herself about to explode. All of a sudden there was a sudden jolt and a man cleared his voice to interrupt them; she had completely forgotten about Hunter's driver and the fact that he was in the car with them. She should have felt embarrassed, but she was still dazed from what had happened.

Hunter slowly moved back to his seat showing no signs of embarrassment either. He adjusted his trousers and buttoned up his shirt, not looking at Annalise. He leant forward and said something to his driver. He then stepped out of the car into the cold, leaving Hunter and herself in the car, alone.

Friday, 19 June
Hunter

He had asked James to wait outside while he tried to work out what had just happened and how he was going to leave it with Annalise. His emotions were mixed, it had been incredible kissing her and oh god did he want more. Her lips were so soft and the way she used her tongue to explore his mouth was on another level. He had instantly aroused by her touch. He had been turned on before by other women, but with Annalise, it was like being on ecstasy.

She had sent electric shocks through his body, and he felt like he couldn't get enough of her. He wanted to touch her all over her body and make her just as high as him. He remembered how she reacted when he touched her breasts, the way she relaxed pushing her body harder into his like they were trying to merge themselves into one. The connection they had was out of his comfort zone.

He never knew that he could feel this way just by kissing a woman. Annalise had an effect on him that he wasn't sure how to handle, but he knew that he wanted to do it again, but something deep inside him was still trying to say no, trying to stop him from getting into unknown territory. As he came back to the present moment, he noticed that Annalise was sitting looking out of the window, and he wondered what was going through her mind. Was she feeling the same as him or was she regretting it? They both had agreed that nothing was to happen, but they obviously couldn't keep away from each other.

H he didn't know how or where to go from here. Could it just be a casual thing? He wasn't sure it would be for her, and when he thought about it more, he didn't know whether he could just let it be a casual thing either. Annalise had made him feel alive again. These past 2 weeks had opened him up to feel that he never knew existed. The only problem was she had a daughter, and he didn't; he couldn't be part of a family.

Hunter sat back down next to Annalise and turned to face her.

"Annalise."

She slowly shifted her body to face him, and he could almost see the anticipation in her face, but there was also sadness in her eyes. She obviously thought she knew what he was about to say.

"Hunter, you don't need to say anything. I know what we agreed earlier, and this was just a moment of passion, we have both been drinking and the tension has been building between us both that it was bound to happen. But now it's done we can both move on and carry on working together professionally."

Hunter sat there not knowing how to respond to Annalise's comments, is that what she really thought or was she just saying that for him. Her body had given him the impression that she wanted more, but maybe she was thinking of her daughter's needs rather than her own. He looked at her deeply trying to figure out what was going on in that head of hers, but she wasn't giving anything else away. She readjusted her dress and started to do her coat back up; she straightened her hair and leant forward to open to door.

He reached out and grabbed her hand; he couldn't let her go like this, but what else could he say to her? He was still unsure of what had happened and what he wanted from her. He removed his hand again and sat back in his seat pressing the bridge of his nose to release the tension that was building up in his head.

"Annalise."

She turned back to look at him leaving the door to the car open and letting the cold air enter the car.

"Hunter, you don't have to say anything, like I said before it's fine, it was a one-off, and we will just remain professional from now on. I better get inside and let Katherine get home."

Annalise exited the car and walked into her house saying good night to James on the way past. Hunter wanted to call after her, but by the time, he managed to pull himself together to say something; she was already inside the house. James sat back in the car, turned to Hunter and looked like he was about to say something, but saw the look on Hunter's face and decided not to. He turned back around, turned the engine on and proceeded back to Hunter's apartment.

Hunter just sat looking out of the window reminiscing about what had just happened between him and Annalise and how she had just dismissed it. He felt confused about it all. He was going to take a step out of his comfort zone and ask her for dinner on Saturday night before he left for Australia, but that didn't go to plan.

He wanted to see how they were away from work to see if they still had that connection and actually got on with each other, that way he would know for sure. If it was just an attraction that they had then he knew that it would fizzle out, and he could move on with his life and if it wasn't, then that was something that he had to deal with.

Now back in the warmth of his apartment, he headed to the kitchen for a beer; he needed something to relax him and to get his head straight. He walked over to his office that was dark but lit from the lights of London and just sat there deciding on what to do next. This was so unlike him! Normally he would just forget about the woman who he had just been with and move on, but this was Annalise, and it had been different with her from the moment he had met her. He wondered what she would be doing now.

He thought about texting her, but he was unsure of how to start the conversation after their previous ending. She had blatantly said that it was a one-off and that they would be professional from now on, but Hunter wondered whether that was really what she was thinking. There was no way that he could just go back to normal after that kiss, it had rocked him hard, and he needed to see where it went. He would have to push the daughter out of his mind for the moment and see what happened with Annalise first. He decided to send her a quick text.

[TEXT MESSAGE]

Hunter: *Annalise, I hope everything was OK when you arrived home? I hope you enjoyed your evening.*

He waited for her reply. His phone lit up, as he slowly opened it up his eyes sparkled with warmth as it read from Annalise.

Annalise: *Hunter, everything went well with Katherine, I'll definitely be using her again. I had a really great time tonight, it felt so nice being out with people my own age again. I feel uneasy about how we left things tonight.*

Hunter: *Annalise, that was never my intention. You left before I could say anything to you.*

Annalise: *I just saw the panic in your eyes and thought I would make it easy for you, Hunter.*

Hunter: *Let's just say that it wasn't the ending I had planned for tonight. However, it was definitely a positive one! I was trying to wrap my head around it all and then when I was able to speak, you had already gone into your apartment.*

Annalise: *So what were you going to say to me?*

Hunter: *I was going to ask you out for dinner Saturday night before I left for Australia.*

Annalise: *Oh! Are you sure you want to take me out? You don't have to feel obligated to just because we kissed.*

Hunter: *Annalise, if I didn't want to do something then I wouldn't. I want to take you out and so I am asking you. Are you going to accept?*

Annalise: *I would need to get a babysitter again, let me check to see if Katherine can babysit again. Can I let you know tomorrow morning?*

Normally Hunter got an answer straight away when he asked someone to join him for dinner, but he had to remember that Annalise had other priorities, and he wasn't sure if these priorities would fit into his life, but it was only dinner.

[TEXT MESSAGE]

Hunter: *I'll be waiting for the answer to be yes.*
Annalise: *so demanding Hunter!*
Hunter: *You haven't seen half of my demands yet!*

And he truly meant it, the next time he saw her he would be in control of the situation in the restaurant and in the bedroom!

[TEXT MESSAGE]

Hunter: *Let me know in the morning if you can make it and I'll make a reservation for 8:00 p.m., I'll pick you up.*
Annalise: *I'll text Katherine now, so she gets it for when she wakes up in the morning. Night Hunter.*

He hoped that Katherine would be able to babysit; he needed to see Annalise before he left, and this would be his last opportunity for him. Hunter needed to get some things straight in his head before he went away. He would wait for her to text him in the morning and then book the restaurant; he had a great little place in mind, which was quiet and secluded. He sat back in his chair and finished the last of his beer; he felt a weird sense of happiness; and he couldn't remember the last time he actually felt happy in his personal life, this was his heart he was dealing with, not his head, and it unnerved him.

All he could do was see how tomorrow night went and then decide on what he needed to do. Australia would give him the distance that he needed; he just hoped that his head would be clear and on point ready to close this major business deal. He decided that it was late enough and his brain needed to switch off; he shut down his laptop and left his study heading to his bedroom for some sleep, it was a new day tomorrow, a start of something different and unusual for him.

Saturday, 20 June
Hunter

Hunter woke early again; he wasn't training with Tyrell until 7:00 a.m., but his body naturally woke at 5:00 a.m. every day due to that being his normal training time. All he could think about was that Kiss him and Annalise shared last night. He checked his phone to see if she had texted him about dinner, knowing that she would still be asleep and that it was unlikely of Katherine to have replied as well. No messages.

He would just have to wait a little longer. He needed to keep his mind occupied so decided to do some work for an hour before heading to the gym; he could sort some final details out for his Australia trip. He checked his emails and noticed that he had received several from the Sydney office about his visit; apparently, the other company had several demands that they wanted them to meet and Hunter was unsure whether they could meet them all. He knew that Hunter recruitment was on a much smaller scale compared to this organisation, but he still had to stand his ground on some things.

Otherwise, all these larger organisations would walk all over them, and he had worked too hard for that to happen. Hunter replied to a few of them just stating that they would have to have a meeting to finalise some details first. Apparently one of the demands was that they did background check for every person they put forward to the company for an interview, including a police check and Hunter knew that that would take too much time and money. He checked the clock and noticed that it was now 6:15 a.m., and he needed to leave to meet Tyrell; he would finish off his emails this afternoon when he had more time to dedicate to them.

As he pulled up to the gym, parked his car and headed to the gym door he noticed that it wasn't open yet. He was only 5 minutes early; he knew that Tyrell trained someone else before him on Saturdays, so where was he. He wondered what had happened, maybe the guy had cancelled or postponed, but normally, Tyrell would text him to bring his time earlier, which he hadn't done. Hunter decided that he would wait another 5 minutes and then call him; hopefully, everything was OK.

It was now 7:10 a.m. and still no Tyrell. Hunter pulled out his phone ready to call him when a car pulled up right outside the gym doors. It looked familiar, but he couldn't quite place it and then he remembered that it was the girl's car from the other day, the one that he had asked Tyrell about. Tyrell stepped out of the car and headed towards Hunter already apologising before he got to him.

"I am so sorry Hunt, time got away from me."

"I thought you trained Marcus before me on Saturday's, did you forget about him as well?"

"Nah, he cancelled. I was going to text you, but then something else came up, that's why I'm late."

"Everything, alright?"

"Yeah, nothing to worry about, just have a few things going on that's all."

"Well, if there's anything I can do, let me know."

"Thanks, Hunter, all good for now."

"Well, in that case, open the door so I can kick your arse for keeping me waiting for 15 minutes!"

"Hunter, we all know that is never going to happen."

"One day Tyrell, don't go dropping your focus. I'll attack when you least expect it."

They both headed into the gym, Tyrell waving to the girl as she drove off. Hunter wrapped up while Tyrell turned all the lights on and set up the gym ready for their session. Hunter quickly checked his phone to see if Annalise had called or texted him but nothing, surely; she was up by now.

"Hey! No business while you are in my gym, put the phone down and start skipping."

"It wasn't business."

"Oh, really? Personal? That's unlike you! Is it this woman from your work again? What's been happening?"

"Her name is Annalise, and it's nothing that concerns you."

"Everything concerns me when it's in my gym, and because you aren't saying anything you can also give me 50 burpees."

"If you think that's going to make me talk, you obviously don't know me well enough."

"I know you enough Hunter, probably the only one that does."

Hunter thought about what Tyrell had just said, and he was right, Hunter had never let anyone get close to him. Tyrell was probably the only one, and he still didn't know everything, only the outer surface and that's how he liked it. Tyrell had never pushed for more info and would always wait until Hunter was ready to talk. They had become good friends over the years, having a lot in common with boxing but also with what had happened to them both during their childhood. Hunter knew that whatever he told Tyrell would never leave his lips.

As they finished up their session, Hunter stepped out of the ring and headed to check his phone again. Tyrell had told him to focus a few times and knew that something was up. When Hunter finally checked his phone, he noticed that he had one new text message from Annalise, as he opened the text and read it he instantly felt relieved. Annalise had said that Katherine was happy to babysit, and she would be ready to be collected at 8:00 p.m. Hunter instantly grew a smile on his face and his heartbeat returned to normal, well as normal as it could when it involved Annalise.

"Well, someone is pleasing you; I don't think I have ever seen you smile like that!"

"Just some good news that's all."

"Well, it must be a woman as you don't get that happy even if it's work-related. So is it your PA or someone else?"

"Her name is Annalise; do I have to keep reminding you?"

"Well, you must like her a lot if you are correcting me."

"I'm not sure. I know that we have a connection, and we had the most amazing kiss last night, but that's as far as we have gotten. I'm in unknown territory and I'm trying not to freak out!"

"Hunter, just relax! It was just a kiss; you have had plenty of them. Why is this one so special?"

"I know, but it's different with Annalise. I don't know how to explain it, Tyrell. But I'm freaking out as I've never felt these feelings before…. Plus, she has a child."

"OK, so she has a child but does that have to be your problem yet. You have only just met the women; you could go on a few dates and then it could fizzle out. Just try and go with the flow…"

"Since when have I ever just gone with the flow Tyrell? I like to be in control of situations and right now I don't feel like I am. I don't do families or relationships and I'm worried that that's what she is after. In fact, I know that's what she is after, but I can't stop myself from being around her. It's like I am drawn to her; she is all I can think about and well after that kiss last night; she is all I want."

"Stop stressing Hunter, just see how it goes and then decide what to do. You put too much pressure on yourself."

"Well, I do run a highly successful business Tyrell, if I didn't put so much pressure on myself half of the things wouldn't get done."

"All I'm saying is that you need to find a balance, Hunter. Working non-stop isn't good for you, maybe this Annalise will be good for you, even if nothing comes of it."

"Trust me, something will come of it. That's what's freaking me out."

The conversation with Tyrell had just confused Hunter; even more, he needed to stop overthinking everything. It was just one kiss and one date, that's all. He would simply see how it went tonight and then decide. He checked the time and realised that it was getting on, and he had some work to do before tonight's dinner.

"Don't forget I am in Australia from Monday, so will text you when I am back. I have to run got a few things to do before tonight."

"What's happening tonight?"

"I'm taking Annalise on a date."

He could see that Tyrell was trying to bite his tongue and not inflame the situation, but his smile gave it away anyway.

Hunter had called the restaurant and confirmed the booking for 8:30 p.m., it still gave him enough time to collect Annalise and drive to the restaurant. He had never taken a date to this restaurant before, it was more of a sanctuary for him, a place where he would go to eat alone and enjoy the food and good wine. The restaurant made him feel calm and relaxed, everybody knew him there and welcomed him each time like they were welcoming a family member, and for Hunter that was the only time he ever felt part of a family. This was a fairly big deal for him to be taking Annalise to this place, but if he was going to give this a try, then he needed to enter into the darkness and try and let the light shine through.

It was now 7:00 p.m., and he was finishing getting ready; he had had his shower and styled his hair. He had opted to wear a smart pair of dark denim jeans with a crisp white shirt, and a pair of dark brown suede boots. He was definitely trying to impress Annalise but didn't want to make it look too obvious and this was the outfit to do that. He wondered what she would be wearing; he had told her that the restaurant attire was smart, so he picked that she may wear a dress.

Whatever she wore he knew that he would find her irresistible, but he had to keep his hands off her at least until after the meal. He needed this to be more than just passion, his gut had already told him that it was, but he wanted to have a proper conversation with her; he wanted to find out about her past. Hunter knew that something had happened, and he wanted Annalise to open up to him. He just hoped that she didn't want to know the same about him; he wasn't ready to tell that story yet.

Hunter had decided to drive tonight; he needed a clear head so he could work everything out. He didn't need alcohol clouding his judgement. He had decided to take the Aston Martin, one of his favourites and a classic car. He hoped that it would impress Annalise; although from what he knew of her so far, he wasn't sure she would be impressed by a car. He wanted to impress her more than anything, but he just hoped that she didn't think he was being showy with the car and the restaurant.

He turned the engine off and sat looking at her house. Even though the curtains were closed he could see some movement in the light, and he knew that her daughter was still up and that it only meant one thing… that he was going to meet her. Hunter knew that it would just be a brief interaction with her, but the thought of it still scared the hell out of him. He never really knew any children apart from himself when he was growing up, but then again, he was different to most children he knew.

Maybe if Annalise's child was like him then he would know that the best thing to do was to leave them alone. As more fear crept into his mind, he just had to be brave and go up to the house. He stepped out of the car and walked towards the gate to her house, as he opened it and proceeded to the front door, hesitating slightly before knocking on it. He could hear noises inside and someone said that they would get it; he hoped that it was just Annalise so that they could exit as quickly as possible.

His worst fears came true when a little girl who looked just like Annalise opened the door with a huge smile. She was wearing a pink onesie and her hair was hanging down loosely. She was bouncing from one leg to the next and looked like she was super excited about something. Hunter cleared his throat and was about to talk when the little girl spoke first.

"You must be my mummy's date; would you like to come in? We were just playing hide and seek, well that was until the doorbell rang, and we had to stop, but I still have an idea where Katherine is hiding. KATHERINE! I'm coming to get you!"

The little girl then ran off back into the house leaving Hunter standing just outside the front door. He decided to enter and stand in the hallway unsure of what just happened. He was nervous that the girl was going to ask him questions, but she seemed too interested in playing her game, which was lucky for him.

"Penelope, would you stop running around, and it wasn't very polite of you to leave Hunter standing outside."

Hunter could see Annalise proceeding down the stairs as she shouted out to Penelope, which he presumed was the child's name.

"Sorry, Mummy, I did invite him in, but then I had to go and find Katherine before the time ran out."

Annalise was nearly at the bottom of the stairs, and she was shaking her head to Penelope's reply but smiling at the same time.

"Sorry about that; she gets very excited, especially with this particular game. Although I shouldn't really let her play it so close to bedtime."

Hunter was trying to listen to what Annalise was saying, but all he could think about was how amazing she looked. She was wearing a fitted red dress that accentuated her bump and breasts. Her hair was tied up tonight in a low bun, and she had left some loose pieces hanging down around her face. She looked gorgeous! And that dress was doing nothing for his sanity.

All he wanted to do was run his hands all over her body and rip that dress off right now. He returned his gaze back to her eyes and noticed that her cheeks were slightly pink; she started pulling down her dress and fiddling with her hair, slightly nervous.

"You look amazing Annalise. You should stop fidgeting though, you don't need to feel uncomfortable with me."

"Sorry. I mean thank you, Hunter, you look very handsome yourself."

They both just stood there looking at each other trying to decide what they were doing next when Penelope came hurdling in and ran straight into Annalise's legs.

"Penelope, slow down! You nearly knocked me over."

"Sorry, Mummy. You look pretty in that dress, like a princess. Is this man your Prince?"

"Penelope, his name is Hunter, and we are just friends. I told you not to think everything is a fairy tale. Right well, we better get on our way, be good for Katherine and make sure you go to bed when she tells you to. You have had a busy day, and I don't want you getting too tired."

"Can I watch some TV though?"

"Only if Katherine is happy with that?"

Katherine had now entered the hallway and was leaning against one of the door frames. She looked at Hunter and instantly started blushing.

"Katherine?"

"Yes, sorry, yes that's fine with me."

"Great, well I won't be home too late. Shall I text you when I'm on my way back?"

"No rush, take your time."

"Thank you again for looking after her; she has really warmed to you."

"Anytime!"

Hunter was standing there feeling a bit awkward, unsure of what to do or say, and he could tell that Annalise knew how he was feeling. He couldn't get Penelope's comment out of his head 'prince', this was only going to end badly if Annalise had the same thoughts as her daughter.

"Right shall we go Hunter; we have a reservation to get to."

"Yes, we better go just in case we hit some traffic."

Hunter opened the door and stepped out of the house appreciating the cool breeze to help cool down his body. Annalise followed him out as he proceeded to the car.

"You're driving?"

"I thought it might be nice to drive, I don't always get the chance to take the Aston out, and it is a special occasion after all."

He noticed that Annalise had started blushing again and was waiting outside the car awkwardly.

"Sorry, let me get the door for you."

"It's OK, I just didn't know if it was unlocked or not."

"Here you go. Mind your head as you get in."

Hunter got into the car and started the engine.

"Ready?"

Annalise just gave him a nod. He could tell that she was nervous; he wondered if she was naturally like this or just around him.

"Annalise, you don't have to be nervous. Let's just enjoy tonight, it's a chance for us both to get to know each other more, that's all."

"Sorry. It's just been so long since I have been on a date, I don't want to mess anything up."

Hunter chuckled at her comment, if anything it was him who would mess it up. If only she knew how nervous he was, which was so unlike him. He took one of her hands and rubbed her knuckles, instantly feeling the atmosphere change in the car. Her breath caught, and he knew that there was still so much chemistry between them.

"You are not going to mess anything up, I promise. Just relax."

He then let go of her hand before it escalated into something more and turned the engine on, heading straight to the restaurant.

Saturday, 20 June
Annalise

Annalise couldn't stop playing with her hands, Hunter's touch had just made her more uneasy, and she was struggling with her nerves. As soon as she saw him waiting in her hallway she was taken aback by his good looks. She felt it every time she saw him, but tonight, it was accentuated. He was dressed differently. His attire was smart, but it also showed her a different side of him, away from work.

Now that they were sitting in a combined space together with just the gear stick between them, she could feel the heat and chemistry ignite. The whole of her body reacted instantly to him, even before he had touched her. She just hoped that she could get through dinner because all she really wanted to do was to lose herself again in a kiss, it's all she could think about since the other night. She imagined how it would feel again to have his lips touch hers, would it be like last time or was the passion just a one-off, surely not after how she was feeling right now.

The car ride to the restaurant was quiet, they both seemed preoccupied in their thoughts and Annalise wondered if Hunter was thinking the same as her. She looked over at him quickly not wanting them to lock eyes and noticed that he was deep in thought. His eyes were fixated on the road ahead, but she could tell that he was somewhere else. His jaw seemed tense, and he was frowning slightly; she hoped that he wasn't having second thoughts about asking her out.

Annalise knew that it was intense when he picked her up with Penelope running around, but she hoped that for tonight he could just focus on them and nothing else. As she sat there admiring his features, he suddenly looked at her. She felt like a rabbit in headlights and instantly turned to look out of the window, hoping that he wouldn't say anything, and she was relieved when he didn't. Instead, he gently touched her cheek with his soft hand and stroked it slightly.

His touch sent shivers through her body, and she gazed into his eyes. There was a shift between them, this time it was deeper than chemistry.

As they pulled up to the restaurant, Annalise waited in the car until Hunter came around to let her out. She had insisted on getting out, but he wanted to be a gentleman and open the door for her. He gave the valet his keys and then took her hand and walked them into the restaurant. As soon as they entered, she was surprised by the familiarity that was shared between the staff and Hunter.

They welcomed him by name and Annalise first put it down to him being a regular customer of the restaurants, but when she looked closer at the situation, it was like they were family. The way they interacted with him and the way he responded to them, he had the same smile that she had only seen once or twice when he was truly happy about something. Hunter then stepped back and took Annalise's arm and introduced her to the maître d, who was called Franko.

"Hunter, you have brought a lovely lady to dine with you tonight."

Annalise wondered how often Hunter came here, quite a lot if they knew him well.

It was nice for Annalise to see Hunter relaxed and laughing, Franko obviously meant something to him.

"Let me show you to your table, I have put you on a very special one for tonight, very romantic! Have a look at the menu and wine list, and I will send Charlie over shortly to take your order."

"Thank you, Franko."

"Sorry, about that, I thought they may be more discreet, but obviously, they are excited to see me dine with someone."

"I think it's sweet; you obviously seem very comfortable here, and he seemed very kind."

"Yeah, this place has that feeling to me. I suppose that's why I love coming here, always have."

"Well, thank you for bringing me here and sharing it with me."

At that point, Hunter reached over and took Annalise's hands, looking her straight in the eyes. He seemed happy and relaxed, which made her do the same. They sat like that for a few minutes just appreciating each other's company. Annalise could have stayed like that all night, but Hunter pulled them out of it saying that they should look at the menu before Charlie came over.

The food looked amazing when Charlie brought over their entrée's. Annalise had never been anywhere this fancy before, and she would have felt intimidated if Hunter wasn't there.

"Oh, wow! This food looks amazing and smells just as good."

"It's one of their specialities, it has been on the menu since I started coming here. Actually, it's probably one of the reasons why I kept coming back, that and the staff."

"They all seem very friendly, almost like family. How long have you been coming here?"

"About 6 years now."

"Wow, you must really love the place. I don't think I've ever been to a restaurant like this before or tasted food as good as this."

"I'll make sure to tell Jamie that you like his cooking."

His eyes glistened with humour, and she wondered what he was smiling at; he then reached over and wiped a small amount of sauce from her lip. Annalise instantly felt embarrassed; his touch had unnerved her; she was feeling like she had control and then just one simple touch, and she was a mess again. She looked at him and decided that if he could do that to her, then she would do the same to him.

She knew that she had an effect on him; she just didn't use it to her advantage. Annalise touched her lips and proceeded to wipe any excess sauce away, but this time she dipped her finger slowly into her mouth licking the sauce off, every moment looking directly into Hunter's eyes. She noticed that they had become dark and his pupils dilated; he shifted in his seat and ran his hand through his hair, his cheeks became flushed and his eyes kept looking between her lips and her eyes, not knowing what to do next.

"There is nothing more I want to do right now than to lean across this table and kiss you, Annalise, especially with you teasing me like that."

She felt pleased with herself, but she felt exactly the same as he did. She had no control when it came to Hunter, and she knew that if he did lean across the table right now, that she would have no willpower to stop herself from kissing him back. Even if there were all these other diners around them.

"Hunter, I'm not teasing you. You said I had sauce on my lip, so I removed the excess, I think it was you who started it."

They were both smiling at each other and Annalise felt her heartache. Hunter made her smile and brought out a fun side of her that she had forgotten about.

Before the situation could become any more heated, Charlie interrupted them by removing their entrée plates and replacing them with their main course, topping up Annalise's wine at the same time. Hunter had already had a small glass and changed to sparkling water since he had to drive back. Annalise was now on her third glass, and she had to remember to pace herself; she wanted to stay in control of the situation; she still had so much that she wanted to learn about Hunter.

Once they had finished their main courses, Hunter had decided to leave the dessert as a surprise; apparently, it was something that he always ordered. His face lit up even when he had confirmed the 'usual' with Charlie. Annalise was excited to see what it was, Hunter had great taste, and she couldn't imagine that changing when it came to food.

They were alone again with no food to distract them, Annalise thought it would be the perfect time to ask him about his family, that's if he even had a family. The more she thought about it, the more she realised that she didn't actually know much about Hunter. So how had she come to like him so much?

"So your family must be very proud of everything that you have achieved, do you see them much?" she didn't look at him when asking the question, unsure of how he would react. Instead, she played with the rim of her wine glass and waited for his response. If he was trying to make her embarrassed for asking the question, he was doing a great job. The longer he left it, the more embarrassed she became.

She wondered whether she had overstepped the mark, but then again, they were on a date and this is how people got to know each other, even she knew that, and she hadn't been on a date in forever. When she looked up at him, he was looking at her, his eyes completely blank with no emotion, it was like he wasn't even there. Annalise kept looking at him and decided to reach over and touch his hand, hoping that it would bring him out of it. As her hand gentle grazed him, he flinched and instantly pulled his hand back as he had just been scolded.

"I'm sorry, did I overstep with that question? I was only wanting to get to know you more."

"It's fine."

But she knew that it wasn't. He had turned cold and defensive, not like the Hunter that she had grown to know recently.

"To answer your question, no I don't see them, it suits me fine."

"Has it always been that way?"

"For as long as I can remember, yes. But it keeps me focussed on the business and what I want to achieve in life."

"Which is?"

"To keep growing the company and expand to more countries. I want to be number one worldwide. It will take time and dedication, and I am willing to give it my all."

"I'm sure you will, you have achieved so much already. You should be very proud of yourself."

"Work has been my life."

Hunter was now looking straight into her eyes, making sure that she knew how serious he was.

"Work is good, but there are other things in life as well, you should be able to enjoy things outside of work."

"I don't have time for anything else."

"So what about you, will your family be coming to visit you now you live in London?"

He was trying to steer the conversation away from him and put the focus on her, which made Annalise uncomfortable and sad. Even though things had been different between her and her parents for years now, it still made her sad every time she thought back to her childhood. The close relationship they had, they were the 3 amigos, and she still missed it so much. Even more, she missed that Penelope had grandparents that didn't want to know her. Hunter reached over to her, obviously noticing the change in her face.

"It's OK, you don't have to answer if it upsets you."

Annalise wiped an unexpected tear away from her face and apologised, shifting in her seat to try and compose herself. She was sure that it was the wine that had made her extra sensitive tonight, but she didn't want to cry on her first date in years.

"You don't have to apologise."

"I just get a bit sensitive when the topic changes to my family. They aren't really in my life much nowadays. I feel more sad for Penelope. I'm an adult and can deal with it, but she doesn't understand why her grandparents don't want to spend time with her. She used to ask all the time, but I think she has just learnt to accept it now."

"Do you mind me asking why you don't see them?"

She was unsure if she wanted to divulge more when he had just shut her down on his life, but maybe if she opened up then he would. She needed to take a risk and let someone in for a change. Maybe Hunter would understand, or maybe he would judge her. Either way, it just felt right.

"It's a long story, but I can tell you the short version of it for now. OK, well…. I was super close to my parents growing up, we did everything together, I was the apple in their eyes and butter wouldn't melt! I was all set to go to university and study law. It had always been a dream of mine and theirs, and they couldn't have been prouder, they told all their friends and family members and put me on a pedestal.

"When I went to university my life changed, I supposed I grew up, and it made me realise I had been cooped up in a bubble for such a long time. It's not that I didn't like it, it's just all I knew, but it was time for me to have some fun. I started going out to parties, bars and meeting friends, and then I met this guy called Dylan. I hadn't had much attention from boys before, so when Dylan started showing me some, I liked it. We started hanging out more together and got on really well.

"So then one night he invited me to his dorm room and said that all his roommates would be out so we could be alone. Anyway, let's just say one thing led to another, and I lost my virginity that night. It was a big deal for me, but I honestly felt that Dylan was the one. In the morning when I woke, I instantly felt different and excited to see where our relationship would go from then on.

"We had both made a commitment to each other, I thought that it meant that we were now official, but Dylan had other thoughts. He completely changed and said that it was fun, but that we shouldn't hang out anymore. I found out later that apparently, that's what he did; he meets girls, spends time with them just so he can bed them. Well, you can imagine, I felt so ashamed and upset. The first people I wanted to talk to were my parents, but I couldn't tell them what had happened, they would be so angry."

Annalise paused to catch her breath not realising that reliving this story brought up all kinds of emotions that she had pushed aside. Hunter gave her a reassuring smile letting her know that she didn't need to rush the story and to take her time.

"Let's fast forward to a few months later and basically I found out that I was pregnant. I know you must think that I was a stupid kid ending up pregnant after losing my virginity!"

Hunter reached over and grabbed her hand.

"Annalise, I do not think that at all, I do however want to find this Dylan and punch him for what he did to you."

"Well, basically, I started getting bigger and was finding it hard to cover up. I think deep down I was trying to not accept it, but one day I felt Penelope kick, and it changed how I felt instantly. I decided that it was time to tell my parents, so I picked up the phone and called them. I thought that they would be supportive like they had always been and help me with it all, but I was wrong. They were angry, they were disappointed, and they were ashamed of their little girl who was not a little girl anymore. I had completely shattered their dreams of me becoming a top-notch lawyer!"

"So they just turned their back on you and your daughter?"

"Pretty much. They helped me at the start as I had to leave university and move back in with them, but they couldn't even look me in the eyes. They would make remarks about how I had ruined my life and that I should give her up for adoption. At first, it hurt me, but after a while, I just started to accept that we were not a family anymore and that Penelope was now my family. And it's been like that ever since."

"I'm so sorry Annalise, it must have been an awful time for you. You should be so proud of yourself for bringing Penelope up on your own. Did you tell Dylan about the pregnancy?"

"Yep. Once I told my parents I went to tell him to see if he wanted to be part of Penelope's life, but he didn't want anything to do with me or Penelope. He basically said that I was one of those girls who fell pregnant so I could live off his money and do nothing with my life. So he has never been in her life. She does ask about him, but I just say that we are better off on our own and that one day someone special will come into our lives and be the best dad to her."

She thought that she saw panic in Hunter's eyes, but before she could say anything more, they were interrupted by dessert, and Annalise actually felt relieved of the distraction.

"WOW! This looks amazing, what is it?"

Hunter's eyes glistened with excitement.

"This Annalise is the best dessert ever! It's a base of chocolate caramel brownie, then a layer of lemon cheesecake and topped with baked meringue and served with French vanilla gelato and hot caramel sauce. It's like having 3 desserts in 1!"

"It sure looks that way. Is this a speciality?"

Hunter leaned across the table just missing the dessert and whispered that the chef only makes it for him, that it's not even on the menu. Just being that close to Hunter made Annalise's heart rate increase.

"Well, they must really like you to do something like that, I'm sure most restaurants don't do special orders that consist of 3 desserts."

"You'd be surprised the persuasion I have on people and what money can make people do, Annalise."

She didn't know what that comment implied, but it made her realise that she would never be someone like that or do something for cash either. Hunter must have known that his comment didn't sit well with her just by the look on Annalise's face.

"Have I offended you, Annalise?"

She didn't want to ruin the night so decided not to make a comment.

"Not at all. This dessert is amazing, make sure you get some before I finish it all!"

She tried to push the thought out of her head, but she knew that Hunter was in a different league to her. He may not make her feel that way, but it was true; he was a successful businessman who had made millions, lived in the expensive part of London, drove flash cars and dined at fancy restaurants. This felt like she was Cinderella and when the clock strikes 12:00 p.m., that she would return back to her normal life. Not that she had a problem with that, she loved her life with Penelope, It just made her sad that she would never win the prize of Hunter, and even if she did, she wasn't sure if he would want her and Penelope.

They had said their goodbyes with Hunter taking a few more moments to talk to the staff while Annalise waited in the lobby. They were both sitting in silence with just the sound of the busy London traffic around them. Annalise knew that she had been quiet ever since leaving the restaurant, and she knew that Hunter could tell that something had changed, yet he hadn't asked her anymore since they had finished dessert. As they pulled up to a set of traffic lights waiting for the light to turn green, she could feel his gaze on her, but she couldn't look at him.

It just reminded her how much she wanted him. Instead, she kept looking straight ahead wishing the light would turn red so that his concentration had to return to the road. It felt like hours, and she was starting to get restless almost ready to give in when the lights finally changed. He sped off driving in and out of the traffic, it was like he was angry about something.

Annalise didn't think she had said anything to make him that way, or maybe it was the lack of words she had said, but Hunter didn't seem like the type of person not to say anything. He always spoke his mind. As they pulled up outside her house, a lot quicker than she had expected due to his driving, he turned the engine off, and they sat there in the dark for a moment before he turned to face her.

"Annalise. Will you just look at me, please! I don't know what's wrong, but you have been avoiding it since we finished dessert."

She slowly turned her body to face him but still couldn't bring her eyes to look up until she felt his hand slowly touch her chin, and he gracefully lifted her head so that it was in line with his. His eyes were dark and determined and his finger was now sliding over her bottom lip.

"Maybe if I kiss you, you will tell me what's wrong? I don't like seeing you look sad, Annalise."

She just sat there in silence looking into his eyes almost begging him to kiss her, feeling like that may be the last time she feels his lips on hers. She just wanted to lose herself one more time. It was like he could read her mind because the next thing she knew, his lips were on hers, exploring her mouth.

He was trying to get closer to her, trying to make everything better without realising it. It was like he needed her, they both needed this. They both came around and pulled away, and even though their lips weren't touching, their eyes were still locked together.

"Hunter, I don't know if this is going to work. I've had a lovely evening and you have been nothing but a gentleman all night, but I don't know where else it can go. You live a completely different life to me."

She wasn't sure what he was thinking, his face wasn't giving anything away that was for sure. It was like he was absorbing the information before he responded.

"Annalise, is this why you have been quiet?"

She didn't want to confirm or deny it, so she just didn't answer.

"I'll take that as a yes if you aren't going to answer me. I thought we got on well, has something changed for you?"

"No, I mean yes…. I mean look at you, Hunter! You are gorgeous and way above my league. You also run a successful business, have money and live a lifestyle that is completely different to mine. What could I possibly offer you?"

"You shouldn't think so little of yourself, Annalise. You have a lot to offer, and you are beautiful."

She was taken aback by his comments.

"You think I'm beautiful?"

"Annalise, I thought that I had made that clear to you, have you not noticed that I can't stop looking at you or wanting to touch you whenever I am around you. Yes, we live a slightly different life from one another, but I'm a simple man at heart. I am not sure what the future holds for us, it's all very new to me too and I've been battling with it all myself, but then something changed, and I just thought why am I fighting this when it feels so right. We have a connection Annalise and tonight showed me that we have more in common than I do with anyone else, and for the first night in a long time, I laughed."

"Yes, that does seem rare for you."

She knew that she was teasing him, but she wanted to lighten the atmosphere.

"Well, I have my moments. Anyway, what I am trying to say is that I want to give it a go with you, see where it takes us."

"And what about Penelope?"

"What do you mean?"

"Well, it's not just me you would be taking on, it's her as well. We come as a package, and I know that you said that you don't do families."

He was silent for a moment and broke their engagement; she instantly felt sad that he hadn't answered straight away, but she also knew how hard for him this would be. She didn't know his childhood, but she knew that it wasn't a great one and that he was overcoming some kind of demons.

"Well, maybe we could just do us for a bit until we both figure this all out. How does that sound?"

"I can manage that for now."

Her heart was all over the place, skipping, jumping, doing cartwheels; she was definitely falling for this guy. In this split second, she didn't care about anything else, there was no doubt in her mind, just how she felt presently. She reached over and grabbed his head pulling his lips down to hers, his shocked reaction at her forwardness inspired her more. Her hands were in his hair, and she was kissing him even more deeply than she had before, letting all her anxiety seep away and soon returned desire.

He responded the same by unclasping his seatbelt and pulling her closer to him; she was now almost laying on him. His hands were feeling the shape of her body, every inch of her curves was being explored like he was tracking his route on a map. She just took every moment in and enjoyed it.

She had never felt like this before, so powerful and powerless at the same time, what was he doing to her. She felt brave and started to undo his shirt so that she could touch his bare chest, but he grabbed her hand. She stopped and looked at him with confusion, her mind all hazy.

"I think this needs to go inside."

"What?"

"Annalise, every part of me wants to lose myself in you right now, but I'd rather do it in a bed than in an uncomfortable car seat."

She looked at him asking if he was sure.

"But what about Katherine?"

"What about her?"

"She will see you."

"And?"

"Well, what if she tells Candice and then she tells someone else and then the whole office will know that we are sleeping together and then I'll get the sacked."

"Calm down! For starters, we haven't slept together yet, and two I own the company, you will not be getting sacked."

"Yes, but I'll be the cliché, you know how the PA always sleeps with the boss!"

"No, Annalise, I don't. This will be the first for me, I don't make a habit of getting involved with people at work."

"OK, I have an idea. What if you wait in the car while I go and say night to Katherine, and then I'll signal you once the coast is clear?"

He was smiling at her, and it made her heart glow; she kissed him quickly before letting herself get caught up in the moment again.

"Wait for my signal."

Saturday, 20 June
Hunter

Hunter waited for Annalise's signal, unsure of what had just happened. He was still trying to slow his heart rate down while coming to terms with the fact that he was about to take his and Annalise's friendship to the next level. Normally it was just sex to him, nothing more. It had always been that way. No emotion. No attachment.

But from day 1, it had been different with Annalise. There was a connection that he had never felt before like he was drawn to her. She made him smile, which was a rare emotion for him, but he was starting to like it. It still scared the hell out of him, going into the unknown, but he felt that Annalise was feeling the same, they just had to take it one step at a time and get other to know each better.

As Hunter thought about the evening, he felt for Annalise after she had told him her story of how she had gotten pregnant. She was still so young at the time and her parents had basically disowned her after they had found out. He knew how that felt, but his parents had hated him from day one. It must have felt awful for her having a special bond and then that bond is broken.

He could see the hurt in her eyes, even now, years after the event she was still trying to deal with what had happened but kept putting on a brave face for the people around her. That's the type of person he could tell that she was, strong and independent. She was determined to make a better life for Penelope and herself; she had taken a huge leap moving to London, just the two, but it seemed like it was working out for her; he just hoped that he didn't ruin anything for her. He just couldn't commit to anything right now, even though he knew that she wanted the whole fairy tale ending, and he still couldn't offer that.

He needed time himself to get his head around things, but that could wait till another day. Right now, all he could think about was getting Annalise naked and doing all the things to her that he had imagined doing. Why was she taking so long! He was starting to get impatient; he didn't like waiting for things, especially sex.

He saw Annalise's front door open, and Katherine walk out, leaving in the opposite direction to where he had parked the car. He waited for Annalise to come out, but there was still no sign of her. It had been a good 5 minutes and Hunter was starting to get impatient. He decided to go and see where she was. As he knocked on the door, he heard footsteps coming and the front door then opened.

Annalise stood there looking more beautiful than ever; she looked flushed and slightly anxious trying to cover herself, obviously wondering whether she had made the right outfit change. She was wearing a black silk-fitted bodysuit with a loose black silk robe and there was lace material over her breasts exposing her nipples. He could see that she was aroused by how her nipples were standing strong and hard, trying to expose themselves through the material. He just wanted to take them in his mouth and suck them hard, until they were red and tender. The way that she was looking at him, made him realise that she felt the same.

"Annalise."

Her name came out in more of a whisper than his normal voice. He had nothing but desire right now.

"God, you look beautiful. That outfit is making me so turned on right now, Annalise."

Annalise blushed and looked to the floor, Hunter wished she would take his compliments and own them. He stepped closer, taking her chin and pulling her head up so that she was looking at him, faces millimetres apart. Desire took over him, and he kissed her so hard that he thought he may break her. His hands slid down her back feeling the softness of the silk and skin at the same time; he touched her right nipple and heard her make a sound of pleasure.

Her whole body was melting into his; she was savouring every single touch and kiss. Hunter moved his head down towards her breasts and started licking one nipple at a time, sucking harder until he could hear her begging for more. His hands moved to her bum, and he lifted her up so that she was straddling him. Still no eye contact, just the sound of both of their arousal.

The way that she was touching him, he knew that she was feeling every single bit of this, just like him. They were in sync together, relishing in their passion. He pinned her to the wall, her legs wrapped around his, his hardness pressing into her. His hands moved to her head, and he kissed her with everything that he had. Her hands were in his hair, then his chest, and then on his stomach, and as she got lower, he could feel her hesitating.

Hunter knew that this was a big deal for her; she hadn't been with someone for so long, and maybe she was scared of messing it up. But that would never happen in his eyes; she had already done things to him that no other women had ever done, and they hadn't even had sex yet. He touched her cheek and looked at her in the eyes, reassuring her that everything was OK.

"Hunter."

She could hardly speak, and he knew the feeling.

"Don't worry Annalise, we can take it slow."

He started kissing her softly starting from her mouth, slowly working to her neck and felt her body relax again.

"Hunter, it's not that."

"Oh, then what?"

"Let's take this upstairs, I'm just worried we may wake Penelope up, and I don't want her walking down here and finding us like this."

He thought about Penelope and panic started to set in; he pushed it away instantly trying to focus back on the moment.

"Are you OK? You have gone a bit pale."

"I'm fine Annalise, I just want you. Now!"

He picked her up and started to climb the stairs, getting her to direct him to the door, which leads to her bedroom. He managed to open it with one hand and found his way to the bed. Although if it was up to him, he would have just taken her then and there on the bedroom floor. He placed her down and sat up to look at her; she was beautiful, and she didn't even know it. Her body was perfection.

The way her body had curves in all the right places, her breasts were full and ready, and her eyes looked at him with desire and hope. What was he doing? Maybe this was too much; he knew that this was more than just sex for her? He had felt that he had never felt before, and he needed to get rid of them for the moment and focus back on what they started downstairs. He pinned himself on top of her; giving her just enough room to move, he then proceeded to kiss her slowly and gently all the way down to her body. He unclipped the buttons to her bodysuit and slowly used his tongue to give her nothing but pleasure.

She screamed out his name and thrust her hips up towards him. This just turned him on more, and he loved that he was making her feel like this. He removed Annalise's clothing and then proceeded to remove his, so they were skin on skin. Her whole body was soft to touch, and with every touch he gave, he could see the hairs stand up like he was giving her mini electric shocks.

"Hunter. Don't stop."

"Trust me, Annalise. I'm not stopping anything."

He raised his body and slowly entered himself into her, feeling every bit of flesh as he did. She was tight, and it felt like nothing before. She groaned with excitement and thrust him in harder, making him lose control. They moved in sync together, both pushing harder and harder each time.

Beads of sweat dripping down them and just the sounds of their hearts beating and their lungs expanding. Hunter felt overwhelmed with passion; he couldn't handle it anymore; and he needed his release. As he sped up, throttling into her again and again, his mind going into the dark, he felt her hand on his chest and a faint whisper.

"Hunter, I need you to slow down."

He only barely heard what she had said, why did she want him to slow down, was her not enjoying it now?

"I want this to last a bit longer than a few minutes, and if you carry on what you are doing then it won't."

"I just want you. I need you, Annalise. It just feels so good, I can't…"

"I know Hunter, that's why I want it to last. I want you to make…"

She stopped in her tracks and Hunter looked at her; he hoped that she wasn't going to say what he thought she was going to. He didn't do that; he just did sex. Dirty, hot, sweaty sex, that was all. He wasn't capable of the other thing. He looked at Annalise and searched in her eyes, panic almost setting in from her comment. He didn't know what to do; he was too aroused to stop, but then he couldn't do it the way that she wanted him to.

She must have sensed his change in mood and instantly started kissing him passionately again. Her hips started to pick up speed, and she was soon grinding him, harder and faster than before. His rhythm was back, and he was starting to get lost in it again. He sucked her nipples, biting on them hard, his hands couldn't control themselves and moved from her face to her breasts to her hips; he just wanted every single last part of her. They were both to the point of boiling over, one last move, and it brought them both to an organism. Nothing like he had ever felt before.

They both lay there breathlessly, trying to recover from what had just happened. Neither of them speaking, just lying in each other's arms. Silence started to fill the room and Hunter started to come back to reality. His heart rate was slowing, the sweat reducing from his body, his mind clearing from what he could only describe as coming down from ecstasy. What had just happened was mind-blowing for him.

He had had a lot of sex before, but this wasn't just sex, this was like nothing he had experienced. The way Annalise had made him feel was on another level, and he was pretty sure that she felt the same. He could feel her heartbeat slowing on his body and wondered if she was falling asleep, Hunter lay there thinking about the words that nearly escaped Annalise's mouth earlier. She had soon stopped herself from finishing off her sentence, but it had made him feel uncomfortable and upset for her.

He had been upfront with her from the start, and all those feelings had changed, and he was still unsure whether he was capable of ever being in Love or even saying the word. When he was with Annalise, he had hoped, but it was like being in a different world with her, where he could do and feel anything. The connection that they had was definitely like no other, but he had to be realistic; she obviously wanted and felt more; she made that clear just now. He thought that he was feeling OK about everything until she was about to say that she wanted him to make love to her.

She didn't finish off her sentence, but Hunter knew what she wanted to say just by the way that she was looking at him. He was unsure whether he should bring it up or just leave it; he didn't want to make her feel uncomfortable and to be honest he didn't really want to have that conversation. He stroked her hair, and she moved slightly reacting to his small touch.

"Hmmm."

She moved her head from his chest and looked up at him, her eyes still misty and glazed, her cheeks flushed, and she had a smile that would light up a whole football field. She looked even prettier than normal, just lying there with nothing to hide behind. She was looking at him like she was going to say something but then decided not to and leant up and kissed his lips. Instantly the connection was back, but before it turned into something more, Hunter relaxed and changed the pace. He made sure that this kiss was more sensual and passionate; he wanted to reassure Annalise that everything was OK, although he was unsure of what was going to happen next for them.

"You are so beautiful, even more so than normal."

She looked embarrassed and looked away from him.

"Annalise, stop it. You need to take a compliment and start believing in what I am saying to you."

"I am completely exposed Hunter, so am a little nervous. I haven't been in this position for many years. And well, I am lying here with you. I mean look at your Abs!"

There was humour in her voice and Hunter felt relieved; he didn't want to be serious right now.

"Well, I work hard for them, I'm glad you appreciate them. And if you haven't noticed, I am also lying here completely exposed as well. Embrace it, Annalise; what just happened was amazing. I'm still feeling the high from it."

He rolled over and pushed her on her back, lying on top of her pinning her down so she couldn't move. She started to giggle but soon stopped when she noticed Hunter's intense look. The atmosphere soon changed in the room; he wanted to keep a clear head, but how could he when she was lying there naked under his control. He was unsure of what was going to happen next, but right now he didn't care.

He just wanted to be with her and enjoy what was happening tonight. Hunter lowered his head and started to kiss Annalise on the lips, working his way towards her neck, hearing her moan after every kiss. He felt her body relax and her hips push up towards him. They were in sync, and it just flowed without having to say anything to each other. They were each other's high.

Hunter lay staring up at the ceiling, the room silent except for Annalise's soft breathing as she drifted deeper and deeper into sleep. He was too energised for sleep; normally, after sex, he would go and do some work, but he couldn't bring himself to leave her. It was the first time that he had ever felt like this, normally sex didn't mean anything, but with Annalise, it had been different. He was unsure of the feeling but knew that it felt good.

He didn't know what this meant for them, but for once in his life, he felt happiness. But with happiness came all other emotions and attachments, and he was unsure whether he was ready for these new feelings to come into his life. He looked down at Annalise; she looked so calm and still; her cheeks still rosy from the last couple of hours. He stroked her hair making sure not to wake her, and she looked like she needed some sleep.

He had never just laid with a woman before. Even when he was a boy; he never received hugs or cuddles from his mother; he had become accustomed to not having any affection from his parents. This had obviously influenced how he was today with other people, some thinking that he was very cold, but how were they to know what he had gone through as a child. It just wasn't in his nature to be an affectionate person; he knew how to block his feelings and become someone else in scenarios.

That was until Annalise had come into his life. As soon as he had seen her, he knew that he was in trouble, who would have thought a few weeks ago that he would be lying there in her house with her body sprayed all over his and him actually enjoying it. Definitely not Hunter.

He felt Annalise move and her hand come up to his face; she stroked it gently like she was trying not to hurt him. She had concern in her eyes and looked at him deeply.

"Hunter, are you OK?"

"Yes."

"You didn't seem OK a moment ago. I looked at you and your face was pale, and it looked like you were in pain. What were you thinking about?"

Hunter knew how his face must have looked when he was thinking about his parents, but he wasn't sure whether he was ready to tell Annalise about his childhood. He had never told anyone the whole story; he didn't want to feel exposed after all of these years.

"Just work Annalise, nothing for you to worry about."

"Hunter, it didn't look like work to me. You looked scared, and I know you don't get scared when it comes to your business."

"It's nothing Annalise, trust me."

"Hunter, I have completely exposed myself to you tonight. I told you about my parents and Penelope's father. I have given myself to you physically and emotionally. I need you to do the same. I need to understand the real you. What makes you Hunter Maguire?"

"I don't think you are ready for that just yet, Annalise."

"You will be surprised how much I can handle. I'm not a weak person Hunter. I need you to do this for me."

Hunter felt the nervousness in Annalise's voice in the last part of her comment. She was obviously worried after she had given herself to him if there was a 'them'. He wanted to reassure her again; he didn't want Annalise feeling vulnerable, but it would mean opening up to her. And that was a hard thing for him.

"I don't know whether I can."

"Open up Hunter, I am not here to judge."

She was looking at him with pleading eyes. Pleading for him to show her how he felt. Telling her his childhood and how it shaped him into the man he was today, would mean that he was exposing himself to emotions and hurt. He had been so strong all of these years; he didn't want pity from anyone. He didn't need it. He needed people to respect him for who he was now, how he had made something of himself. Without family.

They both lay still, unsure of who was going to talk first. Hunter decided that he needed to put his emotions to one side and focus on Annalise, and her needs. And she needed this from him.

"I suppose you want to know about my childhood?"

"Is that what you were thinking about just then? You looked in pain Hunter, was it really that bad?"

"It depends on your scale of bad. Is it bad that your parents wished that they never had you, and made you know that on a daily basis? Is it bad that I use to hide away in my room for days scared that if I left it that they would be remembered that I was still alive? That the verbal and physical abuse would start again."

Hunter could hear the anger in his voice and tried to calm himself down for Annalise's sake.

"Oh, Hunter, that's horrible. You were just a child; how could they treat you like that."

"As I got older, I started acting out more at school. Getting into fights on purpose just to get attention from someone. I didn't care if it came from me being bad. I was used to the abuse that I thought didn't matter either way. The worst would be when they got drunk, it would just heighten their emotions.

"My mum, if you can call her that, would say how she wished that she never fell pregnant and she should have gotten an abortion. Then she would start on my dad, about how he should have worn protection, and then they wouldn't have this mistake."

"What was your dad like?"

"Just as bad, even worse. He was the physical one to me. He used to throw anything and everything at me. Trying to get a rise from me, just so he had an excuse for it all. But, when I didn't retaliate, he would punch me, kick me to the floor. Leaving me there covered in blood."

"Did no one say anything about your bruises?"

"No one cared. I was a bad kid at school, a lost cause as the teachers would say. Even if I did say something, they wouldn't have listened."

"What about other family members?"

"I don't have any. Well, not that I know of. It was just me and my parents."

Annalise reached up and kissed Hunter longingly on the lips, trying to almost wash away the past. He knew that it was her way of showing him that she cared, but to him, it felt like sympathy and that was one thing he didn't need.

"Do you see them at all now?"

"No. As soon as I was old enough, I left home and started working on my business. I wanted to show them that I was better than them, show everybody that I could make something of myself. I met Tyrell, my current boxing coach; he made me channel my anger into boxing; he has helped me a lot and here I am today. The Hunter that is lying here with you now."

"Well, he has turned out to be the most successful, intelligent, charming and good-looking man I know. But seriously Hunter, thank you for telling me your story. I know that it wasn't easy, but I feel like I know you that little bit more now."

"Just as long as you don't share your knowledge with anyone else Annalise. I have never told anybody this. I am still unsure how you persuaded me to tell you."

"Maybe my body had something to do with it."

The smile on her face made Hunter relax; she looked sweet and innocent, but there was also passion in her eyes. He felt more connected with her if that was even possible. What was this woman doing to him?

Sunday, 21 June
Hunter

Hunter must have fallen asleep; he can remember having sex one more time after he had confessed his childhood sins to Annalise. They laid in each other's arms; he heard Annalise's breathe slow and knew that she was asleep, but he thought that after everything he wouldn't be able to sleep, but he had had one of the best night's sleep he could remember. He woke early, the sun only just coming up, lighting the room slightly with speckles of the sun. He loved this time of the morning, knowing that most of London would still be sleeping, it was the quiet before the storm.

Normally, he would be getting up, finalising his plans for the day before heading off to training. But, this morning, he was wrapped up by Annalise's body all over his, the sweet smell of her smothered all over him, and he couldn't help but smile. Last night had turned out to be one of the best nights of his life. This woman had some kind of power over him, but he had never felt happier laying in her bed right now.

The house was silent, and Annalise was still sleeping, so he decided that he would have a quick shower before she woke and then would take her out for breakfast. He left tomorrow so wanted to spend a bit more time with her before he went away. He slowly crept out of the bedroom and headed for the bathroom. He turned the shower on and stepped into the hot steamy water, letting it hit his skin like rain hitting the trees.

His body aching from all the exercise that they were doing last night. He finished his shower, dried himself, put the clothes that he wore last night back on and crept quietly back towards Annalise's bedroom. As he got closer, he could hear voices coming from the room, and for a minute he wondered who Annalise was talking to. She was obviously trying to be quiet, but he then made out that it was a little girl. In the height of emotions from last night, he had completely forgotten about her daughter.

He was unsure whether to keep heading towards the bedroom or quietly head for the door. He knew that would be a bad idea, but Hunter wasn't sure if he was ready to have another encounter with Annalise's daughter. He had only just come to realise that he had told Annalise last night about his childhood; he wasn't sure that he was ready for another step. He was standing in the hallway deciding what to do when he heard her bedroom door open and the little girl was heading his way. Annalise shortly behind her with slight fear on her face.

"Penelope, will you come here."

Before Hunter could do anything, the little girl was standing in front of him. She had long dark messy hair from where she had been sleeping on it, big bright brown eyes staring up at him, a pink onesie with unicorns all over it and a smile that reminded him of Annalise. Come to think of it, she was the spitting image of her.

"Are you Mummy's new friend? Did you have a sleepover? I want a sleepover, but Mummy won't let me yet, and she said especially no boys. But why are you allowed to stay?"

Hunter was confused and tried to take in everything that she was saying in.

"Penelope, stop asking Hunter questions. He has only just woken up; he doesn't need to be interrogated by you."

Annalise looked at Hunter, miming that she was sorry.

The girl, who he was reminded of was called Penelope, and she was still looking up at him, waiting for an answer. He was unsure of how to answer that question. He couldn't really say what he and Annalise had been doing last night, which definitely wasn't for children's ears. But he knew that he had to answer; he would just treat it like he would in business. Straight to the point, matter of fact, no emotion.

"I am Annalise's, I mean your mummy's friend. She kindly let me stay on the sofa last night."

"Why?"

"Err because my car broke down."

Hunter hated lying, but it was a must in this situation, to avoid further interrogation.

"I know that you didn't stay on the couch."

"And how do you know that, Penelope?"

179

Annalise had now cut in, obviously trying to diffuse the situation and avoid embarrassment.

"Because I saw him lying in your bed this morning."

"And how do you know that?"

"Because I went to come in and jump on you to wake you up, and then decided I better not when I saw him."

"Oh!"

Annalise looked just as embarrassed as Hunter did. Both of them felt like they had been caught out by their parents, when in fact it had been a 7-year old.

"Right, you need to get dressed Penelope, and I will make us all some breakfast."

"Oh, actually, I was going to take you out for breakfast, Annalise."

"Hunter, that would have been lovely, but I have Penelope. Why don't I make us all some breakfast downstairs instead?"

She looked at him and her eyes said sorry. He felt annoyed; he had planned it all in his head; he was going to take her to this quiet little French patisserie in Chelsea, they did the best little pain au chocolate that he knew Annalise would love.

"Penelope, go and have a shower and meet us downstairs in 20 minutes for breakfast. I will make us some pancakes with lots of blueberries and maple syrup."

Penelope raced off, obviously excited about the pancakes. Hunter knew that he had no decision in this matter and that his romantic breakfast was off.

"Sorry, Hunter, I would have loved to of gone for breakfast with you, but I just don't have anyone to look after her. Plus, I have been out twice this weekend, it's not fair to leave her again."

He wasn't used to not getting his own way, and it took him a moment to put it aside. Annalise then stepped closer and stood on her tiptoes, kissing him softly on his lips, reconnecting them again but pulling back quickly before it became heated and turned into another scene from last night. He knew that she was trying to make everything OK.

"All good Annalise, I will have to shoot off shortly though as I need to get ready for my trip tomorrow. I still have a lot of work to do."

Hunter knew that his comment wasn't exactly true. Yes, he had work to do, but it could wait. He just felt uneasy spending time with Annalise and her daughter. He wasn't ready for that just yet.

"Stay for some of my famous pancakes at least. I know you're busy, but you have to eat."

And before she could let him answer, she had headed downstairs to start on breakfast for them all.

As Annalise started clearing up the breakfast plates, Hunter sat there and watched her discreetly. She was in her element in the kitchen as she glided from one side to the next, and she definitely knew how to cook, those pancakes were amazing. She danced around the kitchen quietly singing to herself, unaware that he was watching her. She looked more beautiful every time he saw her.

Last night was amazing, just the two of them, he had never felt that close to someone enough to open up to them about his childhood, but it was so easy with Annalise; he knew that there would be no judgement. He felt like a weight had been lifted off his shoulders and didn't realise how much he had been carrying by himself for so long. Strangely enough, talking about his parents had actually given him a bit of peace, he was scared that he may get angry again, having buried it for many years, this being the fuel for his success.

He still had that burn deep inside and wanted to thrive more than ever, but he felt relieved to finally talk to someone about it. Almost getting approval that it was wrong in someone else's eyes that he wasn't the bad child after all. He wanted acceptance from someone else and Annalise had given that to him, just by listening.

As he sat there mulling this over, feeling content for once in his life he noticed that someone was now sitting next to him. In the corner of his eye, he noticed that this person wasn't very tall and more childlike and was now staring at him with a huge grin on their face. As he slowly turned to look at her, he remembers that he was still at Annalise's house, sitting in her kitchen, now sitting next to her daughter, Penelope. Panic started to set in, and Annalise was nowhere to be seen.

"So how do you know my mummy?"

He had this. How hard was it to talk to a child? He dealt with children on a daily basis, if you could put some of his employees in that category.

"Umm, well. Your mum and I. Well, we work together."

"Do you sit next to each other?"

"Not exactly."

"So what do you do together? Mummy says that she works in a huge building, which is filled with lots of pretty things."

"Well, I am your mum's boss."

"Oh, wow! Mummy must be very special if you are staying at our house."

Hunter didn't know where this conversation was going but didn't know how to divert to another subject. He didn't want to have to explain to a child what went on in his life.

"Penelope, what are you doing today?"

"I think Mummy might take me to the park. Would you like to come with us?"

Hunter couldn't think of anything worse than spending time at a park filled with screaming children.

"That's very kind, but I have some work to do before I go away tomorrow?"

"Where are you going?"

"I am off to Australia; do you know where that is?"

"No. But it sounds far away. Will Mummy not miss you? Are you coming back?"

"Yes, I am coming back. It's only a short trip."

"Mummy will still miss you. We never have visitors stay, so you must be special. Will you come and stay again when you get back?"

"I'm not sure yet."

"Please come and stay. Mummy looks so happy. You must be the Prince that she has been waiting for. I've been reading all about them in my book."

Hunter didn't know how to respond. He just sat there quietly hoping that the girl would stop talking and that Annalise would come back in the room soon. He had no idea where she had gone.

"You could be Mummy's prince charming, and we could all live happily ever after together, just like the ending in my book."

Hunter's face drained. Prince charming! He almost started laughing; he was far from a prince. Fairy tales didn't enter his life and neither did happy endings. What had happened in the space of 24 hours? How was he now sitting here, with Annalise's daughter talking about fairy tales? He was brought back to reality; this was precisely why he didn't get involved with people and especially people with children. What had he been thinking, emotions had clouded his judgement? If this is what her daughter was thinking, what was Annalise thinking? Maybe that's what she wanted all along.

He knew that's what she wanted secretly even though she hadn't said it. He had just ignored it, thinking they would deal with it when they came to that crossroads, but it was happening now. In the space of 2 weeks, he had met her daughter, had breakfast with them like a family and was being invited to the park with them, like a family.

And now her daughter was asking if he was going to be their prince charming and live happily ever after. That was one thing that wasn't going to happen. Not now. Not ever. He didn't do happily ever after. It wasn't in his genetics. They never happened in his eyes. He couldn't be a part of this.

Hunter immediately got up from the table, the little girl still looking at him and headed out of the kitchen. On his way out, he bumped into Annalise as she was entering. She must have seen his face as panic set into her eyes.

"What's happened, Hunter? Where are you going?"

"I'm sorry Annalise. I can't do this."

"Hunter. Wait! Please let's talk about this, what happened?"

"Annalise. I told you that I don't do families, and I don't do happy endings. I'm sorry I can't do this. It's not what I want. It's over."

And with that Hunter left the house, closing the door behind him leaving Annalise staring after him.

Sunday, 21 June
Annalise

What had just happened, her mind was spinning out of control, and she felt like she was about to faint. Her brain turning over so quickly that she couldn't keep up with it! Emotions and feelings have been thrown around all over the place, how could her morning start so perfectly and within a few hours turn to this. What had happened in the time that she had left the room and returned a few moments later. She had left Penelope in the room with Hunter, but surely Penelope wouldn't have said anything to make Hunter react the way that he just did; she was just a child, what opinion from a child could change an adult mind like that. She retraced his words.

"I told you that I don't do families, and I don't do happy endings. It's not in my genetics."

Had Penelope said something to him about families? She knew that Penelope went off on her fairy tales sometimes, but that was just imaginary. Why would he think too much into it, maybe it was a mistake inviting him for breakfast with them both, too much too soon? She knew that it might be pushing the boundaries a little too much, but after the amazing night that they had last night and the words he had shared with her; she thought that they were getting somewhere. Annalise's mind was still racing with a thousand thoughts, and she decided to ask her daughter what had happened.

"Penelope darling, what did you say to Hunter just now in the kitchen?"

As Annalise entered the kitchen, Penelope was just sitting there playing a game, so innocent to what she may have said to frighten a grown man.

"We were just talking about fairy tales and happy endings."

"But what exactly did you say to him? Can you remember for me?"

"I just said that he could be your prince charming, and we could all live happily ever after, just like my books."

"Oh, Penelope."

"Did I say something wrong, Mummy? Did I upset your friend?"

Annalise's heart ached, in more ways than one. She was angry but more at Hunter for reacting the way that he did, Penelope was just a child. Yes, she shouldn't have said that to him, but she had nothing but good intentions, Hunter should have spoken to Annalise before storming out like a grumpy teenager. She was angrier with him.

"Maybe next time speak to Mummy before talking about prince charming and happy endings, maybe keep it between us."

"OK, Mummy. I was only trying to make you happy."

"Oh, Penelope, I am happy. How could I not be when I have you in my life."

She embraced Penelope into a giant hug letting her know that it was all OK, but deep down Annalise knew that this was the end of something that could have been amazing for Hunter and herself.

Annalise didn't know what to do; she had been pacing the house for the past couple of hours thinking about Hunter. She hadn't heard anything from him, but then again, he did say that it was over, so she probably wouldn't. As reality started to set in she soon started to realise that it wouldn't just be Hunter who wouldn't be in her life anymore, it would mean that she would have to get a new job. What had she done! This was one thing she kept telling herself, but did she listen, no.

What had she been doing getting involved with her boss, how stupid could she have been? It was all so cliché! What was she going to do? She had rent to pay, bills to pay, Penelope to look after, and she had only been in the job a few weeks, this wouldn't look good with the temp agency? Should she wait to hear from Hunter about her job, or should she just email her notice that way she could say to the agency that it wasn't the right fit for her and hopefully they would have something else for her instead?

But who was she kidding, it was the perfect job for her, not just because of what happened with Hunter, but she loved the offices and the people who worked there; she was good at her job and actually like the industry even though it was completely know to her and very fast-paced. Oh, god what was she going to do!

As Annalise sat there contemplating what to do, she knew that she had to be strong for Penelope's sake; she had to put her first. She would email HR her resignation letter, then contact the recruitment agency to see if they had anything else. She would be happy to work out a weeks' notice so they had time to find someone else, plus Hunter was away so even though she would have to have contact with him via email at least she wouldn't have to see him face to face. That way she could leave before he got back and never see him again as if it never happened.

Feeling relieved that she had a plan, she went to her computer and started typing up her resignation letter; she also decided to draw up an email to the recruitment team, that way they would both get it ready for Monday morning. As she hit send on her emails, she turned her computer off and decided to go and watch a movie with Penelope. Annalise felt drained both physically and emotionally and all she wanted to do right now was cuddle up with her little girl and lose herself in some Disney film where she didn't have to think too much about what was going on. As she entered the lounge room, she looked at Penelope just playing with her toys on the floor completely content and Annalise couldn't remember a time when she looked this happy.

Before they had moved to London, their lives were so up in the air and Annalise knew that she hadn't been in the best frame of mind, which she knew had affected Penelope. She was always angry or upset, mainly because of her parents and their attitude towards Penelope and herself. Since moving to London, it was like a weight had been lifted from her shoulders, and even though she had made some bad decisions already, she felt happy in herself and the life that they were building in London.

"Penelope, should we watch a film together and snuggle on the sofa?"

Annalise saw the excitement in Penelope's face and knew it was more about the film than snuggling with her mum, but it didn't matter either way.

"Yes yes yes! Can I decide what we watch?"

"Yes, but we are not watching *Frozen* again, Penelope. You have seen that film too many times."

"Oh, but I love that film… can we watch Inside out?"

"OK, you can put that one on."

They both settled on the sofa and snuggled under a blanket. As the film started, Annalise didn't realise how tired she was, with last night's antics and then the emotional roller coaster this morning, tiredness started to kick in, and she found her eyelids becoming heavier and heavier.

Annalise woke to the sound of her phone; she wasn't too sure how long she had been asleep, but the credits of the film were rolling, so it must have been nearly a couple of hours. As she looked down at Penelope, she noticed that her eyes were closed, and she was fast asleep as well. Annalise reached for her phone and noticed that there was an email from Hunter.

Her heart started beating faster, and she just stared at the screen unsure of what the email would read. She wondered whether it would be about how he reacted this morning, but why didn't he just call her, why would he do the cowards way out and email her. Well, she was about to find out, as she apprehensively opened up the email and read his words, her mood instantly changed.

[EMAIL] 03:25 pm

From: Hunter Maguire
Subject: Resignation
Date: 21 June
To: Annalise Smith

Annalise, I am very disappointed to hear that you have emailed your resignation to our HR department. Try and be rational about this, you need this job.

Hunter
Hunter Maguire
CEO, Hunter Recruitment

She was fuming by his words, how dare he say to her to be rational about this situation, and that she needed this job. Fair enough she did, but it wasn't up to him to make that decision for her.

[EMAIL] 05:15 pm

From: Annalise Smith
Subject: Resignation
Date: 21 June
To: Hunter Maguire

Mr Maguire

Thank you for your email. I am unsure as to how you have heard about my resignation so soon. But yes, you are correct, I have decided that it would be best for both parties if I moved on from the organisation. I am not being irrational, quite the contrary really. I am sure that the recruitment agency can find me something else quickly. I will of course work a week's notice, so it gives you some time to hire another person and do a handover.

Regards,
Annalise.
Annalise Smith
Personal Assistant to Hunter Maguire, Hunter Recruitment

Annalise knew that her tone and response would annoy Hunter, but she didn't care. He had not only upset her, but she hated it when people tried to tell her what she needed to do. His next email came a bit too quickly.

[EMAIL] 05:25 pm

From: Hunter Maguire
Subject: Resignation
Date: 21 June
To: Annalise Smith

Annalise,

Is this really how you want to play it?

Yes, I do think that you are being irrational, you need this job! You have told me this before. I don't want to go into details over email, but I will not accept your resignation, we will talk about this when I am back from my business trip. In the meantime, please carry on with work as usual.

Hunter
Hunter Maguire
CEO, Hunter Recruitment

How dare he tell her what to do? He had to accept her resignation she had put it in writing, and she will work out the weeks' notice and then leave; he couldn't do anything else about it.

[EMAIL] 05:30 pm

From: Annalise Smith
Subject: Resignation
Date: 21 June
To: Hunter Maguire
Hunter.

I will not retract my resignation letter and will be leaving in one week from tomorrow (Monday). Please do not tell me what I need or want, you do not know anything about my life. I will be able to manage; I have done all of these years without your help.

Have a safe trip and please correspond with me for any work-related matters while you are away.

Thanks,
Annalise
Annalise Smith
Personal Assistant to Hunter Maguire, Hunter Recruitment

She waited for another email, but nothing else came from him. Who did he think he was telling her what to do; he may be her boss, but that was all? Actually, she didn't even know what they were before, they had never established that. At the end of the day, she had only been on one date with him and had slept with him, well a few times, but that was all.

Who was she kidding, it was more than that for both of them? They had a connection, something that only they knew and now it was all over, in a blink of an eye, saying the words aloud hit her hard. It was over. The words finally hit home and sank in, tears turning into sobs and before she knew it she was crying uncontrollably, Penelope stirred and looked up at her.

"Mummy, are you OK? Why are you sad?"

Annalise tried to calm down and compose herself; she shouldn't be crying like this in front of her daughter.

"Sorry, darling, Mummy was just crying at the film, that's all. You know what I get like with sad films."

"But this film has a happy at the ending Mummy."

"Oh, yes, it is. I'm crying because I'm happy for them. That's all."

She pulled Penelope in for a bigger cuddle and kissed the top of her head, her tears drying up, and she was able to speak without lumps forming in her throat.

"Shall we get takeout for dinner? And continue our girly night?"

"Yes! Can we have pizza?"

"Yes, but you have to go and put your PJ's on first as this is a PJ party and anyone not wearing their PJ's doesn't get any pizza."

Penelope raced upstairs before Annalise could finish her sentence. She secretly just needed a minute to compose herself; she needed to be strong and crying in front of Penelope wasn't doing that. After giving herself a talking to, she ordered the pizza even though she didn't really have much of an appetite and set up another DVD, deciding to go for frozen this time as it was Penelope's favourite. Annalise tried to push Hunter out of her mind, but all she kept thinking was what he was up to.

Was he feeling upset like her, his email didn't sound like he was? He was probably too busy getting ready for his trip and sorting out work to be thinking about her; he would probably meet someone else while he was away in Australia anyway, all the women over there are supposed to be beautiful, with blonde hair and tanned bodies. What did Annalise have over them, nothing? She just had excess baggage that Hunter had made clear he didn't want. So that was it, there was no future for them, and she needed to deal with that.

It had only been 2 weeks she could easily get over him and try and find someone who accepted her and Penelope as a duo, it was his loss really. Even though she said these words to herself, she couldn't help but feel sad about it all, but before she could start crying again Penelope came racing into the room dressed in her PJ's and jumped back on the sofa ready to recommence their girly night.

Monday, 22 June
Annalise

As Annalise's alarm sounded, she hit the off button on her phone having been awake for a while now. To be honest, she hadn't slept well at all, all she had been thinking about was Hunter. She hadn't heard anything from him since their email conversation yesterday, but then again why would she; he was probably at the airport by now or even on the plane. She couldn't quite remember the time of his flight but knew that it was early. At least she didn't have to face him when she went into the office this morning, which was at least something that eased her mind.

She would go and see HR first thing to confirm her resignation and then contact the recruitment company to let them know and see what else they had for her, they always seemed busy with different roles so Annalise hoped that there would be something in the pipeline for her; she just hoped that leaving Hunter recruitment wouldn't put a red mark against her name. Hunter was away so they couldn't ask his opinion anyway, and she knew deep down that he wouldn't say anything to jeopardise her getting another job.

Annalise got out of bed and went to wake Penelope up so she could get ready for school; she then had a shower and made breakfast for them both. It felt strange that this time 2 weeks ago; she was getting ready for her first day at Hunter recruitment and now she was going in to confirm her resignation. She had such high hopes and yet again she had ruined it. She was so angry for letting herself get involved with her boss, what was she thinking. She had kept telling him that nothing could happen, but in the end, they both had given in to the feelings that they had, it was inevitable.

As she was finishing breakfast and trying to hurry Penelope out of the door so she could get to work on time, her phone pinged, and she noticed that she had 1 new email. Unsure of whether to read it before getting in the car, she decided to open it just in case it was important. As she hit the button to read, she realised it was from Hunter. All it said was that he was now about to board the plane so will be on limited internet during the flight and that he would reply to any emails when he could.

It was such a generic email that she had to double-check who he had sent it to, and to her surprise, it had been sent to the whole office. She felt another sharp pain hit her hard in the heart; he was just moving on and not even pretending to care about her or what they had. It was just business as usual for him.

She wanted to reply to him, but she didn't know what to say; she just wanted some kind of communication between them, to know that he was feeling just like her and not coping very well. She decided that it would be better if she just left it and only contacted him when she needed something for work. If he could put his feelings to one side, then she would try as well.

When Annalise arrived at the offices, she dropped her bag at her desk, turned on her computer and decided to go to HR to talk about her resignation. As she walked towards their offices, she felt nervous about it, wondering if Hunter had spoken to them yet. Come to think of it he never answered her as to how he found out. As Annalise arrived at HR's department, she couldn't hear anyone in there but knocked anyway, maybe they weren't in, yet it was still early. To her surprise, she heard someone answer her and her nerves instantly kicked in.

"Come in."

Annalise entered the room to see Jo, the head of HR sitting at her desk talking to someone on her mobile phone; when she looked up, she showed Annalise a warm smile, and she animated for her to sit down on the chair opposite hers. Annalise sat there looking around the office trying not to listen in on the conversation; she couldn't quite work out who it was as Jo just seemed to be nodding and saying yes; eventually, she came off the phone and turned her focus on Annalise.

"Annalise, how are you this morning? You must be here to discuss your email that you sent last night?"

"Yes, that's correct. I just feel that it's not quite working out here for me."

Annalise knew that she was just blurting information out, but she was unsure if she didn't say it quickly that it wouldn't come out at all.

"That's a shame, I have heard nothing but great reviews about you. Especially from, Hunter."

Annalise was shocked at Jo's last comment when had Hunter given feedback on her.

"Oh, really?"

"Yes. When I forwarded your email to him last night, he called me at once and told me that I wasn't allowed to let you go. That you have been a great addition to the team."

Annalise just sat there looking at Jo, unsure of what to say next.

"Obviously, I told him that we couldn't keep you here unless you wanted to stay. So the decision is up to you, but just so you know, we all think you fit in great and you would be missed."

Annalise had it all planned out in her head, and now speaking to Jo, she was unsure of what to do. Could she stay here and work for Hunter, would it be too hard to be that close to him and not be able to do anything about it. Maybe she could speak with the recruitment agency, and if they didn't have anything for her, she could stay until they did. Annalise knew that it wasn't fair to mess people around, but she had to think about herself, plus Hunter would be away for the next week so it gave her time to decide properly.

"Would I be able to think about it?"

"Of course. Would you mind me asking what has brought this all on? Is it the hours, the workload, your relationship with Hunter?"

Annalise felt like she was a rabbit caught in headlights, what did Jo's last comment mean? Her relationship with Hunter.

"Umm… no no everything is great. I suppose I was unsure if I was doing a good job or not, Hunter never really has given me any confirmation that he was happy with my work."

"Well, now you have it, so take it from me, you must be doing a good job if he calls up HR to tell them not to let you go."

Jo gave her a look that made Annalise feel like she knew what was going on between them, but how could she, they had both been so careful. Plus, Hunter had said that HR would have a field day with it if they did ever find out.

"Thank you, Jo. I'll let you get on with your work. Thanks for your time."

"Anytime, Annalise."

Annalise's day had been pretty quiet; she still hadn't heard from Hunter but knew he was still on the plane with limited internet. She was still so confused, it had only been 24 hours, but it was the hardest 24 hours for her; she still couldn't get her head around Hunter just finishing it. He had been so open with her that night, and she thought that they were getting somewhere but for him to just run as soon as something didn't quite fit with him, was a coward's way out. Fair enough he had been upfront with her from the start, but so had she; he knew that she had a child, but it still didn't stop him from getting close with her; he hadn't even given her time to talk to him about it all.

That morning had just been a bit stressful with Penelope seeing them together. It was only breakfast; it wasn't like she had asked him to move in with them or marry her. Maybe she was better off without him if he ran as soon as things got tough. He had shown his true colours, it was just Hunter and his own world. He couldn't handle anything more; she could understand because of his background, but surely, there is a time in his life where he needs to start letting people in, let people care about him, just like she did.

Annalise more than cared about him, she had started falling for him. She knew that it sounded stupid; she had only known the guy for a couple of weeks, but when you know, you just know. She had been cautious at the start, but her feelings just couldn't be hidden; she had always been led by her heart and not her brain.

Annalise decided that as she wasn't very busy that she would head home a bit earlier today, no one would really know that she had gone early anyway, Hunter wasn't here, and for all, they knew she had cleared it with him. As she started packing up her things and turning her computer off, her desk phone started to ring, deciding if she should answer it or not, she decided that she better answer just in case it was something important.

"Hunter recruitment, Annalise speaking."

She froze as she heard the person on the other end of the phone talk. It was Hunter.

"Annalise… hello?"

Realising that she hadn't answered him the first time, she pulled herself together.

"Yes. Sorry, I was just preoccupied. Aren't you supposed to be on a flight?"

"I'm at my layover, should be boarding again soon."

"Oh, right. How was your first flight?"

"Fine. You know what these long plane journeys are like, tiring and boring."

"Actually, I don't, I've never been on a plane."

"What? How have you never been on a plane, Annalise?"

"Some of us don't run successful businesses and can jet-set all over the world."

She knew that her voice had risen, but he always managed to get under her skin.

"It's for business Annalise, not pleasure."

"Fine."

"OK, well, I can see that you are not in a good mood, so I'll get to the point of why I'm calling."

"I'm in a perfectly good mood thank you very much. Maybe it has something to do with the person I am speaking with and how they are trying to make me feel inferior to them."

"Come on Annalise, I would never do that. Anyway, I need you to call the hotel that I am staying at and let them know that I will be late with my check-in. I have to go straight to the office when I land, change of plans."

Annalise knew that she was started to sound childish and remembered that Hunter was still her boss, and this was still her job; she needed to be professional.

"OK, will do. Anything else?"

The phone went silent and all she could hear was Hunter's breathing. Annalise wondered what he was thinking about.

"Nothing. I've now got to start boarding so I'll speak to you when I get to Australia. There won't be too much for you to organise while I'm there, but I just need you on standby. Oh, and Annalise, I am glad that you decided to stay."

"Um… well I'm still not sure yet, I just said to HR that I would think about it."

"Well, I'm glad you are still thinking about it. You are a valued employee."

"An employee, is that it?"

"Come on, Annalise, let's not talk about this now."

"Well, we couldn't talk about it when you were here, as you just ran off."

Her voice was definitely raised higher than normal by this point.

"I have to go Annalise…. I'm sorry they are calling me to board. Speak soon."

And with that, the phone went dead, and he was gone, and Annalise was left feeling deflated again.

Wednesday, 23 June (Australia)
Hunter

Hunter had arrived at his hotel late last night, it had been a long flight to Australia, which was strange for Hunter as he normally didn't mind flying, especially with being able to sleep in the luxury of first-class. But, this time, he had other things on his mind starting with the letter A. He had to call Annalise when he was laid over in Dubai airport just so he could hear her voice; he had been happy to hear from HR to say that she had decided to stay with the company, and he knew that he wouldn't have been an easy decision for her either. Hunter knew how much Annalise had felt settled and was happy that she was making a life for her and her daughter, but he couldn't be in that life.

Hunter thought back to the amazing night they had together; he had opened up to Annalise about his childhood and in a strange way it had lifted the load and his mood. She didn't judge him once, and he felt that he could tell her anything. That's what he liked about Annalise; she was so strong and independent, and she didn't even know it. Hunter remembered the conversation with her daughter about him being the 'prince charming' in their lives, and it all started to hit home hard for Hunter.

How could he ever be someone's prince charming? He wasn't built that way? Even his parents had said that he was a waste of space, and even though he didn't believe that, he knew that he was incapable of loving someone. He was never meant to have a family or be in a committed relationship; he thought that he may be able to with Annalise, but after that day, he knew in his heart that he couldn't. He needed to move on and forgot about what had happened with them; he could turn their relationship around and be professional again; he knew how to block things out; he had had many years of experience. But why could he not stop thinking about her? He was thousands of miles away and still she was the only thing he could think of which was frustrating him as he needed to be on his A-game to close this deal off before heading back to London again. It was time for him to be the Hunter Maguire that he knew and liked.

As Hunter arrived at the Sydney offices, which were located in the main CBD close to Sydney Harbour, he looked at the scenery around him. It was autumn in Sydney and even though the sun was shining, there was a slight cold breeze in the air, which reminded him of London. He had never visited Sydney before, let alone Australia. But he had heard good things and Sydney was one of the top profiting offices within Hunter recruitment.

As he entered the building, headed to the lifts and pressed for level 53, he could hear a few people around him talking about the stock market, how they were finalising deals and could be in for a high bonus this quarter. He looked at the expressions on their faces, they were excited and filled with drive. He remembered that face all too well; he was exactly the same at their age, eager to learn, eager to make money and make something of himself. He missed the chase, the excitement that came with gaining a new client, making a new placement, and winning a new tender.

He still got some of the excitement, but it was on a different scale; he had the whole business to think about now; and he was more in the back end of things and only really got involved if they needed him, that's why he was excited to be in Sydney to make this deal work. If Hunter recruitment managed to get the number one bank onboard for Australasia, it could mean massive things for the company. It wasn't all down to him, but he was the deciding factor, so he needed to pull out all the shots on this occasion.

As he entered the lobby of the offices, Hunter noticed the view from the reception area, it overlooked the harbour, and he was mesmerised by the sun reflecting off the crystal clear blue water, it was almost relaxing him into his subconsciousness. He was soon snapped out of it when the lady behind the desk started talking to him.

"Welcome to Hunter recruitment, do you have an appointment today?"

The girl behind the reception desk was fairly young and had an English accent, she had long blonde hair, which was tied up in a neat ponytail, blue eyes and was smiling at him in a very pleasing way. He wondered whether this was how she was with all of the people that came into the office or just him. She was dressed smartly, which he liked; it gave the business a good image when the staff presented themselves well.

"Yes. Can you let Dave Mitchell know that Mr Maguire is here to see him?"

The girl looked slightly embarrassed as if she should have known who he was and treated him in a different manner.

"Of course, Mr Maguire, I know that Dave is expecting you. How was your flight?"

She was now trying to make small talk, but he really wasn't in the mood to discuss pleasantries.

"Long."

She could obviously feel his tone and quickly picked up the phone to tell Dave that he was here to see him. Before the girl could ask any more questions, Dave was coming out of an office door and heading straight towards him.

"Hunter! Long-time no see, how was the flight?"

Hunter had always liked Dave; he was slightly larger with more of a round body and was easily a foot shorter than Hunter, and Dave had a warm and friendly tone to him, almost like a teddy bear. Clients loved him with his great sense of humour and charming personality. But what Hunter liked the most was that when things needed to get done, Dave did them. No one took him as a fool that was for sure.

"Rebecca, can you set Hunter up with a key card for the office, full access please. I'll give him the tour, which office have you located for him?"

"In the Bentley office. Hunter, let me know if there is anything else that you need while you are visiting us, and I can arrange it for you."

"My PA in London is on hand so she should have everything covered."

Dave started walking towards the main office door ushering Hunter to follow him.

"So I thought I would show you around the offices first, then grab some lunch down at the Harbour. You can then get some rest before tomorrow's big meeting. We need to win this deal Hunter, if we get this bank on board then it could mean big things for us."

Dave was basically telling Hunter not to mess it up, in the politest way possible.

"Dave, stop worrying; I have it all under control. It's not like I haven't done this before, remember who set this company up."

"I know, I know. I'm just super excited about this one Hunter. So once Dominik arrives at the offices tomorrow, I have everything set up for the presentation, I will start it off and then you could finish it with everything about the company including growth plans. Then I have booked for us to go to

Rockpool dining for dinner and drinks and then let's see where the night takes us."

"Sounds good Dave, I'll just follow what you have planned."

"Are you going to explore Sydney while you are here?"

"I'm only here for 4 days, I don't think it leaves me much time. I have a few other negotiations going on right now as well, so I'll just be sorting them out before I head back. I might have to stay in Dubai on the way back for a few days. I don't really have the time, but one of the CEOs of a large oil company wants to meet me to discuss doing business with them."

"Sounds interesting. Good money involved?"

"I wouldn't be doing it if there wasn't."

"Very true. Right let me show you to your office and then I'll show you around and introduce you to some of our top consultants."

"Sounds good."

It had been a long day and Hunter was glad to now be back at his hotel room. He was staying at the Intercontinental hotel, which was not too far from the offices. His room was very spacious, and he had a spectacular view of the harbour, Annalise had definitely done well with booking this place although he knew that it was costing him an arm and a leg. Hunter laid on the bed feeling drowsy from the red wine he had consumed at Lunch.

Dave had taken him to an Asian fusion restaurant called Mr Wong that was amazing; apparently, it was one of the best Asian restaurants in Sydney and you could tell because the place was completely booked out. He just hoped that Jet lag wasn't going to get him before this meeting in the morning.

He looked at the time and wondered what time it would be in London, it was around 9 hours difference so would be 7:30 a.m., his mind went straight to Annalise and what she would be doing. He wondered whether he should call her, not knowing what he would say; he decided not to. It was probably the alcohol that was making it feel this way. The best thing for him to do was sleep right now, his brain and his body knew it.

Thursday, 24 June (Australia)
Hunter

Hunter woke from his sleep, the curtains still open and the light from the city shining through his room. His head was slightly fuzzy from the wine and for a moment he had forgotten where he was. He rolled over and checked his phone, 3:00 a.m. Why did he have to wake up this early? He needed to be on form for the meeting today. He rolled onto his back and closed his eyes again, trying to drift back to sleep, but it wasn't working, his brain was now active and thinking about all of the things that he needed to get done.

He could get up now, finalise his proposal for today's meeting, then send some emails and then it would be a reasonable time, and he could have a workout before heading into the office. He liked to get in early anyway, before anyone else. He didn't know why, maybe it was the calm before the storm, seeing the den before the wolves came in, but he just liked the quiet.

As he lay staring up at the ceiling knowing that he should get up, his mind went back to Annalise again. He had been dreaming about her, about them, obviously an erotic dream from the reaction in his pants. He couldn't help feeling like he would love for her to be lying next to him right now; staring at the amazing views he had, he doubted that they would be too interested in it if they were laying here naked together.

He would definitely be doing something more personal with her. Hunter wondered if he should call the office, but Annalise would probably not be there; he could always call her mobile instead. He reached for his phone and before he knew it he had hit dial on her number; as he waited anxiously for her to answer, wondering whether she would answer at all, he finally heard her voice.

"Hunter, is everything OK?"

"Sorry, to bother you, Annalise, I know that you have finished work for the day, but I just needed to speak with you."

There was silence down the phone, and he wondered what she was doing or thinking.

"Annalise, are you there?"

"Yes, I'm here. What did you need to talk to me about?"

Every single possible thing was going through Hunter's brain right now, but he couldn't tell her why he was really calling her. He had finished it with her; he knew nothing could come of them so why couldn't he just let it go and let her move on.

"Um. Sorry, my mind has gone blank."

"Hunter, are you OK?"

"Yes, sorry, it's a mix of a hangover and jet lag."

"A hangover, did you go out last night?"

"Long lunch date, too much wine, that's all. I just need to get some water down me and hit the gym and I'll be fine."

Annalise didn't respond, so he carried on talking.

"The hotel is nice, thank you for arranging it, I have a great view."

Her tone was cold when she finally spoke.

"That's what you pay me to do Hunter, I am your PA."

"Annalise, take some credit. I'm just saying thank you. How was the office today?"

"Fine. You had some emails come through to which I have responded, and I have cc'd you in on them. Nothing too serious, but I thought that you didn't need to be hassled by them, so I just sorted them out."

"Oh, OK, who were they from?"

"Tom from the accounts department just wants to know about the final fee for the Mini Cooper deal and James from the Singapore office about setting up a Skype interview when you are back. Oh, and a message from someone called Rosie, she wanted to know why you were avoiding her texts and phone calls."

Annalise's tone had turned to frost after her last comment. Why was Rosie emailing him and why did Annalise have to see the email? He had told Rosie to never call or email his work details; he should have just texted her back before flying to Australia to say that he wasn't interested in a reconciliation.

"OK, thank you. Did you reply to Rosie?"

"Yes. I just said that you were currently overseas on a work trip and that you would respond to her when you got back."

"OK. I'll sort it. Annalise?"

"Yes."

"She isn't anybody; she means nothing to me. Just a friend."

"Your personal life doesn't interest me, Hunter, I am an employee, that's all."

"Annalise, you don't have to be like that. You are more than an employee."

"Was. Past tense Hunter, you made that clear when you walked out on me the other day and ended things."

"I'm sorry Annalise, I didn't mean to upset you. I told you why I can't continue with us, you want the happy ending, and I can't give you that."

"That's fine Hunter. I know where I stand. Was there anything else as I need to sort dinner out for Penelope?"

"Yes, sorry. I have to make a stop in Dubai on my way back, I have another business meeting that I need to attend. Could you find me some accommodation and extend my flight for 2 days?"

"Will do. I will email you the details."

"Thank you. Have a good evening, and I'll speak to you soon."

There was no reply and the phone went dead, Annalise was angry, but she also sounded upset. He knew that he had hurt her when that was the last thing that he ever wanted to do. Why couldn't he be strong? He knew it was wrong to get involved with an employee; he made it clear to his employees that it wouldn't be tolerated and then Annalise comes along, and it all goes out the window. And now, it was all messed up, not for him; he still had his life and business, but he had made it worse for Annalise, and he hated it. He would apologise properly when he got back to London and hoped that they could work together again.

Hunter had finalised the details for his proposal today, sent his emails and finished his workout at the gym, once he was dressed and quickly ate some breakfast he decided to head into the office, making his way by foot as it was such a lovely day and hoped that he wouldn't get lost on the way. He was the first one there, the whole office was silent, and he was thankful for the peace and quiet so he could go over what he was going to say today. He knew that he had this one in the bag, but he wanted to make sure that it was exceptional, Dave had given him the background on Dominik, and he knew that he wouldn't take any bullshit from them; he wanted the truth in numbers and how Hunter recruitment was going to value their business.

Hunter's belly was fired up, and the adrenaline was running through his veins; he loved this feeling, it was pure excitement. Slowly people started trickling into the office one by one, laughing, talking, some with heads down trying to escape the day ahead; he then saw Rebecca the receptionist heading his way with a warm smile on her face, and she knocked and then entered his office.

"Good morning, Mr Maguire, do you need anything before your meeting this morning?"

"Coffee would be good."

"Certainly, I will get Annalise to get it for you."

"Annalise?"

Hunter's face almost drained from the blood rushing from his head, was she here? No, of course, she wasn't here, his mind was just playing games with him, and the jet lag was hitting him harder than he thought.

"Yes, Annalise is our receptionist."

"I thought that you were the receptionist?"

"No, I am Dave's PA, I was just covering the desk yesterday while Annalise was on her break."

"Oh, OK."

"I'll let Dave know that you are here, and your coffee will be with you shortly."

"Thank you, Rebecca."

"Anytime, Hunter."

As Rebecca left his office, Hunter wondered how today was going to go. He hoped that they would win the deal, celebrate and then he could get on with some other work. Part of his job was to entertain his clients, and even though he liked to do it when he was younger; he much preferred to be at home drinking a whiskey and looking out on the view of his apartment balcony. He was a simple man at heart.

Dave knocked on his door, entering without Hunter even answering; he could tell that he was nervous by the way he kept pacing the office and touching his hair, Dave always had an energetic vibe, but today, it was enhanced, Hunter just hoped that he wasn't like this in the meeting he needed Dave to be on form.

"Dave, will you stop pacing my office and just calm down."

"Sorry, Hunter, I'm excited and nervous at the same time."

"Me too, but I need you to be on form today. Like you said yesterday, this could be massive for us. We need to win this deal for us and the company."

"I know, I know. I'll be fine, I just want to get it over with, get in the mix already and do my showcase."

Dave was now starting to relax and even started dancing around the room.

"OK, Dave, you can stop with the bipolar personality. We have this in the bag. What time is Dominik coming in for the meeting?"

"Ten-thirty in the morning. We have an hour. I need to make some phone calls, meet you in the board room in half an hour? We can go over some final details before he arrives."

"Sounds good, see you then."

Dave headed out of Hunter's office and down to his, passing Rebecca on his way out who was in hand with a large coffee.

"Here you go Hunter, I thought you may need a large one, you seemed a bit tired when I first came in, probably from the plane journey."

"Thanks, Rebecca, you read my mind. Just what I need."

"You are welcome. How long are you staying for Hunter?"

"I leave in a couple of days, have to stop over in Dubai on my way back for some more business, then back to London."

"Busy man, you must get lonely travelling on your home. Do you have a family at home?"

"Its fine, I get used to it. No, I don't have a family, I prefer to be alone."

"No one prefers to be alone."

"Well, I do. It suits my lifestyle."

"And what lifestyle is that?"

"Work."

"And social?"

"I only do social if its work related."

"Well, that's boring."

"To some, yes, but not me. How do you think I grew this business? Hard work, with little playtime."

"Yes, but everyone has to have some fun."

"Maybe."

Hunter wondered if Rebecca was trying to flirt with him.

"Well, if you find yourself wanting to live on the wild side while you are here, let me know. I know of a few good places to go where they serve the best food and wine. Here's my number."

Hunter looked at Rebecca as she was writing her number down on a piece of paper, it was without doubt that she was attractive and obviously she was very confident asking him out in a subtle way, but she wasn't necessarily his type. He knew what his type was. Annalise was his type, but he couldn't go there. Maybe he would take Rebecca up on her offer. As she handed over the piece of paper, he took it in his hand and placed it in his trouser pocket.

"Hopefully I'll hear from you."

She turned on her heel and headed out of the door.

Hunter put the piece of paper in his suit jacket pocket and looked at the clock. It was now 9:40 a.m., and he only had 20 minutes until he had to meet Dave in the board room; he still had a couple of emails to reply to which were fairly urgent so decided to quickly get on to those.

Hunter walked out of the meeting feeling liberated; this is why he had gotten into this business and made it successful; he just gave one of the best presentations of his career and won the business of one of the top global banks. This was going to be a real asset for the company, especially for Australasia, with so many good things to come. Now it was time to take Dominik out and celebrate with the team, and he was so ready to let his hair down. He needed to stop thinking about Annalise and start thinking about the business and what better way to do it than celebrate this win.

"Right, drinks on me. Dave where are we going?"

"I've booked Rockpool for dinner, but we can go for drinks at the Opera bar first, sound good to you Dominik?"

"Yes. As long as Rebecca can come with us?"

"Absolutely. Rebecca are you keen?"

"Do I ever turn down an offer of champagne and fine dining Dave?"

"Ha, never Rebecca, that's why I employ you."

Hunter looked at Rebecca, and she smiled at him, playing the game all too well. She knew how to play these clients and make them happy; he just hoped that she knew where to stop. This was a professional business at the end of the day. He didn't want her feeling that she had to do it, but she seemed like she knew how to handle herself.

Hunter was so energised from the meeting; he needed to have a cold shower and to have a change of clothes before heading out again. He wanted to talk to someone other than the group about the business that they had just won; he wanted to talk to Annalise.

"I just need to head back to the hotel quickly and get changed, meet you at the bar?"

"Don't be too long Hunter, we will put a beer on ice for you."

"I won't! Less than an hour I promise. Meet you there."

As Hunter headed to the hotel, he thought about ringing Annalise and telling her the good news, but their last conversation had ended badly, and he wasn't sure she would even care. He decided that it would be best to have a shower and get changed and then head out again before he changed his mind and called her.

As Hunter walked down to the Opera bar, there were groups everywhere, it seemed that Sydney was just like London and that every night, there was a weekend night. As he managed to push past the crowds of people, he spotted Dave in the corner of his eye and headed straight for him.

"Right, it must be my round!"

"Hunter, you're finally here."

Rebecca came walking up to him with her hands on her hips like she was about to tell him off; she had obviously had a couple of champagnes already as her cheeks were slight flushed, and she seemed more friendly than normal.

"Yes, sorry I just had a few emails to reply to before heading here."

"Always doing business."

"Well, it is my business, it won't run itself."

Dave joined the conversation passing Hunter a beer, Dominik following behind him.

"Dominik, cheers to our new adventure together, may we make money and grow together."

"Cheers to that. I have nothing but faith in your company Hunter. I have always heard good things and today you confirmed those for me."

They all clinked glasses and laughed as they did, celebrating the night ahead. Hunter knew it was going to be a long one.

The night had definitely been a long one, Hunter was making his way back to the hotel on foot, which he had decided was a good idea when he had left the bar. He had left the rest of them at the karaoke bar to finish off celebrating and entertaining Dominik who looked like he was having an amazing time.

He and Rebecca had actually hit it off and Dave was more than happy being the third wheel for the rest of the night, as long as it made the client happy. As Hunter headed back to the hotel there was one person that he wanted to speak with more than anything and that was Annalise. He didn't even contemplate the time that it might in London or even what she might be doing and just hit dial on his phone, waiting for her to answer.

"Annalise, is that you?"

He knew that his words were slurring his words and tried to put on the most sober voice he could find.

"Hunter?"

"Yep, that's me."

"Are you OK?"

"I'm fine. You?"

"Are you drunk?"

"Nope, I'm not drunk. Just fine. Are you?"

"Are you sure? What have you been up to tonight?"

"We won that big company deal so we have been celebrating."

"That's amazing Hunter, well done. So you went out and celebrated with alcohol that means you are drunk."

"I miss you, Annalise."

He didn't care what he was saying, it was the truth, and he just needed to let it out, and it felt good. It was probably the alcohol that made him say it aloud, more like Dutch courage.

"Hunter, you are drunk."

"Maybe, but that doesn't stop me from missing you."

"You don't know what you are saying."

"I know how I feel, Annalise!"

"Hunter, I don't have time for your games."

"No games being played here."

The phone went quiet and Hunter tried to focus on where their conversation was going. The alcohol was hitting him harder now and his head was spinning; it reminded him of why he never drank past the point of being merry; he knew his head was going to hurt in the morning.

"Hunter, give me a call tomorrow when you have sobered up and know what you are saying."

He could hear the slight anger in her voice and wondered why she was being like this with him; he was only telling her the truth, wasn't that what she wanted to hear.

"Annalise, I thought that this is what you wanted?"

"What?"

"For me to miss you, miss us."

"Hunter, I don't want you to miss me, I want you to be with me. I wanted you to push past your insecurities and be the person that you were trying to be. I know that you are scared and that's understandable with your past, but I thought that it was different with us. I thought that we had a connection like nothing else and the minute things start to go down a path that you are uncertain of, you run."

"I didn't run, I walked."

"Are you finding this funny, Hunter?"

"Not at all. But I didn't run. Yes, I ended it, but I ended it and then walked out."

"You may not have ran physically, but you ran mentally and that's worse. I don't need another man in my life to let me down when things get tough. I need someone who wants to be a part of my family, which includes Penelope. So it's probably best that we didn't get any further in 'this' than we did."

Hunter tried to think about the words that Annalise was saying, but his head just couldn't focus; he looked around him and knew that his hotel must be around here somewhere. All he wanted right now was his bed and to sleep this drunkenness off.

"Annalise, I have to go, I'm trying to find my hotel and I'm a bit lost."

"Have you been listening to anything that I've been saying, Hunter?"

"Sorry, what? God, I'm sure my hotel was around here somewhere."

He knew that Annalise was talking to him, but he couldn't focus on the words coming out of her mouth; he was just thinking of how lost he was.

"Goodbye, Hunter."

And before he could say anything else the phone line went dead, and she was gone. He tried to think back to what she was saying, something about him running, but most of it was a blur. Stupid alcohol. He should have never phoned her while he was like this, but he just wanted her to know how much he missed her.

The more he thought about it the more he started to realise his feelings for Annalise; he had never missed anyone since he could remember, but he missed everything about Annalise. He knew that he had some stuff to sort out in his head, but first, he just needed to find his way back to his hotel room. He would call her in the morning to sort everything out.

Friday, 25 June (UK)
Annalise

Annalise had gone to bed early that night but hadn't slept very well at all; she had tossed and turned all night thinking about Hunter, her job and now she felt shattered. She rolled over to check the time, her alarm hadn't gone off yet and with the start of daylight creeping in through her curtains, it must still be early. She had one missed call on her phone from Hunter; unsure of what time he had tried to call her she was glad that she had put her phone on silent before going to bed, she really wasn't in the mood to hear any of his excuses, especially in the middle of the night. Annalise slowly got up and stretched her legs out; before placing them on the floor, she caught a glimpse of herself in the mirror and was shocked at how tired she looked.

Hunter and this scenario were starting to take their toll, and it had only been a few days. She decided to have a shower, wash her hair, and cover her face in make-up to hide the black circles under her eyes and then go and get Penelope up for school. She would make her something nice for breakfast to apologise for being so miserable the last few days, it wasn't Penelope's fault and Annalise hated taking it out on her. She put the phone back down on her side table and decided that Hunter could wait for now.

Feeling refreshed and rejuvenated from the shower, Annalise got dressed and went downstairs to make herself a cup of tea. It was only 6:30 a.m. so she thought that she would let Penelope sleep a little longer. Deciding on making Penelope her favourite… pancakes, she started prepping the mixture and washing the berries to go on top so it was all ready to go for when she was ready for school. While Annalise had a little time to herself she decided to email Jo from HR and see if she could schedule a meeting for when they both got into the office this morning that she would send an email to the recruitment agency to let them know

209

that it wasn't working out for her at Hunter recruitment and see if there were any other positions going at the moment.

Hopefully, they would call her today; either way, she really didn't want to be there when Hunter got back, and it was just easier this way for them both of them. She would finalise Hunter's travel details for Dubai, write up some handover notes and then leave within the next few days, it was a sought after company so she knew that the role wouldn't take long to be filled. She had been so lucky in getting this role, they had gone out on a limb for her, and she really hated letting people down, but she had to think about herself and Penelope. Surely, Hunter wanted to work with someone who he hadn't been involved with as well; he wouldn't have to try to avoid them or feel awkward around them, it was best for them both.

"Penelope, it's time to get up I've already let you sleep longer than normal."

"I'm tired Mummy, can I just stay in bed today?"

"I've made you your favourite for breakfast so hurry up and get dressed and you can enjoy it with me before going to school."

"Are we really having pancakes for breakfast? Yes!"

Penelope jumped straight out of bed and ran to the bathroom to wash and get ready for school, Annalise headed back downstairs to start making the pancakes and heard her phone ringing in the kitchen. As she raced to get the call it died off just before she could answer, not recognising the phone number she then received a text message informing her that she had one new voicemail. As she started to listen to the voicemail she realised that it was Jo from Human resources, she had received her email and was happy to meet with her at 10:00 a.m. Her tone was slightly frosty, which was strange considering how nice Jo had been the other day, maybe she was stressed about something else; anyway, Annalise would meet with Jo and give in her resignation and then start to finalise everything at Hunter recruitment before she said goodbye for good.

As they were driving to Penelope's school Annalise could hear her phone ringing and wondered who it would be this time. She had already called Jo back and getting her answerphone had left her a message saying that she would come to her office at 10:00 a.m. Maybe it was the recruitment agency following up on her email; she would call them back before heading into the office so she had some privacy. She heard the phone ring off and then start ringing again, whoever it was they were either being impatient or needed to talk with her desperately.

"Mummy why does your phone keep ringing, does someone important need to talk to you?"

"I'm not sure darling, it might just be Mummy's work wanting to discuss something. I'll call them back once I've dropped you off at school."

As they pulled up to Penelope's school and Annalise kissed her goodbye and waved to Penelope as she ran through the doors of her classroom, it made her heart warm knowing that she was so happy with the school. Penelope had made lots of new friends and didn't stop talking about how much she liked her teachers, the school and her friends. It was so nice for Annalise knowing that she was finally settled and enjoying it, it hadn't always been that way when they lived in Norfolk, too many people knew their business and would make fun of Penelope for being different to the rest of them.

That was the tipping point for making Annalise relocate them; she could handle herself, but when it affected Penelope, it was time to say goodbye and move on and so far she didn't think that she had done a bad job, well except for the whole Hunter fiasco. Before setting off and driving to work, she decided to check her phone just to make sure that it wasn't anything too important, as she checked her phone it read that she had 4 missed calls from Hunter, 2 voicemails and a text message, what on earth had happened for him to reach out to her that many times. He knew that she wasn't at work yet, but then again, he was in Sydney so probably got the time difference mixed up. Knowing that it must be something urgent for him to call so many times, she just hit redial before even listening to the voicemail or text message.

He answered straight away.

"Annalise, where have you been? I've been trying to get hold of you."

"Sorry, Hunter, I've been driving Penelope to school. What's the matter, has something happened with the deal?"

"No, that's all good as far as I'm concerned. Why?"

"Well, you called me 4 times in the space of 10 minutes. I thought it must be something urgent."

"It is. I wanted to talk to you."

"About what?"

"Us."

"There is no us, Hunter. Remember you finished it and walked out."

"That's what I wanted to talk to you about. I shouldn't have run away like that, it wasn't kind. I normally have more patience, but this is out of my comfort zone Annalise. I need you to give us another chance."

Before Annalise could even contemplate his words, she had to finish this conversation quickly. She had already made up her mind and had to stick to it. She didn't really want to tell him before finalising it with Jo because she was worried that Hunter would change her mind, but it had just come out.

"I'm leaving, Hunter."

"What! Don't do this, Annalise, because of me. You have responsibilities, I don't want you worrying about getting another job. You can keep this one."

"Hunter, we both know how hard it would be for us, well for me at least. I can't work with you Hunter, I need to get over you and move on. I need to start thinking about Penelope and putting her first."

"But that's what I wanted to talk to you about. I miss you, Annalise. I miss us. I want us to give it another go."

"I'm not sure Hunter that it would work out. We both want different things from life, I've realised that over the past couple of days."

"I know my job is full-on, and I have to travel a bit, but we can make it work. I just want to give it another go. Say that you will, and we can sort the rest out when I get back."

"And what about Penelope?"

"What about her?"

"We come as a package, Hunter. I can't have you running when you get scared again. I need you to talk these things through with me."

The phone was quiet like he was contemplating something over in his head, Annalise was going to check that he was still there when he spoke again, this time his voice was cold and again the Hunter that she had just been speaking to had disappeared.

"I'm sorry Annalise, you are right. I am being selfish, I want you, but I'm still not sure if I want to be part of a family."

"Well, that's settled then Hunter, it's Penelope, and I or nothing at all."

"I'm not sure Annalise, why can't it just be us for a while."

"Because it can't. I can't keep talking about this Hunter. You need to figure out what you want in life and be happy with that. You obviously don't want a family or commitment and that's fine but don't hurt people by making them think that you do. I have to get to work. Goodbye, Hunter."

And with that she hung up the phone and started crying, letting all the heartache out knowing that she wouldn't be seeing Hunter Maguire again.

Annalise arrived at the building and headed straight to her office trying not to bump into anyone she knew; she really wasn't in the mood to talk to anyone right now, and she felt that she would start crying at any moment again. She tried to sort her make up in the car, but anyone would know just by looking at her that she had been crying from her bright red and puffy eyes. It was now 9:30 a.m. so she still had a bit of time before her meeting with Jo; she decided that she would make a start with finalising Hunter's travel arrangements for Dubai, the flights were all sorted, but she still needed to confirm the hotel that she had requested.

She decided to send them another email and flagged it as urgent. Ten in the morning had crept up on her, and she was feeling nervous about speaking with Jo, again unsure of how she was going to react with her. As Annalise got up and headed down to Jo's office she noticed that the door was open, and she could see that Jo was on the phone with someone again. Knocking quietly so she didn't interrupt her but loud enough to make her aware that she was here for their meeting, Jo ushered her in and to sit down, whilst whispering that she would be with her in a moment.

"Sorry about that, Annalise; it's go go go as soon as I set foot in this office."

"I can imagine that you must be extremely busy with all the employees. Do you deal with the other offices as well?"

"No, thank god. That is definitely too much workload for me. Each country has their own HR department, I just look after the UK."

"That's still a lot of work though."

Jo just nodded and closed something down on her computer before returning her attention back to Annalise.

"So what did you want to talk to me about Annalise?"

"I've thought about our talk the other day and decided that I would like to go ahead with my resignation."

Annalise instantly felt a rush of relief just by saying the words.

"Only if you are sure? Like I said before, we love having you on board with us and you are doing an exceptional job. It will however leave us in the lurch slightly."

"I'm happy to work out a few days' notice until you find someone else."

"Is there really nothing that we can do to make you stay? It has only been just under 3 weeks, I'm sure if you gave a few more that you would feel more settled."

"Unfortunately not, the role is just too full on for what I am looking for right now. I have a daughter to look after and after just moving here, I need to focus on her for a while and at the moment, I'm not."

"I understand that completely having kids of my own. There's a very fine line between a work/life balance."

"Yes, I need to keep working on that one."

"OK, so I will finalise your resignation and speak with your agency to see if they have anyone else who is suitable and available immediately. If you could speak with Hunter about anything else that he needs finalising before you leave and then if you can write a handover for the next person. It's going to be tough for Hunter with the change again, but he will just have to deal with it."

Annalise felt bad for leaving them with not much notice, but she knew that Hunter would understand.

"I am really sorry about all of this, my intention was to never leave you with short notice."

"Don't be; we women need to put ourselves first every once in a while. I hope you find something more suitable, Annalise. Shall we say next Wednesday will be your last day with us? We should hopefully find someone by then. If you could leave all your passes and keys on the desk before you leave and if I don't see you again, I wish you all the best."

"Thanks, Jo, and thanks for being so understanding."

Annalise got up from her chair and headed out the door feeling relieved like a weight had been lifted. She just hoped that she didn't have to speak to Hunter again before she left; she would just email him with all the final details. Hopefully, he wouldn't make it hard for her after their conversation this morning.

Friday, 25 June (Australia)
Hunter

Hunter's mind was all over the place, what had he been trying to say to Annalise on the phone. Whatever he was trying to tell her, it hadn't come out correctly, and now things were even worse. He had basically said that he just wanted her and not her child, which was kind of true. God what did he know, how could relationships be so hard and confusing this is why he had never had one before.

He had always kept it so simple, no commitment so no feelings, well for him anyway. Annalise didn't even seem upset on the phone; she just acted like it was a business deal that hurt him. Had she moved on that quickly or was it all an act. He knew that she must be feeling something otherwise she wouldn't be threatening to leave, or was she being serious. He needed to find out from Jo; he really didn't want her having to leave just because of their situation, they could make it work somehow.

They were both professionals and could push this all behind them. What was he talking about? He had been away for less than a week, and he already missed her how was it going to be seeing her every day in the office and not be able to just kiss her or touch her, it would drive him insane just like it did when she first started working for him.

Hunter needed a plan; he would finish up with Sydney then head to Dubai to tie up the deal there and then when he was back he would speak to Annalise about her role with them and see if he could even relocate her into another team. Yes, that would work for the both of them; he could still see her around the office, and she wouldn't have to worry about finding another job. But first, he needed to speak to Jo and make sure Annalise hadn't seen her resigning. He picked up the phone not even contemplating the time right now and pressed the dial.

"Jo, it's Hunter; has she been to see you yet?"

"Hunter, how's the trip going? And has who been to see me?"

215

"Jo just tell me, Annalise."

"Oh, yes, she has been in to see me."

"And?"

"She has decided to leave us, I've already spoken to the recruitment agency, and they have a couple of people who they think would work well here. I'm am going to meet a few of them later today and then make a decision. Obviously, if you don't like them then we can find someone else, but we need someone to take over Annalise's role as soon as possible."

"Not going to happen. Can't we find her another role within the company?"

"Hunter, she doesn't want to stay for some reason. Says that it's too demanding, and she needs something low key. She isn't used to working for a large global organisation, sometimes people just need a smaller environment where it's not so busy."

"That's rubbish, she was handling, and it's just an excuse."

He could feel his temperature rising just thinking about the excuse that Annalise had told Jo when he knew that deep down she just couldn't handle working with him.

"Why is it an excuse? Hunter do I need to be worried here, has something happened between you two?"

He almost had let slip about him and Annalise but knew he needed to keep in under rap as Jo was still in HR and even though she worked for him; he knew that she wouldn't be happy about the situation.

"Nothing, Jo. I'm just tired and stressed with some projects. Plus I now have to work with someone else again and get them to use to my way of working. Please make sure to get me someone good, preferably experienced with larger companies, I can't have them leaving again before Charlotte comes back from maternity leave."

"Of course, Hunter."

"Keep me posted."

"Will do."

Hunter hung up the phone feeling drained from hearing that Annalise had actually gone through with it. He thought that it was all words on the phone, like some kind of threat, but it hadn't been. He needed to talk to her again and persuade her to stay; he reached for his phone found her number and hit dial.

As he waited in anticipation the phone just kept ringing and eventually rang off to her voicemail, he decided not to leave a message on this occasion and

216

would try her again when he woke up. It was already early hours of the morning, and he was flying to Dubai tomorrow; he tried to get some more sleep pushing Annalise out of his mind and before he knew it darkness had filled his mind and the room became silent with just the sound of his breathing.

Friday, 25 June (Australia)
Hunter

Hunter had said goodbye to his team in Sydney and had made a pact to them that they would be seeing him again next year; he had really enjoyed his time there and getting to know a few more of the employees, they were doing great things, and he had nothing but faith in Dave to keep it all going well. As he now sat in the airport lounge waiting for his flight to Dubai he realised how tired he was, having not slept much over the past few days he knew that it wasn't just down to being busy and socialising but because of Annalise. He had realised in the space of a few days that even though he hadn't known her for very long, that she had made a huge impact on his life in such a short space of time.

And no one had ever done that to him. She made him open up to her without judgement; he had laughed more with her than he had done in years; she gave him hope that he could have a future with someone and open him up to feel that he never thought he could have, and now he had messed it all up by walking out when things got tough. Why did he just run? He would never have done that if it was a business deal; he liked a challenge and would stick it out to the deal was done so why couldn't he when it came to his personal life.

He knew that he was never going to meet someone else as special as Annalise so why was he throwing it all away. He needed to get his head around having a child in his life, and even though she wasn't his by blood he would have to treat her like she was, he would never want a child to be treated like he was. No child should have to go through that emotional abuse in their life. Hunter was so confused, he knew what he should be doing, but right now, he just couldn't follow it through; he must be more damaged than he thought. He knew one thing for sure though that whatever he decided he needed to make a big gesture to Annalise if he was going to commit to her and her daughter.

Annalise had ignored him when he tried to call her at work; he knew that she had just got into the office, but she would normally still answer, instead she had just sent him an email confirmation with his hotel details for Dubai. The email was straight to the point, with no small talk. He knew that she was upset otherwise she wouldn't be leaving the firm without talking to him again.

Jo had emailed him to let him know that they had found someone to replace Annalise called Hillary; she was in her late 40s and had previous experience working as an executive assistant for the CEO of a large global bank, and she was starting on Monday for Annalise to give her a handover for a few days, so Tuesday would be her last day. It meant that he may see her but unlikely as he wasn't supposed to be landing in London until Tuesday evening. Hunter would just have to give Annalise a few days to gain a level head and then he would try calling her again; he needed to see her when he got back; he didn't care if he was being selfish about his needs; and he would see her even if she didn't want to see him.

Hunter's flight was being called, and he watched as slowly one by one people got up and headed for the boarding gate; he was in first class again so knew he had some time before having to be in his seat. He hated getting on the plane and then having to sit there for an hour before take-off, at least he knew that he could sleep on the plane and try and be fresh again for his Dubai meeting. He really didn't have the energy or patients for this meeting but had to do it for the businesses sake. It could open up so many doors for the Middle East, and he had plans to expand and gain offices there, it was a fast-moving country and so much potential he knew that he could make a lot of money if he got in with the right companies.

His flight was now calling final calls so he headed up to the boarding gate and passed over his boarding card, the stewardess smiled at him sweetly and pass his card back to him, gesturing where he needed to go. As he sat in his seat, he decided that he needed all the rest he could get so decided to turn off his mobile phone and laptop until he landed in Dubai, surely no one would need him urgently and there was nothing he could do while thousands of feet in the air anyway. Before he did though, he decided that he would text Annalise just one last time before he got back to London.

[TEXT MESSAGE]

Hunter: *Annalise. I've been trying to call you, but you are obviously not ready to speak with me yet, and I understand that. Please consider meeting with me when I am back in London, I would really like to clear some things up and set us both on the right path again. I miss you. H x.*

He hit send and then turned his phone off.

Tuesday, 29 June
Hunter

It had been a long few days for Hunter with travelling to Dubai on the way back to London, the deal had gone well, and he was due to head back over in the New Year to finalise everything and get the ball rolling. It was an exciting time for the Hunter and the company, his dreams were all starting to come true. He wanted to be the number one recruitment company globally and with these deals happening in Australia and the UAE he was getting closer to it. He had a great team on board and to say a bit thank you for all the hard work this year; he would be giving out higher bonuses and giving a higher budget for the Christmas event. It was still months away yet but time definitely fly's by so quickly nowadays.

Wednesday, 30 June
Hunter

Arriving back late last night from his Dubai flight, Hunter wanted to get in the office early with it being his first day back in the office. He still hadn't heard anything from Annalise, no reply to his text message he had sent on the plane, and he was wondering how much time he should give her. He was tempted to go round to hers last night on the way back from the airport, but he had received an urgent call about finalising some paperwork because one of the consultants had made a crucial error, and it needed to be put through first thing Wednesday morning. His day was looking fairly quiet today so he would try and call Annalise again and if still no reply he was going to go round there tonight whether she wanted to see him or now. He had things that he needed to say, and she was going to listen to them one way or other.

As Hunter sat in his office staring out on to his view of London he was intrigued to meet his new EA and hoped that Jo had chosen well, he couldn't go through hiring another person if Hillary didn't work out it was all becoming time-consuming for him, and he didn't have time to keep showing someone how he liked his calendar or meetings set up. He knew that Charlotte had just given birth to a baby boy and wondered whether she would consider coming back early, maybe he would run it past her when she popped in to see them all and show off baby jack as she had mentioned in her email. He must remember to get Hillary to send her some flowers and a card to congratulate them all.

As Hunter sat there procrastinating with his work his phone started to ring and to his delight he noticed that it was Annalise. He tried to remain calm and act normal, but deep inside, he was happy that she was finally calling him back, that must mean that she was ready to talk and if she was ready to talk then he had hoped. As he picked up the call he straight away heard the panic in her voice, and he worried that something had happened to her.

"Hunter… I didn't know who else to call. It's Penelope she has been taken to hospital!"

Hunter's heart instantly calms knowing that Annalise was OK, but he was still concerned as to what had happened to her daughter.

"Annalise, what's happened?"

He could hear her sobbing down the phone, and he wanted to comfort her. Instead, he just waited and listened to what she was saying.

"Penelope was outside playing rounder's with some friends when one of the children hit the ball straight at Penelope, and it hit her on the head; she then fell and hit her head on the ground and was knocked unconscious. They are now running tests, and she is coming in and out of consciousness. Oh, Hunter, I don't know what to do, it's my little girl."

Annalise was now sobbing even harder and could hardly breathe. She waited for a response but nothing came. Just silence.

She stopped crying and her tone was almost angry when she spoke again.

"I'm sorry Hunter I shouldn't have called you, this doesn't concern you. I'll let you get on with your day. Sorry to bother you."

"Annalise, enough, what hospital are you at?"

She rattled off the name of the hospital and Hunter quickly wrote it down, knowing that it would only take him 15 minutes to get there. He quickly hung up the phone before Annalise could say anything else and headed straight for his car, passing a lady heading his way. He knew it must be Hillary, but he didn't have time to speak with her right now; she would have to wait. Right now, he needed to be with Annalise; she was more than upset; she felt alone; and he didn't want her to feel that way.

He raced past reception seeing Candice heading his way.

"Hunter, where are you going? Hillary has just arrived, and I sent her down to see you."

"I have an emergency, Candice. Tell her I'm sorry. Cancel all my meetings for today, I probably won't be back in till tomorrow."

"Hunter, what's happened?"

He didn't have time to answer and headed straight into the lift and pressed for the basement level where his car had been parked.

Traffic had been a nightmare at peak hour, but he managed to get to the hospital within 20 minutes; he parked and raced in to find Annalise stopping to ask the receptionist what level they were on. As he exited the level, he saw

Annalise sitting in the waiting room; she looked so frail like she hadn't eaten in days. He face was pale and gaunt, and she had dark circles under her eyes. As he headed over she looked up at him and just started crying, he pulled her up and embraced her taking some of the load from her.

"It's OK, I'm here."

She was sobbing uncontrollably now and Hunter just stayed there, his arms wrapped around her pressing hard so she could feel his presence and let her cry as much as she wanted to. He didn't know how long they had been standing like that, but she soon eased her grip around him and pulled away, looking away from him. He took her face in his hands and positioned it so that she was looking up at him; he wanted to see the pain that she was in and help ease it.

"Annalise, look at me."

"What are you doing here, Hunter?"

"You called me, I wanted to be here for you."

"Why?"

"Because I wanted to, does there have to be another reason? You are upset and need some support right now."

"I didn't want you coming here out of sympathy."

She turned to walk off, and he grabbed her pulling her back into his embrace.

"Stop it, Annalise; stop fighting. We can talk about us later, what's happening with Penelope?"

She looked at him like she was going to push him away again, but instead her body relaxed like she was too tired to fight.

"They are doing tests that are the last I heard. I have been here for hours, Hunter, and they aren't telling me anything."

She started to cry again and sat down putting her hands in her head.

"Right, let me see what's going on."

"They won't speak to you Hunter, you are not family."

That didn't stop him from approaching one of the doctors and demanding some information. The doctor was reluctant at first, but Hunter explained the situation, and he went off to find out for them.

As they both sat there in silence waiting for the Doctor to return, Hunter wondered what had happened to Annalise while he had been away. She looked tired, even more, tired than he looked; he wondered if he had done this to her, what was he talking about of course he had. He had come into her life, messed it up and then left again for her to pick up the pieces. How could he do that to someone he loved.

He stopped in mid-thought, did he just say what he thought he had? How did he even know what love felt like? He had never loved anyone before or been loved by anyone. Maybe he was confused, but he thought back to what Ty had said to him before. How when you love someone, you miss them incredibly no matter whether you are 5 minutes from them or thousands of miles apart, how you want to spend every waking hour with them, that you can tell them anything and be your true self with them, that your heartaches from just not being near them, that you will do anything for them so that they are happy and content.

He felt all of that with Annalise, being away had shown him, but it wasn't until now, seeing her like this that he realised it. He didn't want her to be sad and upset; he want to comfort her and be the strong person she could rely on in life; he wanted to make her smile, feel sexy and confident, but most of all he wanted to be the one person who made her the best version of herself. He needed to tell her how he felt but now wasn't the time, now he needed to be strong for her as he wasn't sure what news the doctor was going to bring back about Penelope.

"Mrs Smith? I have some news on your daughter."

"It's Miss Smith actually. How is my little girl, I want to see her."

"She has just come out of her tests, but she is looking much better, we won't know the results for a few more hours, but if she keeps improving, then I am sure that all the tests will come back good. You can go and see her now if you like; she keeps asking for you."

Annalise broke down into tears again, but these seemed like relief tears; she turned to Hunter and embraced him. He looked down at her and kissed her on the forehead; she instantly looked up at him and the atmosphere in the room changed again. He knew where this could go so he quickly pulled away and ushered her up so that they could go and see Penelope.

"Sir, do you now want to go as well? All family can see her I'm sure she wants to see her dad as well."

Hunter couldn't quite make out what to think to the Doctors comment, the words had a strange feeling but didn't shock him as much as he had thought they would if he ever heard them.

"That's OK, Hunter you can wait here or if you have to leave that's fine."

"The only place I have to be is here Annalise, by your side and Penelope's"

"You don't have to do this, Hunter."

"I want to Annalise. There are some things that I want to talk to you about later, once Penelope has the all-clear."

"And what if she doesn't the get all clear, what I am going to do if my poor little girl has some damage."

"Then we will work it all out together."

As they entered the room where Penelope was in, Annalise rushed to her bedside and gave her a big cuddle not letting her guy for ages, Hunter found a seat and sat in it letting the two of them have a moment.

"Oh, Penelope, I am so glad that you are OK. You had me worried then."

"It doesn't hurt Mummy."

"You are such a brave little girl."

"When can I go back to school and see my friends?"

"Soon darling, we just need to make sure that you are 100% better before going back to school."

"Does that mean that I can stay at home and watch some Disney films with you?"

"It sure does, Mummy doesn't start her new job until next week so she still has some time off, and I couldn't think of anything more I would want to do."

Hunter looked at Annalise surprised at her comment; he knew that she would have to find a new job, but hearing it made it more real.

"Does your friend want to watch them with us?"

Penelope was not looking at Hunter but asking the question to Annalise unsure of her response. It wasn't his idea of fun, but if it meant spending time with Annalise, then he would take it.

"I'm not sure Penelope. Hunter is a very busy man."

"I'm sure I can take some time."

Annalise looked surprised and looked at him trying to figure out what had changed in the space of a few days.

"Penelope, shall I go and get you something from the vending machine? Are you hungry?"

"Yes, please."

"OK, we will be right back."

Annalise gestured to Hunter to come with her, and she didn't look impressed.

When they were in the corridor and out of hearing distance from Penelope Annalise started talking.

"Hunter, I don't know what you are doing, it's one thing getting my hopes up, but it's another when it comes to Penelope's."

"Annalise, I meant it. I want to spend some time with you, with the both of you."

"But you walked out, you said that you couldn't do the whole family thing, that it wasn't in your DNA."

"I know what I said Annalise. But things have changed. I've made some realisations since being away."

"And they are?"

"I've never met anyone like you, Annalise. You have brought out feelings that I never knew even existed for me, a life where I can be part of a family, and it scared me. You have to understand that I have never been part of a family Annalise, never felt wanted or loved by one, not even my own. I always thought to myself that it was my fault that I was the one that caused all the heartache and abuse in my family, but I was wrong.

"It was my parents. I thought that I wasn't capable of love until I met you. You have given me a new lease of life Annalise, and I know it has taken for me to go away to realise it, but I am here now, standing in front of you telling you that I want to be a part of your family if you will let me."

Annalise wasn't saying anything, just standing there staring up at him.

"But what if you walk out again, I don't know whether I can take that chance for Penelope's sake."

"I can't promise that I will know how this all works, this is brand new to me Annalise, but I can promise that I will try my hardest. I love you, Annalise."

The words had come out before he had even realised, but he felt relieved, relieved that they were out. He had loved her from the first day that he met her, but he just couldn't see it as he didn't know what love was, but now, he did he wanted her to know.

"Hunter…."

He waited for her to answer him, which felt like a lifetime; he had just thrown himself into the deep end and was waiting for her to throw him a lifesaver.

"I… I love you too."

Hunter grabbed her face and started to kiss her vigorously not caring who was around them to see; he needed to feel her, to feel their connection, and it felt even more electric than it had done before.

"I think I have always felt that way about you Annalise, but I just didn't realise it."

"I'm glad that you have finally realised it."

And she started kissing him again like she never wanted to let him go, and he didn't care because he felt exactly the same.

Epilogue
Saturday, 31 December
Annalise

Speckles of snow fell from the sky landing on crisp green grass, which had almost turned to white from hours of the same pattern occurring, the sky was clear with shades of blue gracing today's weather and the air was crisp making it a spectacular day to celebrate new year's eve. Annalise sat on the bed looking out of the window, which overlooked the gardens to this most magical property and couldn't quite believe where she was. The gardens were out of this world, the trees trimmed into beautiful sculptures, the grass so pristine anyone would be afraid to step onto it, paved pathways leading the way to magical areas and this weather was adding to its uniqueness.

The building had a historical background and every step you took within the grounds of this exquisite house took you right back to that period. Annalise remembered driving past this area when she was a teenager and how she had always wanted to see what it was like. The house was set back from the main road with a long driveway leading to its grand entrance so she was never able to see its full potential, but today, she had gotten to see it all. She knew that it would be beautiful, but today, it had turned into the most spectacular abode, and she never wanted to leave.

Annalise had woken early again unsure of her feelings this morning. She had tossed and turned all night and was so thankful that she hadn't woken Penelope up who was currently lying next to her in a starfish position. She looked at her beautiful daughter laying there completely content and happy, and it warmed her heart. Just 6 months ago she had been terrified that she may lose the one thing that meant the most to her, but her brave little girl had made a full recovery with no lasting damage.

Annalise remembered how Penelope had wanted to go straight back to school so that she could see her friends, but Annalise wanted her to stay off for at least a week so that she could rest and fully recover. Annalise knew deep down that she was just really worried that it may happen again, and she couldn't go through seeing her daughter like that, completely vulnerable and frail in a hospital bed. It broke her heart. But it was Penelope who had been the strong one out of them both, bringing a smile back to Annalise's face and reassuring her.

Annalise knew that she was supposed to be the strong one with being the parent and all, but she just couldn't even imagine what her life would be like if Penelope wasn't in it. Over the past 6 months, she had started to worry less and didn't rush to collect Penelope from school or phone the school to make sure that everything was OK; she was getting back into her normal routine and relaxing again, which pleased Penelope no end.

Annalise looked at her watch and saw that it was 8:00 a.m.; she had so much to do today, but her mind just couldn't focus. Part of her wanted to stay in bed with Penelope and watch the snowfall onto the grounds while drinking cups of tea and talking to Penelope, but she knew that there were other things for her to be getting on with, and it thrilled her. She was excited about what today was going to bring, not only for her but for Penelope as well. It was a bit overwhelming being back in Norfolk though especially as she hadn't seen her parents or family since moving to London.

She had been unsure as to reach out to them when she knew that she was coming back to the area for a few days, but there had still been a longing in her heart that her parents would forget all the past and start thinking about the future. She had hoped that putting some distance between them all would make things better. Well, she would know in a few hours if things had changed and just thinking about possibly seeing them again made her feel overwhelmed and anxious. She had to push those thoughts to one side for now otherwise she would fall apart before the day had even started, and it was going to be a long day.

Penelope started to stir and rolled over looking up at Annalise, her hair was covering her face, but Annalise could see those big brown eyes and knew that Penelope was also excited about today. Penelope stretched out her entire body and then sprung up onto her feet and started bouncing on the bed, almost knocking Annalise off the bed and spilling her cup of tea onto the floor.

"Penelope… be careful! Mummy's tea nearly got spilt along with me falling with it."

"Today's the day… today's the day… Mummy, today's the day!"

Penelope was trying to make her words into a song, but all that was coming out was a high pitched yell.

"Penelope darling, I know that you are excited, but you need to be quiet in case you wake someone else up."

"Sorry, Mummy, I'm just excited. Are you excited?"

"Of course, I am darling."

Annalise was more nervous than excited at this moment, but Penelope didn't need to know that. Penelope decided to dive off the bed onto the floor and ran to the window squealing.

"And it's snowing… it's a fairy tale Mummy, look!"

Annalise walked over to where Penelope was standing and admired their view again, Penelope was right, it was something out of a fairy tale. It had been years since it had snowed over the Christmas period in Norfolk, but today, it had and Annalise thought that someone was trying to make this day perfect for them.

"Mummy, can we go outside and make snow angels?"

Penelope's face was overjoyed, and she was bursting with excitement.

"Maybe later darling, we have to start getting ready now."

Annalise would like nothing more than to go and play snow angels outside with Penelope, but she had more important things to do right now. She had a schedule to keep if everything was going to go to plan today; she just had to keep her nerves at bay. She decided to go and have a shower and leave Penelope watching cartoons on the TV, it would give her a bit of peace and quiet and some time to get her thoughts together.

Annalise instantly felt more relaxed after having a hot shower; she let the water soak into her skin and made sure she didn't rush; she was probably in there longer than she had time to be, but she was still on schedule. As she headed out of the bathroom and back into the bedroom area there was a knock at the door, she checked her watch and saw that it was 9:00 a.m., which meant that it could only be one person. She headed over to the door almost bumping into Penelope as she charged straight for it before Annalise could reach it first, and was welcomed with a familiar warming smile, and she relaxed once again.

"Candice!"

Penelope ran straight into Candice, and she responded by picking Penelope up by the waist and embracing her into a huge cuddle, screaming her name at the same time. Both of them seemed more excited than she was, but Annalise knew that it was just down to her nerves.

"It's good to see that you are both sticking to the schedule… well at least you have had a shower, Annalise. BUT Penelope… have you been watching cartoons again?"

"Only while Mummy was getting ready."

"Well, why don't you go and jump in the shower, I will order some breakfast for us and then we can all sit down and chill for a bit before we have to finish getting ready."

Annalise thought about breakfast, but her stomach was too full of nerves to eat, all she could manage was another cup of tea… or at least some champagne.

"Yay… can I have a pain au chocolate?"

"Since when do you eat Pana chocolate for breakfast…?"

Candice was looking at Annalise with a smarmy look.

"Well, it's not from my influences, trust me! And Penelope you can have some fruit with that as well."

"OK…."

Penelope disappeared into the bathroom leaving Annalise and Candice on their own before Annalise could say anything Candice pulled out some champagne from her bag and waved it in front of Annalise already reading her mind.

"So how are you feeling? I thought this would help."

"You are a lifesaver… I'm a bag of nerves."

"It's to be expected plus it's your first time back in Norfolk for over 6 months. Does it feel strange being back here?"

Annalise walked over to the window again and looked out taking in the view.

"Strangely not. This was where I grew up, and I have so many memories, not that they are all good ones. It's just so picturesque and quiet, and it was a great place to bring Penelope up, but London is where my heart is now. However, it didn't stop me from wanting to spend the Christmas period here and surprisingly I have felt at peace with it all. I think because we are happy and settled now, I can put the past behind me."

"So do you know if your family are coming today?"

"Well, I did invite them so we will see. I'm not getting my hopes up, but it would be nice for Penelope's sake for them to have a relationship at least, so if they show then that will mean that they are keen to try."

"Well, I'm sure they have missed you both and will make the effort."

Annalise wasn't too sure; she knew how it had been left with her parents, and she didn't think that they were going to change their feelings about her and Penelope.

"Right, you look like you need a glass of this. Let's crack it open, order room service and then start getting ready… only a few hours to go!"

Candice's last comment kicked started Annalise's nerves again, it wasn't that she didn't want today to happen, it was just that it was going to be one of the most important days of her life, and she just wanted it to all go perfectly, especially when all the pressure was on her.

Saturday, 31 December
Hunter

Hunter hadn't slept at all last night, emotions running wild in his head with different feelings springing into his thoughts. He had tossed and turned until he decided to get up and do some work, that's one thing that he could always rely on to get him back on track when he was feeling like this. Over the past 6 months his life had completely been turned upside down, and it had taken him a little while to settle into it; he had at times wanted to pull back, but he was in too deep. Both emotionally and physically.

He had still managed to maintain his routine but with a few extra activities added to his day, which he had come to love. Hunter had seen the business grow dramatically in the past 6 months, they had increased their headcount to an extra 100 in the London office and an extra 250 in total worldwide. The next step was for him to grow the APAC region, and he thought of no one better for the job than Dave from the Sydney office.

He had it all planned out and just had to put the offer to Dave next week after the holidays were over. He never understood why people had to take so much time off over the Christmas period, if it was up to him he would work straight through like he usually did, but he had other priorities to think about now, and it would be more trouble than it's worth to not take time off.

Hunter never thought that his life would come to this, it was never in his plan, but life was strange like that and rather than fight it anymore he embraced these changes, and he was happier than he had been in a long time. As he shut his laptop down, quickly sending an email to the Hong Kong office about finalising a deal, that was the last piece of business that he had to do for the weekend. Now that it was just him and his thoughts; he started to get anxious and even though it was still before midday; he headed to the minibar and pulled himself a whiskey, just what he needed to calm his nerves.

This was a whole new chapter in his life for Hunter, and it actually exhilarated him bringing new challenges and rewards along with it. He never thought that he would be in this situation, and it made him think back to his parents and his childhood. It didn't even cross his mind about inviting them to today's event; he hadn't seen them in over 10 years now, and he had come to terms with them not being in his life. He had made a life for himself and been successful without them; he was on the right track to being where he wanted to be, and it was all down to him and hard work.

There had been a few spanners thrown in the mix, but he had learnt to embrace them and knew that life sometimes threw these into the mix, not to throw him off course but to challenge him and show him that there were other things in life that were important other than work. As Hunter sipped on his whiskey looking out of the window, he could feel his heartbeat becoming stronger and louder; he never got nervous even when he had a big deal to close he had always been confident but today wasn't just about him and that's what made him nervous. It would soon become more than just him.

Showered, freshly shaved and now fully dressed, Hunter looked in the mirror almost not recognising himself. It wasn't because of what he was wearing but because of where he was standing, on this day, in this location, about to step out of his comfort zone and into the unknown. Today was going to bring a whole new aspect to his life and surprisingly he felt content about that.

He had grown as a person over the last 6 months and had been open to new feelings and emotions that he had never experienced before; he had noticed it so he knew that other people in his life had noticed it as well. It had even made him a better businessman with being able to understand people's motives more and being able to delve deeper into their backgrounds and what drives them, it had all been a positive change.

Being pulled out of his thoughts by someone knocking on his door, Hunter smiled to himself, down his whiskey and headed to answer it knowing all too well who it would be.

Before he could do anything, he was embraced into a hug and just stood there not knowing what to do.

"Hunt… how are you feeling?"

Tyrell didn't care about showing affection, but Hunter on the other hand was still learning how to do that. Wondering how long he had to stand there feeling awkward he was relieved when Tyrell pulled away almost sensing how Hunter was feeling.

"Fine. Why?"

"Well, you don't look fine. Nervous?"

"And why would I be nervous?"

"Well, did you ever think that this day would come? I would be nervous if I was you."

"Well, the difference between you and I Ty is that I don't get nervous, I am always in control of my feelings. Nerves don't get to me."

Hunter knew that he was lying, his nerves had hit sky high, but he couldn't let anyone on to that, especially Ty.

"OK, Hunter if you say so."

Tyrell was mocking him, but Hunter let this one go; he didn't want to get into anything today.

"I see you have had a whiskey already, want to poor me one?"

Hunter headed over to the minibar and pulled out two small bottles of Jack Daniels, took two glasses and poured them, passing one to Tyrell. Hunter downed him in one gulp feeling the alcohol hit his insides sending a warm feeling and easing his nerves instantly.

"Woah… slow down Hunter, we don't want you drunk today, and how would that go down!"

"Tyrell, I'm fine. I just need to take the edge off that's all."

"So you are nervous?"

"Tyrell, drop it!"

Hunter's tone was blunt and Tyrell knew not to say anymore.

"So… less than an hour to go, are you all set?"

Hunter thought about how his life would be so different in a few hours' time, and even though he was nervous, he was all set for his new adventure. It brought a smile to his face and warmed his heart; he may not have wanted this before, but he did now, and he knew that was because of certain people in his life.

"All set."

"Right, well we better go down and check everything is ready. I'm ready to meet some women today!"

"Tyrell seriously… can you keep it in your trousers for one day! This is not the day or time OK!"

"I saw a hot blonde downstairs in the lobby, maybe she is coming today."

"Enough Tyrell, most of the people coming today are from the business so you are not allowed to go there… OK?"

"I can't help it if they love my charm."

"What happened to that girl you were seeing from the gym? I thought it was going well."

"She's still away, and we have lost contact recently… anyway, I don't want to talk about it."

"Fair enough. We need to go, I can't be late today."

Hunter looked in the mirror one more time before heading to the door, knowing that when he would return later, he would be a different man.

Saturday, 31 December
Annalise

Annalise was standing looking in the mirror almost not recognising herself; he hair was put in an updo with some small curls of hair falling around her face, her makeup was fresh and delicate just how she liked it. She touched her outfit feeling the soft silky fabric that hung to all her curves, the neckline sweetheart with a lace overlay and small angelic crystals placed delicately on the dress. She had never worn such a breath-taking dress before and had instantly fallen in love with it when she put it on in the shop. Annalise turned around to face Candice and Penelope, and they were just starring at her. Feeling insecure she started to fiddle the dress unsure if she did look as good as she thought.

"Well… do I look OK?"

Candice was now smiling at her and came over to give her a quick hug.

"Annalise, you look absolutely stunning. Breath-taking in fact."

"Penelope followed Candice and came to give Annalise a big squeeze."

"Mummy… you are a princess. I knew it!"

Annalise was overwhelmed with emotion and tried not to cry; she didn't have time to re-do her makeup, in fact, time had gone so quickly, and she was sure that they needed to be downstairs already.

"I feel like one Penelope, and don't you look like a little princess as well my darling girl."

Penelope began to twirl making her dress spin with her, giggling as she did.

"Right, we better get going. Ready?"

Annalise's nerves were still there, and she couldn't talk so just nodded to Candice that she was, and they all headed to the door, Annalise looking in the mirror one last time knowing that she would be different when she returned to the room later.

Sunday, 1 January
Hunter and Annalise

The day had been all that Annalise could have imagined it to be and more; as she walked into the conservatorium with Penelope and Candice just in front of her, she remembered noticing how spectacular it had looked. The glass roof was covered in snowflakes with beams of sunlight shining through which was enhanced by the glistening of the chandeliers on the ceiling. Baby's breathe flowers were placed delicately around the room tied with pale pink ribbons, which matched the colour of Penelope's dress.

Annalise could remember the moment that she saw his face, all her worry and nerves went instantly taken away and her body was filled with love and warmth. The man she was going to be spending the rest of her life had made today possible, and here he was waiting for her to meet him at the end of the aisle, leading her to him by those deep and emotional eyes, the same eyes that had made her fall for him from day one.

Hunter had remembered seeing Annalise for the first time when she entered the conservatorium; she had taken his breath away. How someone could be so perfect and want someone like him, this woman had changed his life for the better without even knowing so. She had his heart from day one and there had been no question in his mind when he asked her to marry him.

He had fallen in love with not only her but Penelope as well. They had become this little family that he never thought he deserved and was still pinching himself on a daily basis that this was all his. As she glided down the aisle, he could see that she felt it too, the same feeling they got when they first met each other, it was still there. His life was about to come complete.

As they both rolled over to face each other, still finding their way out of the fairy tale of yesterday's events, love instantly filled both of their hearts and emotions were running wild in their eyes. Hunter reached over and pulled

239

Annalise into an embrace, trying to merge their bodies together; he kissed the top of her head and heard her relax into him. His life was content, and he didn't want to be anywhere else right now, other than with Annalise by his side.

"Good morning, Mrs Maguire."

Just saying the words made him smile.

Annalise rolled over to face him looking directly into his eyes, leant forward and gently kissed him on the lips.

"Good morning, Mr Maguire."